A LINE OF FORGOTTEN BLOOD

MALCOLM MACKAY

HEAD
of ZEUS

First published in the UK in 2019 by Head of Zeus Ltd

9 7 5 3 1 2 4 6 8

A catalogue record for this book is available from the British Library.

(HB): 9781786697134
(ANZTPB): 9781786697141
(E): 9781786697127

Printed and bound by CPI Group (UK) Ltd, Croydon, CR0 4YY

Head of Zeus Ltd
First Floor East
5–8 Hardwick Street
London EC1R 4RG
WWW.HEADOFZEUS.COM

A
LINE
OF
FORGOTTEN
BLOOD

ALSO BY MALCOLM MACKAY

In the Cage Where Your Saviours Hide

A
LINE
OF
FORGOTTEN
BLOOD

PROLOGUE

There was a bang and her head jerked forward. The world fell into a blur, a feeling of movement and noise but nothing making sense, her brain swamped with shock. The world was slowing but vaguely she knew nothing was slowing fast enough. That was when she snapped back into real time, when her instincts scoffed at her sluggish brain and took back control.

Freya Dempsey slammed her foot on the brake pedal and the car screeched to a stop. She took a few seconds to breathe deeply and consider where she was, what had happened and where she should direct her rising anger. She had pulled out on the corner of Siar Road and Kidd Street and some eyeless halfwit had gone straight into the side of her car. It had to be their fault because the shock commanding her system wasn't willing to move over and make room for guilt. Some idiot had crashed into her and if they weren't already in great pain she intended to do something about that. Traffic was stopping around her and somewhere in the background a committed moron was leaning on his horn as though it might help.

Freya began to swear loudly and prodigiously in the car, as a woman from Whisper Hill would, and she toned it down to a feral hiss as she stepped out into public, as a woman living in Cnocaid should. Nothing felt painful as she stood up, although she was pretty sure she could whip it up into something chronic should the need to lay it on thick arise. She grimaced at the damage to her car and repeated the look when she spotted what had hit her. Now she could see how expensive it was she decided it was definitely their fault.

A man in a dark blue suit and white shirt was getting out of a black car that would have been gliding luxuriously through the streets of Challaid until it crossed her path. Now the front right was tangled up in itself, the bumper pushed into the wheel arch, and the well-dressed driver was looking at her with the sort of anger that promised trouble before he opened his mouth.

He shouted, 'What the hell were you doing? Don't you even look where you're going, or are we all just supposed to play dodgems with you?'

It occurred to her that she hadn't looked carefully because a van had blocked her view, but she shouted back, 'Of course I looked. You must have been rocketing up that road like you owned it, thinking you can drive however you want. You're going to have to pay for the damage you've done.'

His mouth hung open for a few seconds before he said, 'Have you been on the glue or something? That was your fault, you'll pay for that.'

Before either of them could spin the argument round in another circle the back door of the heinously expensive saloon car opened and a man got out. He wore a dark grey suit and white shirt with yellow tie and a long black coat that was open. He had a trim goatee beard and was bald on top, hair shaved short at the sides and wearing gold-rimmed glasses. He couldn't have been much past forty, Freya guessed, and from the second he stepped out of the car it was clear that he not only owned it, he also owned anything else that caught his fancy.

He didn't look angry as he walked over to the woman and young man, instead rather amused. Freya Dempsey was thirty-one and boldly attractive in a way that warned you in advance she was more than two handfuls, so whatever trouble you got into with her was your own fault. The owner of the car seemed to have worked all that out by the time he reached her, and he was still smiling.

He said, 'I am sorry about that, a terrible accident, no one's fault.'

Freya said, 'Not mine anyway.'

He laughed again, turned to his driver and said, 'Will, see if you can get the cars off the road so we don't block the traffic, and deal with the police when they finally bother to show up, their station's only up the road. Oh, and if you see who's been blowing their horn for the last few minutes see if you can stick their steering wheel up their backside and make them spin on it.'

The driver was used to doing what he was told and scurried off, leaving Freya alone with his boss. They stepped onto the busy pavement, ignoring the pedestrians who had stopped to watch the pleasurable spectacle of a minor accident that inconvenienced others but not them.

The smiling man said, 'My name's Harold Sutherland.'

'Oh, wow, so you can afford the repairs.'

The Sutherland family ran the Sutherland Bank, and it wouldn't be a skip into hyperbole to say the Sutherland Bank had a controlling interest in the city of Challaid, and undue influence over the country of Scotland. The bank often seemed to have its hand on the tiller of the entire economy, and the family who founded it still very carefully controlled it. If you lived in Challaid and your name was Sutherland you had no excuse for not being wealthy, and if you sat on the board of the bank you were probably rich to the extent that counting the zeros on your bank account became a long snooze.

Harold laughed at her bad manners and said, 'I suppose so. Can I ask your name?'

'Freya Dempsey.'

'Were you going somewhere important? Perhaps we could call a taxi for you.'

'Nowhere important enough to make me leave my car. You?'

'A meeting, but they'll wait for me.'

The driver had by now moved both cars to the side of the road so the traffic was moving again, crunching slowly over broken glass. He was tall and broad, still in his twenties but with the sort of downturned mouth that suggested he had a lot to frown about and lines on his forehead that gave an equally negative second opinion. He had a narrow face and thin eyebrows, all a little too angular to be attractive. He glared at Harold as he stalked across to Freya and handed her car keys to her without a word.

He turned to Harold and said, 'I've called another car; they'll be here in a minute or two.'

Before another word was said the police arrived and started asking questions of them all, looking to apply blame as quickly as possible. When they heard the Sutherland name the blame rushed with open arms towards Freya, and when an even more extravagant car arrived to help him complete his journey it was all they could do not to take off their jackets to cover the puddle Harold stepped over as he made his way to it. Freya stood on the pavement, abandoned by everyone, including the police who had independently decided not to care about her a millisecond after Harold Sutherland suggested she had done nothing wrong and they should leave her be. All she could do was stand on Kidd Street, shops and shoppers on either side of the road, and wait by her battered car for the tow truck to arrive.

1

IT STARTED, AS OTHER worthwhile stories have, with a phone call. Darian Ross was sitting at his desk by the window of the Douglas Independent Research office on the second floor of a building on Cage Street when his mobile rang. His boss, Sholto Douglas, was downstairs at The Northern Song, the Chinese restaurant on the ground floor, where he was buying them lunch, so Darian was alone. Leaning back with an elbow on the windowsill, looking down into the narrow pedestrianised lane, he picked the vibrating phone from his desk and saw the name on the screen: *Vinny*. PC Vincent Reno, a friend and police contact in the Whisper Hill district to the north-east of Challaid. They did each other favours, Vinny the cop on the toughest beat in the city and Darian the unregistered private detective pretending he was a humble researcher.

He answered the phone and said, 'Vinny, what flavour of favour are you after?'

'A bitter one, Darian. I have this missing person thing, I think she's missing anyway, and I was hoping you might be able to help me out with it.'

The gregarious, barrel-chested copper sounded more sombre than usual, so Darian said, 'Who's the missing person?'

'Yeah, that's the bitter pill, it's Freya.'

'As in your ex-wife Freya?'

'There can be only one.'

'Freya, the woman you've been hoping would go missing for the last five years?'

'Well, we only split up five years ago, so I've been hoping she would go missing for a little longer than that, if we're counting. Now she's gone and I'm buzzing around all over the city like a blue-arsed fly trying to find her, this is just way out of her brutal character. Wee Finn is missing his mother something chronic and my weekends just aren't the same without her verbal abuse to bookend them. Listen, can we talk about this, just the two of us to start with? I've got nothing against Sholto, but I'd rather start with your advice before you bring in the old man for wit and wisdom.'

'Sure. Where and when?'

'How about Misgearan, six tonight, when I knock off. We'll get a room and have a drink and I'll tell you what I know, which will take about half a glass.'

Darian said he'd see him there and hung up, wondering if he'd ever been to Misgearan and not woken up the following morning with a jackhammer dismantling the inside of his skull. It was a tough little drinking den up on Long Walk Lane in Whisper Hill, a place that should and would have been shut down long ago if the local police didn't also use it as their own little alcohol-sodden hideaway. It had long been a favourite of Vinny's.

Sholto Douglas returned with their lunch and they ate at their desks. Darian didn't mention the call to the former detective because there was much they didn't tell each other until circumstances prised their mouths open. That makes it sound like they didn't get along, but they did, very well in fact; it was just that each respected the other enough to see his limitations.

Sholto was a man hitting fifty who had been ecstatic to free himself from the Challaid Police Force and seek employment that better suited his stress-free aspirations. In the one-room office on the second floor of a modern grey building in the Bank district, right in the centre of Challaid, he had set up his private detective business and called it a research company so he wouldn't be held to the legal restrictions of a proper agency. He hired the young son of his former colleague on the force and tried to teach Darian everything he knew about keeping your head down and staying out of trouble.

Darian, a handsome twenty-three-year-old with soft features and intense large brown eyes, looked across the room at his boss, short and chubby, bald on top and with hair at the sides that had won whatever battle they had recently fought with a comb. His white shirt was a size too small for him and the top button was open under his tie, his desk so shrouded in papers that the folders his phone, laptop and foil lunch tray rested on might have reached to the floor for all anyone knew. Sholto played the figure of bumbling innocence well, but he was fiercely loyal and there were sharp edges to his placid mind that cut through his well-constructed image from time to time. Darian wasn't going to bring trouble to Sholto's door; he had done so before and owed his employer better this time around.

They spent the next couple of hours filing separate reports on a man they had been hired to find, a pension fund manager who had apparently fled Challaid with £45,000 of other people's hard-earned cash. They worked out he had only made it as far as his teenage lover's flat in Whisper Hill before she relieved him of the money and made it all the way to Costa Rica with it, one of the Caledonian countries. The only thing she'd left behind was the pension fund manager, and his employers weren't paying to get him back.

They did what they always did: wrote separate reports, one for the insurance company that had hired them which was full of what the customer wanted to hear, and one for their own files containing all the gory little truths and judgements that might prove useful in the future. Sholto always wrote for the client because he had the reserve and diplomacy of a man who wanted repeat clients, and Darian always wrote for their records because he had the bluntness of youth.

At ten past five Sholto said, 'Well, doesn't look like the phone will ring with a lucrative job to rain riches upon us. I might as well go home and mourn the remains of the day with Mrs Douglas.'

Sholto spent roughly forty-six per cent of his working life complaining about a lack of money and clients but the truth was they were doing okay, well-paid, petty jobs that kept them bumping along in the potholes of society. Their work for big companies wasn't often dignified, and as the rich couldn't stomach parting with money those paydays were infrequent, but their heads, necks and shoulders were above water.

Darian said, 'I'm nearly done as well. I'll be off in ten minutes.'

'Okay, lock up behind you, we wouldn't want anyone coming in and stealing... well...'

Sholto had his laptop and phone in his bag; all they left behind in the office overnight was paperwork they weren't scared of others seeing. The good stuff was well hidden now and there was enough on those files to keep gossipmongers and curious coppers up reading all night. The security of those files was absolute and no one other than the two members of Douglas Independent Research staff got unfettered access to them.

He waited in the office for twenty minutes, knowing Sholto wouldn't go straight home; he'd be downstairs in The Northern Song, chatting to Mr Yang and collecting his dinner. All of Sholto's three square meals a day came from there, and they were responsible for his changing shape. Darian waited a few minutes after seeing his boss walk along Cage Street, laptop bag in one hand and white plastic bag with food in the other.

With the door locked behind him as promised, he made his way down the stairs and out through the side door. The Chinese restaurant took up the entire ground floor, the Yang family flat and a talent agency office on the first and Douglas Independent Research, Challaid Data Services and an empty office on the top floor. Growing up, Darian had wanted to be a detective like his father, with all the bustle of a big station, but this was the next best thing. From Cage Street it was a well-worn twelve-minute walk to Glendan Station, he had no car of his own, and then the train up to Whisper Hill to meet Vinny.

DOUGLAS INDEPENDENT RESEARCH

Douglas Independent Research
21 Cage Street
Challaid CH3 4QA

Tel: (01847) 041981

Dear Mrs Gilbert,

I'm writing to confirm that Douglas Independent Research has completed the first phase of our investigation into the disappearance of your employee, Mr Walter Reilly, at the same time as a significant amount of money from the pension fund of your company, PINE Insurance. You will know by now that we have managed to track down Mr Reilly.

I have not included, at this time, a bill for our services as the question of recovering the missing money remains open. In our initial contact you stated that identifying Mr Reilly's whereabouts would be our only role, but as his discovery did not yield the missing money I would prefer to give you time to consider whether our investigation should be extended. My updated report is enclosed with this letter. I await your reply.

Yours Sincerely,
Sholto Douglas
Douglas Independent Research

***

REPORT INTO FINANCIAL AFFAIRS
OF WALTER REILLY

By Sholto Douglas, Douglas Independent Research –
For Roxana Gilbert, Port Isobel New Edinburgh Insurance

This page contains a breakdown of our investigation, and how we were able to find Mr Reilly. Our investigation began by locating Mr Reilly's whereabouts from the moment he was last seen at your office.

- My colleague, Darian Ross, was able to ascertain that Walter Reilly, after leaving your office on Sheshader Street at his usual time of five thirty, had travelled by train from Bank Station to Three O'clock Station in Whisper Hill.
- After extensive inquiries we were able to identify the taxi driver who collected Mr Reilly from outside Three O'clock Station and he was able to tell us the street where he had dropped off Mr Reilly.
- We were able to learn from one of the neighbours which address on Woodbury Drive Mr Reilly had been frequenting in the two months before his disappearance. He had been visiting flat number 3-9, which is owned by Harbour Housing and was rented to a Miss Filis Marrufo, a nineteen-year-old woman from Costa Rica who had been resident in Challaid for seven months.

- Having received no answer from the flat we were able to obtain the help of the owners to gain access where we found Mr Reilly, injured but not seriously, where he had been for two days, now alone.

At this point it became clear the nature of the criminal acts committed but as you have urged us not to contact Challaid Police, as did Mr Reilly, we have not yet done so. Despite finding Mr Reilly we have since continued to investigate the case and have discovered that Miss Marrufo was assisted by a Mr Arturo Salamanca, a twenty-two-year-old Costa Rican national who had earned residency through twelve months' work in Challaid several months ago.

As you know the money was transferred to a small bank in San José where it was collected in cash on Saturday evening. Miss Marrufo and Mr Salamanca travelled on a direct flight from Challaid International Airport the morning after the theft (Saturday) and so would have collected the cash themselves, us not finding Mr Reilly until Sunday evening. While the money has not been recovered we do not consider the case closed, and can work with colleagues in San José to recover it should you so instruct us.

REPORT INTO FINANCIAL AFFAIRS OF WALTER REILLY

By Darian Ross, Douglas Independent Research –

For **Company Use Only**
STRICTLY CONFIDENTIAL.

We were called in on Sunday morning, nearly 40 hours after Walter Reilly walked out of PINE Insurance on Sheshader Road with £45k from the pension pot. They hadn't realised it was gone until it was withdrawn from a bank in San José on Saturday and wasted the next 12 hours with their own security trying to recover the money in the hope the news would never leak out. This made it much more difficult for us and we assumed Reilly and the money would be out of the country already, in San José, something we made clear to PINE executive director Roxana Gilbert when we met in her office. She made it clear that the priority was finding Reilly; she didn't seem to believe he would have stolen from them. Mrs Gilbert believed finding Reilly would find the money, and she obviously hoped to avoid the reputational damage they would receive if they had to report the missing cash in their accounts. The company has had bad PR lately, told off by a parliamentary report, and secrecy mattered more than the cash, although she didn't say so.

The first step was working out where Reilly had gone with the money because even he wasn't stupid enough to return to his own home with it. He was, fortunately, stupid enough to use his railcard, which took him from Bank Station to Three O'clock Station on the 17:52 train on disappearance day, Friday. We were able to find this out after Sholto made contact with source #S-61 who used access to the database showing every journey using a registered card.

A man fleeing the country with his bags packed was unlikely to walk the streets of Whisper Hill so we assumed he had either been collected at the station or had taken a taxi. As usual the taxi drivers were a total nightmare and had to be bribed excessively to open their usually flappy mouths, the only time they ever do shut up is when you need info from them. We paid £100 to recipient #362 to find out who had been working on the evening in question and another £200 to recipient #363 to tell us where he had dropped Walter Reilly. He informed us he was certain he had dropped the man in our picture on Woodbury Drive and that he remembered him because he was a 'twitchy bugger'.

We were sceptical but it only took a short time of checking with people living on the street to find someone willing to tell us that Reilly had been a regular visitor to flat #3-9, and that he wasn't the only man who was. The neighbour, who made no attempt to hide the grudge she harboured against the resident, informed us that a young man stayed in the flat with the young woman who was the only listed occupant but he always left before Reilly arrived and returned only when he had left. The neighbour named the occupant as Filis Marrufo, a Costa Rican national who has not yet completed her 12-month employment period that would enable her to claim citizenship. From the research into her we've done it doesn't seem as though she works at all, and may have a 'paper job', a fake job created by criminal gangs to trick immigration officials into thinking she's earning citizenship here.

We attempted to gain access to the flat but there was no response so we called the owners, Harbour Housing, who sent a member of staff round with a key. She let us in and we found Walter Reilly sitting in the living room, the curtains drawn, cut and bruised and drinking from a bottle of vodka. He was the only person in the flat and a quick search revealed no sign of the money, just his packed bags.

When the Harbour Housing employee left the room to inform her employers their flat had been abandoned and to check if any rent was owed, Walter Reilly told his story to Sholto and me in the living room. He informed us he had met Filis Marrufo at a nightclub some three months previously and that despite the 24-year age gap he had thought she loved him. She appeared to know no one else and was lonely and unhappy in Challaid, wanting to return home to look after her sick mother (he actually somehow believed this) but needing to earn money first. He claimed that stealing the money from PINE Insurance was his idea and that he had planned it all alone. When he arrived at the flat with the cash he found she was not alone, and that she had another long-term lover. Marrufo and Reilly had booked seats on a flight to San José the following morning, the 07:15 flight, and he had already sent the money ahead and could collect it when they arrived. Marrufo's lover is Arturo Salamanca, a 22-year-old Costa Rican national with joint Scottish passport, and he too had bought a ticket on the same flight, unbeknown to Reilly. Marrufo and Salamanca beat Reilly and held him in the flat at knifepoint through the night, flaunting their own sexual relationship in front of him, making him watch them as they had sex and mocking his stupidity. He claims that in the morning they drugged him and left for the airport as he passed out.

While he was clearly drunk, full of self-pity and conflicted about how much he wanted to blame Marrufo, it is our belief that he was mostly telling the truth. Most likely Marrufo picked up a dunce like Reilly who would buy her gifts and help her with cash when needed, and would have looked for ways to exploit him further. When she expressed a desire to find money to return to Caledonia she was probably hoping for him to come up with cash to help her, and likely pushed him towards the plan to steal the money, although he carried out the actual theft all on his own. Marrufo and Salamanca saw their chance and took it.

There is no doubt the money is now in San José, along with Marrufo and Salamanca. We have alerted Corvus Security, the detective agency we cooperate with in the city, and are ready to take the next step in the job of recovering the stolen money. We now await a response from PINE Insurance.

2

TAXI DRIVERS IN CHALLAID would all be millionaires
if there weren't so damn many of them and they didn't
keep picking fights with each other. Our city is built in
a U shape around the bottom end of Loch Eriboll, a
sea loch on the north coast of Scotland. There's a single
rail line that runs through the six major districts, but if
your destination isn't close to the line you either need
cash for a taxi or a comfy pair of shoes because there's
only one branching line which goes to the airport, no
underground and an infuriatingly unreliable bus service
made worse by the recent collapse of one of the local
operators. The taxi ranks outside the stations were
always frantic, but this time Darian decided to join the
battle of elbows at the roadside. The journey to Long
Walk Lane lived up to its nickname and he didn't want
to be late for the meeting with Vinny.

The driver who took him from Mormaer Station
dropped him on Fair Road near the entrance to the lane

because you couldn't get close to Misgearan without running over six drunks and a cop and there was nowhere to turn at the end of the cul-de-sac. Darian paid the man and strolled through the smattering of people already milling around the narrow space between the ugly, flat, single-storey buildings on either side of the road. On the left were the backs of the buildings that faced Fair Road and so were at least pretending to be respectable, but on the other side the buildings fronted the lane and backed against a large metal fence that blocked access to the railway line. Darian had spotted the rear of Misgearan as he whizzed past on the train many times and the only difference between that pitiful blur and the front of the building was the smell of booze, piss and vomit. At any hour you chose to visit the picture of humanity splashed across that place suggested that if the end wasn't nigh then it should be.

The front door led to the bar and the bar was no place to have a conversation, so Darian went to the side door and knocked. It took seconds for Caillic Docherty, the sixty-something manager of Misgearan who saw all and knew all, to open the door. No one had managed to persuade her to tell the stories of all that had passed there, the criminal chronicles of Misgearan, but there would be a lot of people lining up to hear if she did. She let Darian in without asking him what he was there for.

'I'm here to see...'

She was already walking along the corridor, ignoring him, opening the door to a small private room where Vinny was sitting. Darian went in and Caillic closed the door behind him, leaving them alone in a windowless room lit by a bare bulb with a small round table, two chairs and no room for a third.

Darian sat opposite Vinny and picked up one of the two whisky glasses filled from the half-bottle of cheap Uisge an Tuath in the middle of the table. He said, 'This is romantic.'

'Isn't it? You could lose your virginity in here and not be sure it happened, rubbed up against each other like this.'

Every room Vinny entered seemed to shrink around his booming presence, over six feet tall and with the barrel-chested build of a circus strongman. He had a large, wide face with an easy smile and twinkling eyes, pale skin that blushed red with the effort of his ebullient storytelling. He was loud and cheery and a bloody good cop and loyal friend. Among his greatest skills as a police officer was that he didn't take the challenge of life too seriously, but as he took a San Jose cigarette from the pack on the table and lit it, to hell with the smoking ban, he looked unusually serious.

Vinny said, 'You working on anything fun?'

'You call a middle-aged moron running off with other people's pension money only to be shafted by his gymslip lover fun?'

'Round here? I'd call that an average day.'

Darian said, 'So, Freya.'

'Aye, Freya. Saying her name still sends a shudder through me, but it's a different sort now. She's just disappeared and left Finn behind and he's upset about his mother not being around and that's upsetting me. He's with my mother while I'm working; she picks him up from school, which she isn't really fit for, her hip's in bits and she won't go to a doctor. The only thing I've got in common with Sherlock Holmes is that I once fell down a waterfall but even I can deduce the trouble in this. Freya's never gone missing before, never left Finn. She was an unmanageable wife, but I would never knock her ability as a mother, not even behind her back. There's no explaining it, Darian, and it needs explaining.'

'What's the search party so far?'

'I reported her missing to Cnocaid station, that's where her and Finn have been living. They'll keep an eye out for her, up above and out beyond normal because she's connected to me. We look after our own.'

Vinny had said it without thinking and didn't notice Darian's grimace. His experience of Challaid Police was not as optimistic as his friend's, as the son of a detective framed for murder and currently serving a life sentence in The Ganntair, the prison in the city. The year before Darian had also become entangled in a case that centred on a bent cop and his corrupted acolytes, a man now out of the force.

'You want me and Sholto to join the hunt?'

'I do, yeah. The reason I didn't go to the office with this is because I don't have a lot of dough, Darian, so whatever I pay you will be half a peanut at best. Sholto's always been a decent old duffer but he might be able to pluck up the courage to point out that what I'm asking for is charity and what he's running is a business. I know you need to earn.'

Darian took another sip of the rough whisky and said, 'I can keep an ear to the ground free of charge, I've got one to spare. I can ask a few questions for very little, so can Sholto. We're mercenaries, we're not bastards. Tell me what you know.'

'She dropped Finn off at my place on Friday evening, as usual, and she seemed the same as she always did, insufferable. She didn't mention any trouble, but she wouldn't anyway because only my failures get the spotlight. No hint that she wouldn't be back on Sunday afternoon for Finn, that was the routine. She just didn't show, and when I phoned to mock her timing the line was dead, not even voicemail. We went round to her house and couldn't find her. Called her friends and her work but there's been no sign of her. That was four days ago and there's been nothing. Her keeping her mouth shut for four days? No bloody way. It's something bad and every cop that can spare the time is looking and finding nothing. Right now no one has seen her since she left my place on Friday, which makes her miserable ex-husband the last person to see her. It's not good, Darian. "I want her back" might be the last words I ever thought I'd utter but that's Freya, always taking me by surprise.'

They emptied the half-bottle as they talked about Freya and Vinny's marriage. It had been a whirlwind at the start and a natural disaster by the end. As soon as it slowed down they realised they'd been spinning with the wrong person, but by then there was a child involved and that tied them together. They disliked each other with cheerful purpose, each committed to genially attacking the other without ever landing verbal blows Finn could see or hear.

It was after eight when Darian took the long walk to Mormaer Station, the cold night air helping to sober him halfway up and the journey a good opportunity to think of what he was going to say to Sholto. As with all the neatest equations, this one was pretty simple. Vinny couldn't pay them much to help, but there was much goodwill to be won from Challaid Police by helping one of their most popular members. When you're running a private detective agency under the false banner of a research company it pays to have the favour of the local law enforcers. Darian took the train down to Bank Station and walked up to his flat on the corner of Fàrdach Road and Havurn Road.

It was a small, one-bedroom place that easily contained the few fragments of Darian's life that existed outside of work. It was in a good area, though, and from the living-room window he had a view of the loch and the lights crying into the darkness around it. He sat at the table there and thought of Freya Dempsey and the couple of times he had met her. She was unfriendly but interesting, harsh but smart, tough but not wild. People like her didn't just wander off.

3

It was uncomfortable for Darian to be in Cnocaid police station, the place his father had worked, and where the anti-corruption unit Darian had broken apart was still based. Wasn't the same ACU anymore. Most, but not all, of the former officers had been pushed out and its remit severely narrowed, but the memories were the same.

Wasn't much more fun for Sholto who had worked there for years and hated every brick of the building, but it was his idea to go there as a first step in finding Freya Dempsey. Darian had told him everything Vinny knew and Sholto decided the police officially leading the search for her would probably know more, which meant Cnocaid station.

It had been an easier conversation than he'd expected that morning when Darian pitched the case to Sholto, spelling it all out, including the fact that Vinny's trousers weren't falling down because of the weight of the wallet in his pocket.

Sholto had nodded and said, 'He's quite popular, your pal Vinny, among the rest of the force, I mean.'

'He is, yeah.'

'I do enjoy getting paid for my work, but I also like being able to do it without fear of the police shutting us down. We can help him out, but I'm not making it my life's work.'

He had found out the detective with responsibility for the Freya Dempsey search was DS Irene MacNeith, and that pleased him because he had never heard of her. Cops who had worked with Sholto tended not to take him too seriously. They had introduced themselves at the front desk of the building on the corner of Kidd Street and Meteti Road and were waiting for DS MacNeith to come to them.

She was in her mid-thirties, a short woman with dark skin and shoulder-length black hair, large eyes and a squint front tooth. Her expression suggested she was going against her better instincts by talking to them. Those brown eyes were flooded with showers of contempt for the two private investigators she had been saddled with, and that annoyed Darian. In his noble opinion a person serious about achieving their aim didn't turn down help, whoever it came from, but perhaps knowing where it came from was the source of the scorn. She led them into what the plate on the door called a 'family room' where vulnerable witnesses or victims were usually questioned. The only differences between it and a typical interview room was that the table and chairs appeared to have been stolen from someone's kitchen and there was a window from which you had a charming view of the side of the building next door.

As she sat she said, 'I'll be honest with you both, if you hadn't been sent by PC Reno I wouldn't be talking to you. You're friends of his and everyone here seems to be friends of his, too, so we'll talk.'

The blunt tone with which she attacked her mention of Vinny made clear his popularity meant less to her than him being the last person to see Freya.

Darian said, 'Whatever you might think of us we're not bumbling amateurs and anything we do will be done carefully. We're all trying to find Freya Dempsey.'

'Some of the stories I've heard about you, Mr Ross, suggest bumbling would be a generous term, but you are trying to find her and that could be useful to me. I'll give you a few pointers then. There was no sign of her from the moment we're told she left her ex-husband's home on MacWilliam Drive, although the CCTV coverage in Whisper Hill is about as useful as a two-inch stepladder. It's like the Forth Rail Bridge. By the time you're done fixing one vandalised camera the last two repairs have been broken again. Someone's targeting them, probably the Creag gang, and the force have practically stopped funding replacements.'

'So you have nothing to say if she was being followed.'

'No. What we can say is that her car has also gone missing and it didn't leave the city. The Southern Road, Heilam Road and Portnancon Road are all covered by working cameras and the ferry terminal is, too. We can't find her car at all, a two-year-old light-blue Volkswagen Passat, so if you want to help the investigation you can focus on that and let me know how it goes. The registration is CX41 VMT.'

'How many people do you have working on this?'

'Officially? It's one of four missing persons cases that I and two other colleagues are working on.'

'Unofficially?'

'PC Reno has a lot of friends on the force. There are plenty of people in this station with an eye open, hoping Freya Dempsey will come into view, and I'm sure the same is true of officers in other stations. He's a boisterous and talkative person, PC Reno, the fact he's friends with you both is probably further proof of that.'

'You don't sound like you've fallen under his spell.'

DS MacNeith looked at him and said, 'When a woman goes missing do you know what the statistics are on a partner or ex-partner being involved?'

Darian said, 'In this case, misleading.'

'You told me you wouldn't bumble, Mr Ross, but you're already bumbling.'

She walked them back to the front desk and left them without a goodbye. As they headed back to where Sholto had parked his Fiat he said to Darian, 'Well, we found one woman immune to Vinny's loveable roguishness.'

'She seems to hate him. I hope it's not clouding her conduct of the search.'

'Darian, listen. I know it's hard to think about a friend like this, but you have to realise that right now Vinny ticks a lot of boxes he wouldn't want to get trapped in. He's her ex and they got along like a bull and a china shop after they split up. He was the last person who saw her, and the alibi his young son gives him is gossamer-thin. An alibi from an infant offspring isn't exactly the Rolex of cover stories. Right now he's the person at the top of DS MacNeith's list, and he's the only name on ours, even if he did hire us.'

'He's not on my list at all.'

'Then you don't have a list, you have a blank sheet of paper and a lack of imagination. If it wasn't Vinny then we have to come up with someone else who had motive and opportunity.'

'We'll start with the car. If that hasn't left the city then we can find it. We do that and it gives us a thread to pull at.'

As he opened the driver's door Sholto said, 'It does, but until then we have a case where the person who hired us is the front-running suspect. Don't know about you but that's eerily familiar and I don't like it.'

Darian tutted at more memories he wished hadn't been reawakened and got into the car.

4

THE FIRST STEP TO uncovering what had happened to the missing car was to go and speak to someone with an extensive knowledge of under-the-radar vehicles. In the spirit of using a thief to catch a thief they drove over to Bakers Moor and onto Tuit Road, an ugly reminder that not all squalor in the city lived in Earmam and Whisper Hill. These were industrial buildings where the industry was mostly carried out at night when the police were less likely to have their eyes open. It was tucked back against Bakers Hill on the east side, buried in shadows and as cold as the welcome most occupants would give a stranger. It might seem like an odd place for a car hire firm to base itself, but JJ's car hire was a specialist lender to the underfunded, the secretly industrious and the legally unfussy.

As they turned onto the patch of waste ground where the cars were parked they both spotted JJ talking to a rightly nervous young customer. Sholto parked beside a small office building in such disrepair that a solid head-butt could have sent the whole thing tumbling. It was short and flat and as they got out Sholto thought he could see a gap between the window frame and the wall.

Darian said, 'We'd better wait for him. He won't be happy if we interrupt his swindling.'

Sholto took a wander over to the nearest cars, those parked closest to the gate because they looked the most roadworthy. He ran his hand along the top of one and, as he looked at the cardboard sign on the windscreen, said, 'This one looks okay, how do you suppose it's only eight hundred quid?'

Darian shrugged and said, 'Probably various bits of different cars welded together. A lot of them are.'

It was at this moment that JJ arrived, round-faced, jaundiced, like someone had stuffed too much mince into a yellow stocking, with a long scraggly goatee beard that looked like a kid had pinned the tail on entirely the wrong donkey. Every time he spoke he sounded as though he was halfway through swallowing his teeth and determined to finish. He had an optimistic look in his beady eyes as he saw Sholto touch up a banger and said, 'You interested in that one?'

Sholto said, 'Do you have an actual whole car, like the manufacturers and safety testers intended?'

JJ looked hurt as he wiped his oil-stained hands on his oil-stained blue overalls and said, 'I'm sorry, we're just not that sort of company.'

Before they lost him to unethical outrage Darian stepped in and said, 'We need a bit of help from you mate, some information about a car we can't find. It hasn't left the city, but it isn't on the road and we've got some money that says you can't find it.'

JJ, like many avowedly dishonest people, didn't like helping those who were almost police, but a bet with some roguish private detective was just a bit of harmless fun he could profit from. 'I've got two hundred that says I can.'

Sholto grimaced at having to pay two hundred for the information but he stayed miserably silent as Darian said, 'You're on. A light blue VW Passat, twenty fifteen, number CX41 VMT. How long do you think you'll take?'

'Give me a day or two. I'll call you.'

They drove back to the office unsure of their progress. Sholto parked on Dlùth Street at the bottom of Cage Street and they went in through the side door and up the stairs to the office. They sat at their respective desks and tried to find some work to kill the day with. There were often empty periods with little to do and they tried to fill them by doing the things they assumed professionals did.

Darian said, 'Even if we find the car there's a good chance we don't find Freya with it.'

'Or who's behind her disappearance. There are a hundred ways of getting rid of a car in this city that don't leave a spot behind. It'll be the next step on the path and we have to walk it.'

'There is a chance the journey ends with us finding out Freya did a runner because she was sick of this place. We hear she was a great mother and would never leave the boy, but we don't know what was inside her head. She might be shacked up with some lover boy as we speak.'

Sholto nodded. 'Could be, but you heard what DS MacNeith said about women going missing. I've seen cases of men going walkabout because they thought they'd found a better option than carrying on with the life they had here, but women often take a more sensible approach. We should all be braced for bad news here.'

'The odds of her being picked off the street by a total stranger after leaving Vinny's place?'

'Similar to my odds of waking up tomorrow with Miss Challaid next to me and a winning lottery ticket clutched in my sweaty hand.'

'You don't play the lottery.'

'Exactly right. If Freya was picked off a public street then it was almost certainly by someone who had been following her and targeted her specifically, almost certainly someone she knew.'

There was a warning in his tone and Darian thought again about Vinny. He was a mate and had been for a couple of years, one of the most helpful cops he had ever met. Somewhere deep inside Darian's head there remained the vision of the police force he had carried as a child, the tough group of men and women motivated by a desire to make hard lives better in the unfair city of Challaid. A lot had happened in his life to chip away at that belief in the force, but nothing had been able to destroy it yet and that was because of people like Vinny. He represented all that was good about the local police, the ideals a young Darian had aspired to, and he couldn't be guilty of this. Another thing the passing of time had taught Darian was that Challaid had a smaller percentage of good and honest citizens than he had originally thought, and more who were potential targets for their investigative work.

LIBERAL PARTY WEBSITE

Liberalparty.sco

COUNCIL LEADER MORAG BLAKE GIVES SPEECH ON CHALLAID'S ECONOMIC FUTURE

Challaid city council convener Morag Blake today gave a speech to the Morgan Institute, the group representing business leaders in the city, in which she outlined the progress Challaid has made since the Liberal Party took control of the council in the 2015 elections. Speaking after the latest economic figures showed the Challaid economy back in growth, albeit at a slower than predicted rate, she made it clear that not only has the city changed, but the expectations for the city have too. Below is council leader Blake's speech.

'First of all ladies and gentlemen I want to thank you for having me here today to address the Morgan Institute, a group whose tireless work to promote and develop business opportunities, and with it employment, in Challaid I have always had the utmost respect for. I'm sure you will all want to join me in thanking Lamya Khan for her running of the institute and all the staff here at Morgan Hall, a most wonderful setting for this event.

When I was invited to speak to you on the theme of Challaid's economic journey my mind raced back to

Barton Secondary and Mr Smith's history class. I thought of Captain MacDougall being put in a rowboat in the North Atlantic by the crew of his ship after trying to swindle them, and I thought of Jack MacCoy, hanged on Stac Voror for his theft of the city's money, or Joseph Gunn being sent to Panama for his. Our city has a history of holding to account those in control of the finances, and I find it serves me well to remember it all.

All joking aside, there are indeed valuable lessons for us to learn from our economic history, where we have come from informing where we are going. When we talk about Challaid's culture we frequently talk about our language, our great writers, our role in the world, love of the sea and our sport. What we rarely talk about is what allowed all those things to flourish and that helps us to be the success we are today, our sense of entrepreneurship.

Our history is littered with great business leaders, like the Sutherlands, the Duffs and the Forsyths, but that sense of creating wealth from humble beginnings permeates every level, with ingenuity the engine of our economy. Small businesses spring up when they spot the opportunity because they know it is the very spirit of this city to have a go. It's important that we're never afraid to try, so the atmosphere encourages the sort of decision-making that necessitates an organisation like the Morgan Institute. For all our other cultural strengths it is this that provides the foundations every other part of Challaid's identity is built upon.

I want, today, to talk a little about how that spirit of endeavour and creativity has been viewed by people outside Challaid in the past and how it's viewed now. For many centuries we were seen as isolationists, a city on the edge of the map that only interacted with the rest of the world to take money from it and interfere occasionally in the Scottish political process. We were the outsiders. This, I have always felt, was something of a misleading view of a port city, but it stuck. From the Caledonian expedition to the Spanish conflict to the trade wars to the two world wars, Challaid has always done its bit, its men sacrificing all to serve the greater good for Scotland. Indeed, if you even look at the evolution of our city's name to its current, simpler spelling and pronunciation, that was due to our connections with the outside world and our desire to interact more easily. But it was something else said about us that really rankled with me and many others.

People in other parts of Scotland, perhaps other parts of the world, viewed Challaid as a city hard to trust. There was a belief that the very entrepreneurial spirit we celebrate today was something untrustworthy, a mark against us. Many read the poem 'Black Challaid' and saw it as a fair reflection of us, and in a world then so disconnected it was hard for us to argue back. Challaid was seen as a place where business was done in a way the rest of Scotland disdained, and we have long been tarred by that brush.

So what has changed? Not us. We should be proud of the companies that have such a long history here in Challaid, we should be celebrating the work they have done over the centuries to help create an environment where now companies can spring up, employ people and create wealth in our society. What has changed is how we are seen, because we are no longer isolated. In Challaid we have worked harder than any other city in Scotland to make sure all our citizens have access to superfast broadband, to make sure we are front and centre of the technological advancements that are making the world smaller every single day. It is because of that that no one can be misled and we can be seen only as we should be seen, as a bold city that encourages and supports enterprise, which relishes the opportunity to create jobs and prosperity for all of its people.

We don't want Challaid to be an urban museum like Edinburgh, and at the same time we don't want to be always chasing modernity because we've lost the identity we had, like Glasgow. Challaid must be a city that with one hand grips its past and with the other, the future. Ladies and gentlemen, our economic story has been a long one, and much has changed since that first day, when Challaid began as a place to trade, a place to do business, but some things remain the same. Our reputation, ill-deserved, for criminality and duplicity, is gone among all but the most doggedly ignorant, Challaid now recognised as a fine hub for all manner of local, national and international industries. It is together we have achieved this, and together we will achieve much more. Our past is one of bold, enthusiastic entrepreneurship, and our future is too. Thank you.'

5

THE FOLLOWING MORNING was spent hunting down as much information about Freya Dempsey as possible, which was not an awful lot. Darian had met with Vinny to get some more details about who her friends and family were and then made his way back to Cage Street, bumping into Sholto coming out of The Northern Song with their lunch.

As they walked up the stairs to the office together Sholto said, 'The problem with Freya Dempsey is that she is terribly normal.'

Darian already knew what his boss meant, but this was Sholto venturing to spread some of his many years of gathered knowledge around and Darian knew it was best to let him get it out lest the weight of it crush him. 'Vinny would say she was normally terrible.'

'That may also be true, but there was nothing remarkable about her. We're used to chasing after criminals, Darian, people who have gone missing because they have something to run away from. This is different. A woman like Dempsey, the hard part is working out where the start line is, not the finish.'

Sholto stopped to unlock the office door, putting the bag of food down and glancing along the corridor as he did. He was looking at the door of Challaid Data Services, the only other company on the top floor, and he had just opened his mouth to say something about them when he heard the phone ringing in the office. Sholto didn't enjoy hurrying and held pressure in great distaste so the need to rush caused the key to wriggle out of his fingers and drop into the carrier bag of Chinese food.

As he fumbled in the bag the phone stopped ringing and he said, 'If it was important they'll ring back.'

'Or ring Raven.'

Sholto pushed open the door at last and said, 'Now, Darian, you might think that sort of thing is funny but if you can't hear anyone else laughing you've botched the joke and I'm not hearing so much as a chuckle right now.'

Raven Investigators was a company in the south end of Bank who actually admitted to being a private detective agency. They were the biggest in Challaid and the bane of Sholto's life. A company headquartered in Edinburgh with a big budget, lots of employees, many ex-cops, and who had a reputation for playing by the rules and so got a lot of juicy contracts Sholto would have easily fallen in love with. Joking about them was considered to be in very poor taste. No message had been left on the office phone; few ever were because people didn't want to leave recordings of their business with Douglas Independent Research lying around.

'This number is on the private contact list.'

Darian went across and looked at it, not recognising the number. He returned to his desk and switched on his laptop, finding the number on his private file as he tucked into the first of his two Hoisin wraps. The phone number belonged to contact #D-09, better known to the rest of the world as JJ. They each had their own contact list, secret from the other, and Sholto's all began with S and Darian's with D. He picked up the phone and, his mouth stuffed with food, called.

'Yeah?'

'JJ, it's Darian Ross, sorry I missed you just now.'

'You sound like you're talking to me from under a duvet.'

Ignoring the irony of JJ complaining about someone else being unintelligible Darian said, 'I wish. Sorry, let me just swallow this. Right, what's your news?'

'You still ready to pay for that bet on the Passat?'

'Of course. You found it?'

'Bits of it. The thing was broken up for parts a few days ago, some of it was sent for scrap. Wasn't an old car, so the people breaking it knew something was going on but they were far too smart to ask questions. It was MacAskill's garage up in Earmam that handled the dismantling, sent parts to a few places. Only thing he could tell me was that it was a man who brought it in to be broken, late twenties, early thirties.'

'No description?'

'He was being paid to look the other way. He probably took that literally.'

Sholto had stopped eating to listen to Darian's half of the conversation, and Darian knew he needed a bit more detail. He said, 'There couldn't be any clean reason they wanted the car broken apart, could there, JJ?'

'Clean? Well, there's impress your minister clean and there's Challaid clean, if you know what I mean. There's no honest to God reason for it, not a car that new. There are reasons that aren't virgin pure but round here are common enough, this is Challaid we're talking about. Someone gets in a crash and decides to take the insurance company for a ride, getting some extra dough and a nice new car, pretend the old one was wrecked. That happens plenty. A lot of garages play along, diddle the insurers because they've got it coming to them for having such high prices. That's the Challaid way, dozens of scams like that. Don't listen to the politicians, Darian; we're the same city we always were.'

'Okay, thanks, JJ. I'll be round in the next few days for a cup of tea.'

That cup of tea would cost Darian two hundred quid. He put the phone down and looked across at Sholto, who said, 'The car was broken up?'

'Taken to MacAskill's in Earmam by a man in his late twenties or early thirties.'

'No sighting of Freya?'

'No.'

Sholto chewed furiously on a prawn and said, 'If she was picked up outside or near Vinny's flat then let's assume that was someone who got into her car. They wouldn't leave the car behind and take her on their own, that would be too much of a risk for a sensible psycho. Are we really saying that someone carjacked her in Challaid? Got into her own car and did her harm there, meaning they had to get rid of the motor?'

Darian didn't like the direction this was racing in when he said, 'What else are we saying?'

'The police will say, because they prefer to start with the obvious and climb down the ladder from there, it would make a lot more sense to say she didn't disappear outside Vinny's flat but inside it, which meant he could swipe the keys from her pocket and get rid of the car so he could pretend she had left the place. Their second suggestion would be that she was working with some lover boy on an insurance scam gone too far, but they'll start with Vinny.'

While Sholto dipped another prawn in sauce and shovelled the whole thing into his face Darian turned in his chair and looked out of the window, not hungry anymore. Knowing what had happened to the missing car was a step forward, but they were still walking in mud.

6

MacAskill's Garage was, as you would probably expect a wrecking yard to be, tucked away in a dreary part of Earmam. Sholto drove along Purcell Road, narrow with high fences on either side of it that blocked access to a bunch of warehouses and industrial units that didn't want people wandering in off the street and seeing what they were up to. MacAskill's had a large gate for cars, vans and trucks to get through, which was closed and locked, and a smaller one for people, which wasn't.

Sholto parked out on the street and said, 'Looks like we're getting some unwanted exercise.'

They walked in through the gate and found themselves in a valley of car parts, the empty shells of vehicles piled up on either side of them. The innards had been picked clean by the vulture that ran the place and the frames stacked and left to rust in the hard rain falling over Challaid. They were way up over head height so neither Darian nor Sholto could see past them and they led in a straight line to a sharp corner, forcing anyone who entered to walk along the muddy ground for a few valuable seconds before they had the chance to turn and see the building. It felt like the defence mechanism of a paranoid owner so it wasn't a surprise when a dog came hurtling round the corner to check on them. Rather than a snarling security beast, however, it was a border collie with a shiny coat and its tongue lolling out of the side of its mouth. It looked delighted by its newfound company.

Sholto didn't share the joy, stepping back behind Darian and saying, 'Bloody hell, a junkyard dog. That's just what I need, to get torn to pieces in a car graveyard.'

The dog had reached Darian and turned sideways to walk with him, pressing itself against his leg so he would reach down and stroke it behind the ear. As he did Darian said, 'Well, he might be crazy because I think he just wants to be your friend, don't you, boy?'

'It's not his taste I'm worried about, it's his teeth.'

They turned the corner to see MacAskill's Garage ahead on their right, a single-storey brown brick building with a flat roof and two large garage doors that you could squeeze a small truck into if you really needed to. Both doors were open and there were no cars out in the open square in front of the building. There was a large yellow machine opposite the garage that looked like a small crane and a fat green box the size of a shipping container that Darian assumed was the crusher. A man in his sixties with silver hair and blue overalls sauntered out of the garage with a cigarette in his mouth to see what his adorable alarm had gone running to greet.

Darian said, 'Joe MacAskill?'

'Yeah. You the pair JJ was on about?'

'How did you guess?'

He nodded and said, 'You look like the pair he was talking about. Come in.'

Neither of them knew whether to take that as an insult or not so followed MacAskill in without reply. The look he gave them and then the dog as he patted it told them what little cheer he had was reserved for his canine pal, so there was no need to aspire to good manners.

Darian asked, 'Did JJ tell you what we're looking for?'

MacAskill had deep lines on his face, a weathered charm to him. 'Told me you were wanting detail on the cove that brought the Passat for removal, didn't say much else. Said you would pay.'

'Yeah, I thought he'd remember to mention that. We will, if you can help us.'

MacAskill watched Sholto who was nervously eyeing the dog. Every time the animal made eye contact with him it thought it was going to get a scratch so shuffled a little closer, which caused Sholto to move back a half-step and confuse the dog.

MacAskill said, 'She won't bite you. Might lick you to death, but that's about it.'

'Aye, well, I'll be dead either way so I'd rather avoid it.'

MacAskill shook his head. 'Come through to the office, I'll show you what you're looking for.'

On the desk in his office he opened a laptop and switched on a media player, selecting the file dated the day the car was destroyed. He pressed play and they watched in silence as the footage showed the car coming in the front gate first thing in the morning. He opened another file that showed footage from a camera just inside the garage, the man getting out of the car and talking to MacAskill on the threshold. The new arrival was wearing a coat, a baseball cap and dark glasses. Darian paused the footage on the best angle it had of his face but the quality was too poor.

Darian said, 'Can you remember anything about him?'

'He was youngish. Twenties, maybe thirty. He was in a hurry, but that isn't unusual. Local, I think.'

Sholto said, 'A man comes in dressed to conceal and you do business with him, no questions?'

'A man comes in with cash in his hand and he can have on a fat suit, a plastic moustache and a plasticine nose for all I care. I trained as a mechanic, not a minister of the kirk.'

'Would you recognise him if you saw him again?'

'Couldn't say that I would, no. You two can look over that, I'll be outside waiting for you to pay me for my help.'

MacAskill and the dog went out of the office and left them alone to look at the paused footage.

Darian said, 'Could be anyone.'

'Could be Vinny.'

Darian groaned, thought about saying it was too small to be him but stopped, the coat and the angle making it hard to rule anyone out.

Sholto said, 'Doesn't help us a great deal then.'

'I don't think that's likely to be Vinny, too narrow.'

'I'm afraid think and likely aren't going to cut it in court, kid, we need actual proof. I'm going to go out and see how little I can persuade Cerberus's master this is worth. You watch it again and see if your younger eyes can make anything of it. Oh, and save it onto something for goodness' sake. Make sure we have a copy before the dog pees on the laptop or something.'

Darian watched both videos again on his own, trying to persuade himself it couldn't possibly be Vinny and not quite managing.

7

THE MOST IMPORTANT thing about working *with* the police is to act like you're working *for* them. Know your place. Sholto had always intended to ram that lesson home but didn't get round to it in time, instead having to watch as he and Darian were dragged into battle with Challaid Police's rotten anti-corruption unit and sort of won. Since then Sholto had been careful to make sure he mentioned the value of deference towards the good people of Challaid Police at least once a day, twice if the opportunity came along.

As they drove towards Meteti Road and Cnocaid police station Sholto said to Darian, 'Just you remember not to get chippy with her, no matter what she says about Vinny.'

Sholto did what he always did when he was trying to talk and drive at the same time, which was to slow down, and he wasn't winning any time trials to begin with.

Darian said, 'You concentrate on the road now and I promise I'll concentrate on keeping my mouth shut at the station if we make it there alive.'

'I don't know why you always criticise my driving, it teaches you patience.'

As if to dispute the point an irate driver, which could describe most motorists in Challaid, who was stuck behind them, sounded his horn and Sholto was spurred to put his foot down. The drive to the station still took longer than necessary and the adventure of a flustered Sholto trying to reverse the Fiat into a narrow parking space in the station car park could rival any theme park for intensity.

Darian said, 'That wouldn't make a good impression, reversing right into some detective's car. Might even be DS MacNeith's.'

'You know, I'm becoming convinced that there are times when you're not even trying to help.'

They went in through the back of the station and waited while a sulky desk sergeant called DS MacNeith to come down and retrieve her guests. When she did she looked about as thrilled as her colleague by their arrival, but showed them into a cold interview room where they sat across the desk from her like a couple of obviously guilty suspects.

She said, 'So what have you found out about the car?'

Sholto said, 'We found out that it isn't a car anymore, it's a pile of scrap metal and some reused parts. A man took it to a garage and had it broken up on Saturday, less than twenty-four hours after she went missing.'

'Do you have a description of this man?'

'Tall, white, late twenties, early thirties, probably local accent. That's about it I'm afraid, not exactly pinpointing the target.'

She looked at Darian and said, 'Do you think PC Reno could pass for early thirties?'

'He could, but so could tens of thousands of others in this city. There's a chance it wasn't the person who took her, if she's been taken. It might be a third party the car was passed on to afterwards. Some insurance setup, perhaps.'

At the mention of an insurance scam DS MacNeith gave a little twitch. Darian spotted it and said, 'Are you looking at an insurance angle? Was there something to do with the insurance on that car we should know?'

'Not that you should know, but I'll tell you. It was involved in a minor accident out on Kidd Street a couple of months ago, no one hurt, no great damage done. We didn't connect the two events.'

'So she claimed insurance on the car?'

'Not on her own policy, that was the thing. The owner of the other car picked up the tab on his, or theirs, to be more exact. The car was owned by the Sutherland Bank, used exclusively by Harold Sutherland, one of the vice-chairmen, although our record of the crash shows one of his staff was driving it and he was in the back at the time. We've checked all her financial records and she made no personal claim on the car, although there was a receipt for the repairs the bank's insurers paid for.'

'But that doesn't mean there wasn't a scam here.'

'It also doesn't mean there was.'

'Let's say Harold Sutherland offered to pay all the expenses because his driver was at fault and she thought it would be a breeze to swindle him out of some money, pretend the car had been much more badly damaged than it seemed. Maybe she claims a fortune, he smells a decomposing rat and gets the bank security people to investigate so she does a runner. They can be scary bastards, those security people.'

'So who dumped the car for her?'

'A friend. A lover. Could have been anyone that was in on it with her.'

'I know what you're thinking, Mr Ross, you're thinking that if she was trying to hoover the wallet of a Sutherland family member and ran away to hide of her own accord then the next person you want to speak to is a member of the Sutherland family. I know PC Reno hired you and he's your friend, but take my advice as someone smarter than both of you. Don't interfere any further in a police investigation. Some of us in this station have goodwill for Douglas Independent Research for forcing rehabilitation of the anti-corruption unit, but don't assume it will stretch to the end of my tether.'

Sholto jumped in and said, 'Oh, you don't have to worry about that, we're not going to chase Harold Sutherland, not at all. We'll stay well out of the way of smarter people than us, won't we, Darian?'

The kick under the table Sholto gave him was neither subtle nor necessary, and Darian said, 'I won't do anything to get in the police investigation's way. You have my word.'

They left the station having delivered their update to DS MacNeith. Sholto led the way and neither of them said a word until they were back in the car and had driven along the side of the building and back out onto Meteti Road.

Sholto said, 'I wish you wouldn't lie to the police like that.'

'I wish you wouldn't make me. And I wish you wouldn't kick me.'

'Too good an opportunity to miss. So what are you already plotting?'

'I'm going to talk to Vinny and he's going to help me talk to a Sutherland.'

Collected Prophesies of Seer Annasach

CHAPTER 16 – THE CITY OF CHALLAID

Such a place, born in the darkness of a frozen winter morn, and to return unsought, punished for a spirit of wantonness undimmed by the touch of places beyond. On the stone where the first man stood so shall stand another to herald the slip of the sun to ever darkness.

This hill will be riven asunder and men will step inside and such men will disappear from this place.

In this place a prince will be loved by all men, his destiny to sit upon the stone. In the street where I lay in arms a man of peace will strike this prince down with a blade, and mourning will follow.

The last stone of Dubhan Abbey to fall will be the last stone of Challaid to fall, and will be the end of this place.

On the day that greed so holds the rulers of Challaid that true friends are dismissed and distant needs ignored then the punishment shall see the mouth of the loch dry to nothing and this place will have no route to the world, to be forgotten.

A man shall see the edge of the world, and from this evil place bring home with him the devil's laugh, and it shall fill the mouths of the young and the old and will leave no house silent of its horror.

The wealth of kings shall reside in Challaid, but the blood of any that sits upon it shall turn to poison.

The blood of Challaid's brother will poison the world, bringing man from millions to thousands and hastening the dark end.

That the city of Challaid shall stretch beyond the mountains and reach to the lowlanders, and that all men from all the world shall seek it.

Buildings of the city shall rise above the hills and look out to the sea.

Ten score of ships will pour into the loch, thick that the water will be covered and the waves pushed down, the loch made wooded land, and on these ships will be the warriors of three nations, and with coldness to their bones will attack Challaid and its people with axes.

The hero of this place will ensure the glory of the king and country with the blood of people unseen, in lands of power and wealth.

When men of the north hold Challaid to their order winter shall last four years and no crops will grow.

The last man of Challaid will stand on the bank, alone in the place he loves most as the cold water rises around him and he will not move. The water will rise to cover his mouth and then his nose, as he falls below the water at the end of us.

Seer Annasach MacFie was born around 1380 and died in 1426. He was born in Challaid and spent the early part of his life there. He left around 1400, by which time he was already gaining fame for his ability to see events of the future, travelling Scotland to share his gifts with the great houses of the day, including many royals. He was considered a great showman, never revealing his true first name, his long beard and bright blue eyes striking, and his public appearances were said to always draw a crowd. Some of his predictions were characterised by self-interest, suggesting favourable treatment for those who had helped him such as the monks of Dubhan Abbey and the Lord of the Isles, and a hatred of the Scandinavians that had unknown origins. Many of his predictions were petty and inconsequential, relating to the fortunes of the great houses that were offering him shelter at the time, but of those that were genuine he was said to be a passionate guard, going as far as threatening, and perhaps even carrying out, acts of violence against those who doubted him.

8

THERE ARE ONLY THREE parks worthy of the name in Challaid and two of them are barely large enough to contain an exuberant frisbee thrower. It's strange that we have so few green spaces in a city this size. It's been said the reason there's been no call for more is that if you stand on the street in the north-east of Challaid facing south you can look to your left and see Whisper Hill, Dùil Hill and Bakers Hill, look straight ahead and see Stac Voror and Gleann Fuilteach, and look to your right and see Loch Eriboll. You would have to suffer extreme long sightedness to miss the mass of concrete and brick sprawled out between you and those landmarks, but there is a true sense that wherever you stand in the city of Challaid the wilderness is pawing at your peripheral vision.

The one park that lives up to the billing is Sutherland Park, right in the middle of the Bank district and the heart of the city. Major buildings surround it on all four sides, but within the ornate black railings that surround it there are trees and walkways, some rough heather and Loch Bheag, a small patch of water that had been the largest of five before the others were drained and concreted over, even Loch Bheag shrunk from its apparently larger original size. Nothing is allowed to inconvenience the expansion of the rich.

Darian went in through St Andrew Gate, the large black metalwork made from the guns of the ship of the same name that had been on the original Caledonia expedition, directly opposite the Sutherland Bank headquarters on the east side of the park. He walked with the speed of a man who needed to warm up, getting to the white marble fountain dedicated to Isobel Barton where he had agreed to meet Vinny. The cop was there ahead of him, broad and bold, a man built for the rugged area he patrolled and not the genteel surrounds of the park. Here he looked like a brute just waiting for the right target to wander past so he could cheerfully mug them.

He nodded and said, 'Darian, mate, what's the news saying?'

'Maybe something not terrible. We've found out a couple of things that might help us track her down. Did you know she'd been in a minor car crash a couple of months ago?'

Vinny, wrapped in a thick coat, said, 'Yeah, she moaned about something, getting shunted by another driver and it being their fault. Everything is someone else's fault with Freya. She couldn't pin the blame for that shit on me so she didn't say anything else about it. Is it relevant?'

'It's worth looking at. Her car was taken to a garage and broken up for parts a day after she went missing. It might be... did she tell you who she crashed into?'

'No, just that she was definitely a safer bloody driver than them.'

'Huh, that's strange. The car she hit was owned by Harold Sutherland. It was his chauffer behind the wheel but he was in the back at the time. Maybe she didn't even see Sutherland, I don't know, but her not telling you fits with a theory I have. She has a minor bump that's Sutherland's driver's fault and realises she can milk it. Instead of the small repairs the car needed Freya claims for a lot more and panics when they rumble her, gets rid of the car and goes into hiding. She doesn't tell you because you're a cop, and, well, she knows she won't get much but laughter from you anyway.'

Throughout most of that Vinny had been shaking his head like it was caught in the wind. 'No, Darian, no way. You don't know her like I'm unlucky enough to. Freya can be sneaky when it suits her but there's no way on God's blue earth she would go in for scamming people like that, not a single bloody chance. And let's say she did, which she wouldn't, but we'll play make-believe. You think she'd run away from someone challenging her on it? Come off it. You know her at least well enough to understand that if she was caught with bright red hands she would find a way of claiming they proved her innocence. That whole theory is a nonstarter.'

He said the last few words with the sympathetic tone of a cop who knew the feeling of seeing a perfectly good idea being hacked to death by other people's logic. Darian shrugged and said, 'That leaves us with the Sutherland connection. It might be nothing, but the car being destroyed is going to be an angle for the police, I've told DS MacNeith about it.'

'Yeah, she'll dig into it, and I'd rather get my spade in the ground first because given half a chance she'll smash my skull in with hers. Good job I'm the wisdom-spewing mentor of an actual human Sutherland.'

'Your twelve-year-old partner in crime prevention.'

'He's not twelve, he just looks it. He's twenty... something. Come on, we'll take the train up to Whisper Hill and pay him a visit.'

PC Philip Sutherland was twenty-four and a cop at Dockside station in Whisper Hill, traditionally the hardest beat to walk in Challaid. It was said his mega-rich parents had objected to him joining the police force instead of going into the family business of hoarding other people's money and had pulled strings to get him placed in the worst situation possible, thinking he would soon come running back into their welcoming arms. Most often paired with Vinny, he had turned out to be an excellent cop and embraced not only Dockside station but the whole frenetic, absurd, dangerous Whisper Hill experience.

He lived on Chester Street, a short, straight road with four-storey flats on either side that looked like the ugly arse ends of more appealing buildings. It was hard to believe an architect had conceived them to look this way, but somewhere in the council building there would be 1960s designs for them that someone must have shamefacedly signed. Because the city is relatively narrow and was expanded with the sort of gleeful lack of forethought we've turned into an art form we have a lot of short streets, another issue that makes getting around quickly a near impossibility. This one felt like a street designed for bleak experiences and yet nothing was damaged or out of place. When they went into the building it was clean and the hall looked like it had been recently painted a fresh shade of beige.

Darian said, 'Did we stumble through the back of a wardrobe or something because this doesn't feel like a Whisper Hill block of flats.'

Vinny said, 'You noticed that, huh? He doesn't talk about it, wee Phil, but I reckon the almighty family send people round to keep the place spick and span and free from the sort of everyday human grime that interacting with working-class bastards like me might bring. I don't think he likes them doing it, but then he hasn't moved somewhere else, has he?'

Phil was on the top floor and he was expecting them, Vinny having called from the train not to ask him if they could come but to tell him. His flat was small like all the others, two bedrooms, one bathroom and a living area, but there were little hints that this occupant was sitting atop a trust fund that would one day make him incalculably rich. Small luxuries, and the occasional style over substance choice, but nothing too obvious, and nothing worth going out of your way to rob the place for.

In the living area they sat at the small, round dining table and Philip Sutherland, skinny and baby-faced, probably fed up with being called cute, perfect teeth and carefully styled hair, said, 'So what happened with my uncle Harold?'

'Right, well, you know my heartache has gone missing and I'm on the hunt for her, and it turns out she managed to drive her car into your uncle's wagon a couple of months ago. What we hear is that your uncle accepted it was his chauffer's fault and paid out, and then the next thing that happened to Freya's car is that it was ripped to bits at a wrecker's yard the day after she disappeared. I doubt very much there's a connection because the only way there would be is if she was pulling a scam and that's beneath her highness, but, shit, I have to check everything here. DS MacNeith will go calling on your illustrious family about it so I want to go, too. Do you think they'll have any record of what your uncle paid Freya?'

'Bloody hell, yes, they have records for every penny any member of the family or the bank spends. Literally every penny. If a family member threw a coin down a well someone would abseil down with a torch to find out how much it was worth. Pretty sure they have a file somewhere listing every penny of pocket money my father gave me. My mother gave me more because she's the Sutherland.'

Vinny said, 'Listen to this, Darian. Your parents are still married, Phil, so how come you have her surname?'

He didn't enjoy his family traditions being prodded for Vinny's amusement but he said, 'That's how we do it. My father keeps his name but the kids are always Sutherlands. If you don't carry the family name you won't get shares in the bank.'

Darian said, 'Well, you sure screwed up their plans for you. You ever think of switching to your father's name?'

'No, I'm a Sutherland, I'm not ashamed of that. We might be poison but we're still a family and I still get on well with most of them.'

'So why become a cop?'

'I could spend years sitting in boardrooms listening to people moan about pension fund deficits and South East Asian liquidity, or I could have drunken sailors try to punch my lights out and drug dealers try to run me down with their gaudy cars. It really wasn't a difficult choice at all.'

'So could you find out about any payment to Freya?'

'I can, yeah, and I can do better than that for you, Vinny. If you want I can get you a face-to-face with Uncle Harold. He's a good sort; he'll help if he can.'

'Great, let's do it.'

This was the first time Darian had heard Phil speak and he was surprised by how normal he was. He had expected every Sutherland to speak as if he had a bunch of grapes wedged in the back of his throat. Yeah, he had a posh accent, less phlegmy and softer on the vowels than his working-class colleague, but this offspring of the elite was likeable and friendly and he was going to get them a meeting with someone from the very highest branch of the mighty family tree.

9

BEFORE EIGHT O'CLOCK the following morning a group of four men made their way up the steps and through the grand front door of the Sutherland Bank headquarters on East Sutherland Square. This was a family with a perverse obsession with projecting humility while at the same time slapping their name on every damn thing they owned, which was a lot. The group was led by someone who knew the way, PC Philip Sutherland, a man who should have spent his working life inside the building. Behind him were Darian, Vinny and Sholto, three men who lacked the confident air of their leader.

The hall of the Sutherland Bank was colossal, high and wide enough for a Harris's hawk to get lost in and, it felt like, the Isle of Harris itself to just about fit in. As they walked across to the reception desk, staffed by six people, Sholto said, 'I'm sweating like a bank robber here. I should have brought a towel, or a sponge. People are going to be falling and breaking their necks on the puddles I'm leaving, and I can't afford to be sued by the sort of people who work here.'

There were two things that always made Sholto sweat: rich people and dogs. He was safe from the latter here but the former were unavoidable. People tended to think of the Sutherland building as a grand sort of place because it was big and old. The front half of it, which could pass for a cathedral, was built on the site of the bank's previous headquarters in the early eighteenth century, with a huge extension going onto the back around a century later. The only part the public tended to see was that entrance hall, the towering room with balconies around the first- and second-floor levels, and the scale of it could deceive you into believing it was beautiful. The truth was that every part of it was plain. There was no hint of imagination in anything, as though the builders had finished their work and no one had thought to tell the decorators it was their turn. The hall was huge because when it was opened it was a functioning bank the public used so space was needed for them, whereas now it was the reception area for the headquarters of a corporate giant. The reception desk was dark brown and plain, the tiles beneath their feet dark grey and without design, the walls unadorned.

The other three hovered shiftily by the desk while Phil spoke to the woman behind it and told her they had an appointment with Harold Sutherland. He didn't tell her he'd been able to get an appointment at such short notice because he was the man's nephew. Darian looked to his left at the security. Two guards were sitting on chairs across the hall from them, tucked in at the side of the room. They were unobtrusive enough to make sure you didn't feel intimidated, but watching just blatantly enough to make sure you realised that one dodgy move would see you rugby tackled across the tiles, out of the door, down the steps and into the middle of the road.

The receptionist had checked and confirmed they were all entitled to head deeper into the building. As she handed him a security pass she said to Phil, 'If you take the main lifts past the security door up to the third floor and when you get there go straight ahead, eventually the corridor will turn into two open-plan spaces and you want the one on your right.'

Phil smiled, having been raised to be too polite to tell her he knew his way around the building because he had visited many times as a child, and said, 'Thank you.'

They went through security and took the lift up, packed in with four other people as the bank began to fill up with its resident desperate money grabbers. A couple of them looked at Sholto and wondered just what exactly he was so nervous about, and the more he was watched the more erratic his facial expressions became.

Phil led them with the confidence of a man who needed no directions, along the corridor, through another security door and across to the open area he knew his uncle worked from. There were about a dozen desks in the open-plan office, all of them tidy with no personal touches, no pictures on the walls and nothing to suggest this was a fun place to work. Phil led them across to a desk outside an office door where a woman in her fifties was settling in to start a day's work.

Phil said, 'Good morning, Mrs Robin, is my uncle in yet?'

She looked up at him and smiled with the warmth of someone who considered herself closer to family than staff and said, 'Yes, he is, go right in.'

Harold Sutherland's office kept the same glum tone as the rest of the building – no individual tokens and nothing that could be described as decorative or attractive. The closest thing to a luxury was the window with a view of the park, but that seemed accidental as one side of the bank inevitably had to face the nice scenery. Darian was surprised to note that a man who had been club chairman of Challaid FC for nearly a decade didn't have any memorabilia or photos of their triumphs at his place of work.

Harold Sutherland got up from behind his desk and reached out a hand, saying, 'It's good to see you, Philip; it's been too long since you were in the bank.'

'You say that every time I see you and I keep telling you it makes no sense for me to visit a place I don't work at.'

Harold sighed with a smile on his face and obviously

decided not to poke the touchy subject any harder. He had great affection for his nephew and no wish for an argument with him, certainly not when three strange strangers were filing into the room behind him. It took the best part of a minute for handshakes, introductions and everyone to get seated in front of the cheap-looking desk; time enough for Darian to realise that Harold sat with his back to the window so that he couldn't even have that small pleasure distract him while he worked.

'I understand this is about the car crash a couple of months ago?'

Vinny said, 'Yes, the woman involved is my ex-wife, Freya, and she's gone missing since it happened. One notable thing is that her car was destroyed at a wrecker's yard the day after she was last seen, so we're working backwards through its history to see if it might have something to do with all this. What do you remember about the accident?'

Harold nodded, pushed his glasses up the bridge of his nose and said, 'I do remember it well. I wouldn't say it to her because she seemed, well, fiery, but I think it was probably her fault; she pulled out when she shouldn't have. She was exceedingly insistent that she wasn't to blame and I didn't want a scene. It happened on Kidd Street so there were plenty of people around and I thought agreeing to pay for it would take the sting out of the tail. It all only took three or four minutes before a replacement car picked me up.'

Phil said, 'And she made a claim?'

'Yes, she did. I remember signing off on it because it reminded me of the accident. It was, if I remember rightly, about six hundred pounds, but I can have someone dig out the receipt for an exact number.'

That ended any speculation she was trying to rip him off. People didn't go on the run for the sake of fiddling six hundred quid, not even in Challaid.

Darian said, 'Did you have any other contact with Freya?'

'No, I assume I must have given her my office contact details, or perhaps Will, my driver, did, so that she could put the claim in. But, no, that was it.'

'Could your driver have had any further contact with her?'

'Will? I don't know, I don't think so. He's never mentioned her to me again although that doesn't mean a lot. I don't think he appreciated her blaming him for the accident. You could ask him. I can call across the road to Eideard's Tower where the drivers wait. We don't have room for them in here so they're next door. This place wasn't built with the modern needs of the company in mind, I'm afraid, and we have no room left to expand.'

'If it's no trouble.'

He looked at Vinny as he said, 'No trouble at all. I know you've been looking out for Philip while he's been working with you and the family appreciates that. I'll do whatever I can to help.'

A quick phone call and some hurried handshakes and they were out of the office and back in the lift, Sholto beginning to breathe properly again, Vinny and Phil looking like they both understood this was going to be a waste of time and Darian trying to take in the whole robotic, unblinking, unfriendly atmosphere of the place.

10

THEY NEEDED THEIR security passes to get out through
the guarded door at the back of the bank and onto
MacAlpin Road. From there they just had to turn
right and cross the road to Eideard's Tower. It was a
circular building that had gone up not long after the
first part of the Sutherland building in the early 1700s,
and at the time it would have been a tall and majestic
thing. It wasn't built by the Sutherlands; it was instead
a watchtower that served to advertise the paranoia of
Eideard Brann, a man strange enough to be locked up
but rich enough to be dismissed as eccentric and left to
his own devices. In the centuries since it had fallen into
disrepair, then been bought by the Sutherlands because
it was next door, with new buildings around it turning
it into a place of unremarkable size and mediocre
function. Modernity has a habit of trampling across the
past like that.

Disappointing as it was to see a striking old building put to such poor use the simple fact was that no one else wanted to own the watchtower. It had no historical significance, being nothing more than a rich man's curious whim, and its only achievement was not falling over during one of the hundreds of winter storms it had lived through. The cost of keeping it upright was more than the council considered worthy, so the Sutherlands got to own their odd neighbour.

The tower where the drivers waited was a thirty-second walk across the road; they had to be close enough to run to the multi-storey car park opposite the bank and round to pick up the executives at the front door at the drop of an expensive hat. Phil led them into a small reception area that needed its lights on all day because there were no windows, just the light coming in from the open door. As Phil stopped by the reception desk a thick wooden door at the side of the room, that looked like it might have been there since the place went up, opened slowly and a man stepped out. He was in his late twenties and had a sour expression that showed no surprise at seeing them.

He said, 'I'm Will Dent. Come through here.'

Dent spoke with all the joy of a man on death row whose last meal had turned up burned. The four of them followed him into a room that was supposed to be a kitchen because a sink had been added and a microwave stood on a counter, but the madness of its creator was still on display. There was one small, high window near the ceiling, grated and set in the remarkably thick wall. There was a long, sturdy, wooden dining table that filled the room, one wall curving to make it feel smaller, and they all sat at it.

Darian took the lead. 'We just wanted to know what you remembered of the crash you were in with Freya Dempsey a couple of months ago on Kidd Street. All the details you can remember.'

He shrugged. 'It was her fault, that's about all I do remember. She pulled out and hit me, another car came from here to get us, that was it.'

When he spoke it was mostly out of the left side of his mouth, the right appearing to stay half shut, and it sounded like he was picking every word reluctantly. He looked at the faces of the four men staring back at him, clearly under pressure and unsure why it took so many to ask about a minor prang.

Darian said, 'You must remember more than that. I would hope it's not every day you crash into someone. Even your employers don't get to play bumper cars in the streets.'

'I didn't crash into her, she crashed into me. It was only minor anyway.'

Sholto, feeling more at ease with staff than the fabulously wealthy who employed them, said, 'You wouldn't be much of a gentleman if you got out of the car and ignored her and I'm sure you're something of a gentleman. What did you say to her?'

Dent shrugged again, looked to the side and said, 'I can't remember. Told her she shouldn't have pulled out when she did, something like that. That was it.'

Sholto said, 'That was it?'

'Probably, I think so.'

Dent spoke like a man afraid that in every word might lurk the kernel of truth that would choke him. It may have been because he was afraid of saying something that contradicted his boss and got him the sack, or his fear might have travelled from a further, darker place.

Sholto said, 'You must have given her a number, though, so that she could put a claim in.'

'Uh, yeah, I suppose so. A card or something, probably.'

'And you gave her the card, not Mr Sutherland?'

'Maybe, I don't know, I can't remember. Look, that was two months ago, right, and it wasn't that big a deal. I don't know what your problem is here.'

Sholto gave him a smile that was supposed to indicate he knew more than he was letting on and said, 'I don't know why you're getting so worked up. I'm just asking you a few harmless questions. Have you spoken to Freya Dempsey since the crash, any time in the weeks since?'

Quietly he said, 'No.'

'You weren't in contact with her when she called about the claim for her car?'

'No. I'm a driver, I don't handle insurance stuff.'

There was silence for a few seconds before Phil said, 'Okay, thanks, Will, we'll let you go now.'

They had less than they needed but all they were going to get so the four of them left the tower and walked back round to East Sutherland Square. As they marched two abreast Sholto said, 'Of the two thousand or so shifty-looking buggers I've questioned in my time I think he might crack the top hundred and fifty.'

Phil said, 'He was certainly nervous. Might not mean much, might just be scared of losing his job. Uncle Harold likes to keep the same people around for as long as possible, and he pays them well if he likes them. It's a cushy number to lose for a man whose only skill is driving.'

Vinny grunted and said, 'Well, my Spidey senses are telling me he knows more than he's willing to let on, and I think he might be a lead worth following. We have to skip on up to Docklands, though; we have a shift in the pig market starting in half an hour we're already going to be late for.'

He was looking at Darian when he said it, almost with an expression of pleading. Darian said, 'Don't worry, we'll have an eyeball stuck to Dent for the rest of the day and night.'

Vinny and Phil went north in Phil's car to start their working day at Docklands police station and Darian and Sholto got into Sholto's Fiat.

Darian said, 'I'll get a motor from JJ for the day and watch Dent. I take it you're going to call DS MacNeith to let her know about our progress.'

'Don't say it like I'm sticking my tongue in her ear and a knife in your back. This is a good lesson for you. We're not cops, which means we have to suck up to those who are hard enough to inhale the bastards.'

Darian couldn't, and didn't want to, argue. He had more interesting things to do than debate the strategy of Douglas Independent Research with its owner.

11 May 2018
HAROLD SUTHERLAND UNVEILS MACBAIN
PAINTING AT TALL AN RÌGH

A large crowd of dignitaries gathered at Tall an Rìgh on Macaulay Road as Harold Sutherland, chairman of Challaid Art Foundation, unveiled a recently purchased Rachel Macbain painting, *The Gaelic Queen at Camp*. The painting, bought by the charity for the gallery two months ago from a private owner in California for a sum believed to be in excess of two million pounds, was revealed in its new spot in the atrium gallery in a grand unveiling that brought many recognisable faces to the event.

In his speech Mr Sutherland said, 'It is a great honour for Challaid Art Foundation to be able to present this truly special piece of work, not just for what it brings to Tall an Rìgh but what it brings to the entire city of Challaid. Our hope is that it can prove to be another step on our great city's evolution as a place of art and culture, and bring more recognition to the great artists, writers and poets of our history, among them Rachel Macbain. Over the years Tall an Rìgh has been at the forefront of promoting Challaid as a place of real influence in the art world, and with the crowds we anticipate this painting will draw that influence should only grow further.'

The painting has been described as one of the finest

examples of MacBain's bleak style and ingenious use of light, a dark scene of The Gaelic Queen at fireside, only her face and hair clear while the remainder of the scene is partially lit by the fire and moonlight. CAF have justified their spending on the painting by saying they believe having such a piece back in the city where it was painted will draw many visitors to Tall an Rìgh and raise the standing of the city among culture tourists, making such a large outlay worthwhile.

Harold Sutherland, who is thought to have provided much of the funding, is the first member of his family to have taken a prominent role in either the cultural or charitable sector in the city. For generations the generous funding of Tall an Rìgh, and other institutions around the city, came from the Duff, Stirling and MacBeth families, jokingly referred to as the No Sutherlands Club.

'My family has always taken great pride in helping to provide the economic environment in which institutions like this can thrive,' Harold Sutherland told the *Gazette*. 'Our role has always been behind the scenes, and our involvement in CAF, Challaid FC and other organisations doesn't mark a change of policy, merely a moving of the spotlight toward us.'

There has been some criticism of the painting's arrival in Challaid as some have argued such a sum could have been better spent, pointing out that the gallery has failed to instigate a strategy to use the painting to draw more interest to art either through a long suggested but never implemented programme of free visits for schools or with a strategy to attract people from poorer backgrounds.

None of these concerns were evident in the gilded surrounds of the gallery as special guests, including Tall an Rìgh patron Prince Alastair and the arts minister, enjoyed the occasion. The event passed late into the night in high spirits as the always charming Harold Sutherland and his equally impressive staff ensured that one of the biggest cultural events in recent years in Challaid lived up to its billing.

11

WHILE SHOLTO WAS talking to DS MacNeith, Darian was picking up a fourteen-year-old Ford Focus from JJ's yard and paying him for the info previously provided. They stood beside the car and Darian said, 'I'll need her for the night. Might be back tomorrow, or I might keep her longer.'

'That's okay, Dar, there's no queue waiting to use her.'

'Will she last a few days?'

JJ shrugged. 'She's soldiered on this long, so she's either good for a few more months or ready to collapse in a heap underneath you. The fun is in the finding out.'

It was on the third turn of the key that it started and Darian heard JJ give a small cheer that contained a hint of surprise. He pulled out of the yard and headed for Bank and MacAlpin Road where he could watch Eideard's Tower, ready to follow Will Dent into a dark Challaid night. Finding somewhere to park was as much fun as usual in the city. On the fourth time circling the block he saw someone pulling out and slipped into the vacant place by crossing a lane of traffic and nipping in front of someone coming the other way already indicating to enter the same gap.

After an hour his mobile rang, Sholto's name on the screen. 'Hello.'

'It's me, Sholto.'

He always announced himself, seemingly unaware that his name flashed across the screen on other people's phones just as theirs did on his. 'Yeah, how did your squealing to MacNeith go?'

'I got three eye rolls and a curt thank you. If we were twelve I'm pretty sure she would have given me a wedgie.'

'Still time.'

'Well, I found out something that might be of interest to you. Are you still watching Dent?'

'I'm watching the tower, no sign of the driver yet.'

'You might be in for a long night. I just saw that Harold Sutherland has a big thing on tonight at Tall an Rìgh. He's unveiling some grim-looking painting he paid the gross domestic product of Luxembourg for. That starts at half seven, so they won't be finished until... Well, I have no idea how long it takes to unveil a painting, do you? Five seconds to lift the veil and then however long it takes rich people to get drunk and congratulate themselves. But if Dent's working it you could be in for a late one.'

'If Phil's right about his uncle always using the staff he likes then he will be.'

'Phil. That doesn't sound right, it should be Philip. A kid that posh needs at least two syllables. Let me know how you get on.'

It was boring but that wasn't a novel experience for Darian. He had long reconciled himself to the fact that doing a good job rarely meant racing through the city at high speed or chasing thugs down alleyways and over fences. It wasn't until half past five that Dent finally left the tower and when he did it took Darian a few seconds to spot him. There was some distance between them – you don't trail someone by standing close enough to see their nasal hair – but what threw him was that Dent had changed his clothes from the morning. At the interview he had been wearing a shirt and tie, ready to look formal when called upon by his boss. Now he was in a hoodie and jeans. This was not a man on his way to the glamorous unveiling of a piece of fine art. Dent went into the building across the street from the tower where the cars were kept and emerged driving a yellow hatchback, final proof he was no longer working.

The driver went east into Bakers Moor and Darian followed. The traffic was, needless to say, appalling, so it was easy enough to crawl along behind without standing out. Eventually Darian could drop back further because he knew Dent was going home, a flat on MacLean Street. By no means the great heights of luxury his boss occupied, but a sweet spot for a young man working as a driver. Phil had said his uncle paid good people well.

The block of flats he lived in had a small car park at the side which Dent drove into and Darian drove past. He couldn't get too close here; had to make sure Dent didn't spot him given it had been only hours since they'd met. He circled the block and came back, parking in the car park of the flats across the street where he had a good view of the entrance to Dent's building.

Darian sat and listened to his stomach cry out for the meals that had skipped on by. More than two hours later a taxi pulled up outside Dent's building and the man himself strolled out wearing a blue shirt and black trousers. He got into the back of the taxi and it pulled away. Darian tried to start the Focus and it wheezed back at him as if it had a fishbone stuck in its throat. The second attempt was no better but the third brought joy and he pulled quickly out onto the road and managed to catch up with the trademark red of the Challaid Cabs taxi. He trundled along behind it for a few minutes until it stopped outside Transistor nightclub on Martin Road. This area had once been the fast-beating heart of Challaid's party district on the borderline between Bakers Moor and Bank, but as the partygoers had softened so the centre of fun had gravitated over towards the more genteel Cnocaid. By this time Transistor was a still good club in a now mediocre area.

Darian made his way in and couldn't spot Dent anywhere. The place was packed, a couple of hundred people, and Darian moved through the throng, down a couple of steps towards one of two bars. The place was lit in blue and green, the music slower and a lot better at this early stage. Darian could actually hear a woman singing rather beautifully on the track playing. He spotted Dent alone at the longer of the two bars, downing a shot of a clear liquid and demanding another from a big barman who served him before others ahead of him in the queue. That wasn't because of status; it was because the barman was trained to spot trouble and Dent looked like trouble.

Darian went to the smaller bar against another wall and the barmaid nodded to him. She was a woman with a mass of unnaturally red hair and smart eyes who looked too young to be working there.

'Two orange juices.'

The barmaid looked left and right for a companion who wasn't there and then went to get Darian's drinks for him. He took a stool at the end of the bar that gave him a good view of the huge room and sat there sipping steadily, aware he was likely to stand out in a place where most people were trying to have fun.

Dent was perhaps the one other person in the place who wasn't trying to tempt a smile onto his face. He was blowing off abundant steam, and after three drinks he went onto the dance floor and approached the first pretty girl he saw, a young blonde who was dancing with her arms around her boyfriend. Dent butted into the middle of them and started trying to dance with the girl. She shoved him away and her boyfriend shouted something while standing in front of Dent, a fist clenched. In Challaid it's rare to spot a nuanced response to a simple problem; sledgehammers have been used to crack many a nut. The driver laughed at the couple he had upset but Darian couldn't see any pleasure in the pain he'd caused them. He was laughing to save face and walked back to the bar for another drink. This, Darian realised as he started on his second glass, was Dent's plan. Other people were looking to decimate their stress by dancing up close with another person but Dent would get his kicks from something harder.

12

KEEPING WILL DENT in view from the small bar was a challenge, but no more difficult than making sure the girl with the red hair didn't have him thrown out.

For the third time she came across to him and said, 'Can I get you anything else?'

'Another orange juice, thanks.'

She frowned and said, 'You've had three orange juices and you haven't gotten off that stool. You know you're in a nightclub, right?'

'I'll dance, maybe... I'm building up to it.'

'God, after this kind of build-up if you don't dance like Disco Stu it's going to be a terrible disappointment for both of us.'

Despite her very reasonable concern that Darian was some sort of creepy oddball, she got him another orange juice and left him alone. The music was getting faster and louder and further out of step with Darian's more acoustic tastes, but he blocked it out and focused on the reason he was there.

Will Dent was all over Transistor, at the large bar and then on the dance floor, back to the bar and off to the bathroom and back on the floor. He seemed to be making a point to be as annoying as possible to as many people as he could encounter in the crowd, bumping into some at the bar and stepping on people who were trying to dance. It was all so deliberate that even in a place so full of movement and noise it became noticeable to more than just the spy ensconced at the small bar. The barman who had been serving Dent was alert to it and Darian saw him make a call on the phone behind the bar. A minute and a half later two very large men wearing T-shirts with the Transistor logo made their way inside and took Dent by each arm, guiding him to the exit.

That was Darian's cue to leave but he had to play the role carefully. If Dent was on the hunt for a battle then spotting Darian would give him a target. He walked slowly round the edge of the room and out to the main exit, thirty seconds behind Dent and his burly escorts. Out through the double doors and into the street, colder now than when he had come in but louder, life tumbling out of the bars on surrounding streets and trying to fall into the club to round off a night of inebriated entertainment. Dent was over by the kerb where a near-constant stream of taxis was picking up and dropping off, drivers beeping horns and shouting abuse at each other, their industry increasingly heated. It was easy for Darian to skip out unnoticed and move along Martin Road until he found a nook to hide in. He took up position and watched Dent make another attempt at picking a fight.

His drunken indignation was turned towards the two bouncers who had chucked him out, one a completely bald man built like the sort of rugby player who would be banned for excessive violence while the other was tall and thinner, dark and with the sort of matinee idol looks that wouldn't have lasted long on a doorman in Challaid had he ended up sticking around.

It was at that one Dent shouted, 'It's people like you that they shouldn't let… people like you into this country.'

If he'd know what the person he was shouting at would go on to become the abuse would only have been more unpleasant. If there's one thing drunken racists hate more than foreigners it's foreigners that become successful in their new country, and Baran Vega would go on to great success. At that point he was a twelve-monther, earning his dual passport with a year of employment in the city.

The bald man said in a thick Challaid accent, 'It's arseholes like you that shouldn't be allowed in this country, but maybe we can get rid of you one building at a time because you're barred from this one.'

'You can't bar me because I quit. I'm wouldn't come back here if you paid me.'

The two bouncers glanced at each other, laughed at the stupidity of it all and went back inside. The look they gave their female colleague on the door was sympathetic.

Being thrown out and barred was a poor return for his night's aggravating work so Dent was never going to leave it at that. Darian watched from the doorway of Sharik's Pet Store two doors down while Dent looked left and right for the easiest target he could find, which happened to be a young and drunk couple who seemed to be suffering from an excess of gravity as they fought to avoid being pushed to the ground under the weight of it. They found the struggle hilarious as they swayed about, and neither of them was paying any attention to Dent when he walked up to them and punched the young man in the guts.

The girl screamed, 'Hey, that's my Duncan, that's Duncan.'

Dent didn't care that he was punching Duncan. It could have been Prime Minister MacDonald and he would have kept swinging those fists. He got three or four punches in before a couple of other revellers jumped in and pulled him away and the woman on the door ran across. Darian noticed her putting something back into her pocket and guessed correctly it was an alarm to inform her colleagues inside she could use backup. They would be out in a second and Dent would be monstrously outnumbered and outgunned. He was about to become the target in a game of whack the bastard, and he was smart enough to realise it, which was why he started to run.

If he had gone the other way things could have turned out very differently, but he didn't, he ran down towards the pet shop. He didn't spot the young man lurking there, so he didn't see the foot that Darian stuck out and tripped him with, standing back in Sharik's doorway and watching a ruck of people pile on top of the sprawling Dent. It didn't take a beautiful mind to deduce what was going to happen next so Darian slipped away from the rumble on the pavement and made his way back to the car.

The first person he called was Sholto.

'Darian? Tell me you're not still working. Tell me you don't expect to be paid for all these hours.'

'Dent didn't go to work tonight, he went partying, which in his world means getting hammered by both alcohol and doormen. He's about to get arrested outside Transistor on Martin Road. Do you have a number for DS MacNeith? She can use this as an opportunity to question him.'

Sholto sighed down the phone and said, 'I'll call her, persuade her this is worth her time, I'm more charming than you. You didn't get him beaten up, did you? Because you know we're not allowed to make these things happen.'

'He didn't need any help from me or anyone else.'

Darian hung up and tried to start the car, getting a cough of life from the engine on the second try and enough power to trundle back to his flat. He went straight to bed, knowing he would be up early, desperate to find out if the formidable DS MacNeith had cracked open Will Dent and ripped the truth out of him.

Transcript of suspect interview

12 May 2018
Cnocaid Police Station, 18–20 Kidd Street, Cnocaid,
Challaid, CH2 1WD

Suspect – William Dent
Lawyer – Kellina Oriol
Interviewing officers – DS Irene MacNeith, DC Cathy
Draper

10:32: **DS MacNeith** – My name is DS Irene MacNeith,
joining me is DC Cathy Draper, interviewing William
Dent, also present Kellina Oriol. Just to let you know
that this interview is being filmed by a camera mounted
on the wall in the corner over there. Do you know why
you're here, William?

10:33: **William Dent** – I was in a fight, I got arrested for
it. I said I was sorry, but I didn't start it anyway.

DS MacNeith – That's why you were arrested last night in
Bakers Moor and it's being investigated by the officers
at Bakers station. What I'm asking is do you know why
we asked to have you brought across to Cnocaid so we
could speak to you?

William Dent – No.

DS MacNeith – Do you remember Freya Dempsey?

William Dent – Her, yeah.

DS MacNeith – Do you know that she's gone missing?

William Dent – I heard. Some people came. I think they were cops or something, they asked me about her, yesterday morning. You can talk to them about it if you don't believe me. I already spoke to you lot; I don't [unintelligible].

Kellina Oriol – As my client has said, he's spoken to Challaid Police about Miss Dempsey already, and I assume they were operating in an official capacity because it would be unacceptable if they weren't.

DS MacNeith – Sounds like you already know something of this case. So when I asked your client if he knew why he had been brought here and he said no, that wasn't entirely true.

William Dent – I didn't know.

10:34: Kellina Oriol – He didn't. I asked him when I arrived here why he might have been brought across and he couldn't think of a reason. It was his employers who informed me of the visit from the police yesterday.

DC Draper – Your employer.

Kellina Oriol – Excuse me?

DC Draper – Sutherland Bank, they're your employer, too.

Kellina Oriol – They are. Is that some sort of issue?

DC Draper – Does the bank send its lawyers to defend every member of staff arrested for brawling in the street and public drunkenness?

Kellina Oriol – Seems to me we're talking about potentially more serious allegations than that. In answer to your question, the bank sends its lawyers to support any member of staff it thinks deserves help.

DC Draper – In my experience that's not very many.

Kellina Oriol – Then your experience must err on the side of negativity, unless you're less experienced than you look.

DS MacNeith – William, tell me about the morning you met Freya Dempsey.

William Dent – I told you that already.

DS MacNeith – No, the people you told were not Challaid Police officers.

10:35: **Kellina Oriol** – But there were two police officers with the men who questioned my client.

DS MacNeith – They were not at that moment acting on behalf of Challaid Police.

Kellina Oriol – That doesn't sound good, detective, two officers working out of hours.

DS MacNeith – Do you wish to report them?

Kellina Oriol – I may yet.

DS MacNeith – You might want to clear it with your employer, Harold Sutherland, first.

Kellina Oriol – Oh, I know one of the officers was his nephew, and I would imagine he would be thrilled to get the young man he cares about out of the toxic culture of Challaid Police.

DS MacNeith – Would he be thrilled to have a nephew who never spoke to him again?

Kellina Oriol – We appear to be getting side-tracked by family issues that are none of our business.

DS MacNeith – Freya Dempsey. Tell me about the morning you met her.

William Dent – It was ages ago, I don't remember everything about it, not all that clear. She pulled out and hit me, down the road, corner of Kidd and Siar, just down the road from here. It wasn't anything big, just a dent for her. Front to side, though, so our bumper got pulled down into the wheel arch. I called for another car, it was all done in a few minutes and we were gone.

DS MacNeith – So it was her that hit you? Her fault?

10:36: **William Dent** – Yeah, I thought so.

DS MacNeith – But that's not what your boss thought because he paid her costs.

William Dent – Yeah, well, that's the gaffer, isn't it? He didn't want trouble, not out on the street, and he didn't want to have to spend time hanging around dealing with her. Just said he would pay for it so he could get into the new car as soon as it got there and get to his meeting. Getting to that meeting was worth a lot more to him than fixing the car. Every meeting he has would be.

DS MacNeith – And she claimed for the cost?

William Dent – I don't know, I don't handle any of that.

I suppose she must have. Next time I heard anything about her was when the cops came round yesterday morning.

DS MacNeith – Could Mr Sutherland have heard from her?

William Dent – The gaffer? The gaffer wasn't going to waste his time handling insurance claims for a person like her.

DS MacNeith – What sort of person was she?

William Dent – Ordinary.

DS MacNeith – So you know nothing about what happened to her.

William Dent – No.

DS MacNeith – Nothing about the fact that her car was destroyed after she went missing, the same one you crashed into?

William Dent – How would I?

DS MacNeith – You don't seem to like talking about her.

William Dent – I don't like talking to you.

Kellina Oriol – My client has cooperated with you, and if you don't have any more questions of worth then I'm sure he'd like very much to go home.

10:37: DS MacNeith – Where were you in the late afternoon and early evening of the fourth of May?

William Dent – I don't know. I don't know what day that was.

DS MacNeith – It was a Friday. Eight days ago.

William Dent – I'll have been working then.

DS MacNeith – All afternoon and evening?

William Dent – All afternoon, some of the evening, I think. Maybe all of it.

DS MacNeith – And the bank will be able to prove that?

William Dent – My work file will tell you when I signed out for the day, to the second.

DS MacNeith – Good, we'll be sure to check. You can go now, Mr Dent.

END

13

DARIAN ARRIVED AT THE office on Cage Street the following morning shortly after Sholto. He knew his boss was already there because he could smell his breakfast from the top of the stairs, picked up from The Northern Song on the ground floor as he made his way into work each morning.

As Darian closed the office door behind him Sholto, with a gob full of grub, said, 'I have no idea what happened last night other than the fact that every time you go to a party someone ends up getting arrested. That's why you and me will never socialise.'

'Yeah, well, this time he actually wanted to be.'

'Takes a special sort of fool to go looking for an arrest in this city. What got into him?'

Darian sat at his desk by the window. 'I don't know, but it was in there before he reached the club, so it must have been in there before he left work. He didn't work that swanky do his boss was throwing, so he might have been in a huff about that. Maybe he feels like Sutherland set us on him, or maybe Sutherland gave him a bollocking for the evasive way he spoke to us.'

'Or maybe he spoke to Sutherland about her in the same evasive way and the big boss man thinks the driver might be a worthy suspect.'

'Have you heard anything back from DS MacNeith?'

Sholto piled more rice onto his fork and lifted it toward his gaping mouth, grains falling onto his desk, and said, 'Not yet. If he was in the state you say he was then they would have let him sleep it off in the salubrious surrounds of the drunk tank. Let's say they questioned him at Bakers Moor about the attack first thing this morning and then sent him across to Cnocaid. They might not have started talking at him yet.'

'Hopefully she'll get some useful info out of him.'

Sholto nodded. 'She might, but it might not be the info you're looking for. How likely is it that a man who committed a perfect kidnap in near broad daylight would then go and get himself arrested for something as tedious as a drunken scrap outside Transistor?'

'You don't think he's involved?'

'If he is then he's gone from criminal genius to colossal goof in the space of a week. That's the sort of drop in standards that only a witch doctor could bring about and I don't know any living this far north. I do think he's up to something, but I'm beginning to wonder if it's something we care about.'

Darian was about to say something he hoped would avoid decreasing the number of alternative suspects to just Vinny when his mobile rang. He looked at the screen and saw the code that told him it was JJ.

'JJ.'

'Hello, Darian, is it good to talk?'

'It is.'

'I thought I'd call you and tell you a funny wee story about what happened to me when I turned up at work this morning. I wasn't even into my boiler suit when a car comes into the yard and these two spivs in fancy suits get out and tell me they're working for an insurance company and they're looking for Freya Dempsey's Passat. I told them I didn't know anything about it because I did know more about them than they realised. One of them was Alan Dudley, and unless he's changed jobs in the last couple of months I know he works for Raven Investigators, not some insurance company. Isn't that funny? Anyway, I'll see you when you come back with the Focus, if it makes it back.'

Some people, Darian thought as he hung up, were very good at being informants. Like many who worked on the fringes of criminality JJ knew who the threats were, made sure he would recognise them if they showed up in his vicinity. Douglas Independent Research he saw as a potential friend because they weren't official, but Raven were the biggest private investigators in the city, probably the country, and JJ viewed them with a level of suspicion usually reserved for the police.

Darian repeated the story to Sholto who stopped scraping the bottom of the container with his fork to say, 'Raven? Bloody Raven? Who are those pound store Pinkertons working for?'

'The obvious candidate would be Harold Sutherland. He knows about the car, realised his driver was a suspect and decided to dig a little deeper himself.'

If you asked Sholto about Raven Investigators you would likely be on the receiving end of a forty-minute diatribe about them, the highlights of which would be this. The private investigations industry had a good thing going in Scotland until Raven managed to cock it up for everyone. They had, at that point, four large offices in the country, in Challaid, Aberdeen, Glasgow and Edinburgh, although they shut the one in Aberdeen a couple of years ago. They cultivated good relationships with the police and did a lot of their work for big businesses, so they were well insulated from the occasional act of stupidity they were prone to committing. They were, and these would be Sholto's words, arrogant morons, reckless halfwits and a cretinous collection of corrupt clowns. It was their Edinburgh office that ran a little too wild and free, bumping shoulders with alarmed politicians and accelerating the formation of government policy to tighten controls on private investigators across Scotland. It was a policy so quickly thrown together it almost matched one in England word for word. Even though they had shrunk since then, Raven's Challaid office remained the biggest investigator in the city, and on the list of things Sholto could bring himself to hate Raven were in with a bullet at number one.

Sholto said, 'Well, if that lot are involved in this case we're not having anything more to do with it. I don't want to be anywhere near them… Or, no, wait, if they're involved then we need to get all the information we can and get this solved. That'll show them. Or… Murt mhòr, I don't know, I hate them too much to make a decision.'

'If you can get in touch with MacNeith we might be able to get a small lead on them.'

Sholto shook his head. 'If Sutherland hired them then he'll know a lot more about what Dent said in the interviews than we will. But I'll give her a ring anyway, see what she spits out at me. If we could get this wrapped up before that lot, oh, that would be sweet as three bags of sugar.'

Darian smiled and nodded. He leaned back in his chair and thought how sad it was that the investigation was a challenge to them, a process about finding a truth, while for Finn Reno it was about waiting for someone to tell him why his mother had disappeared. It wasn't that Darian and Sholto didn't care, it was just that for them Freya Dempsey was a part of their week, whereas for Finn she was a huge part of his life.

14

DARIAN SUSPECTED SHOLTO didn't want him to hear the phone conversation with DS MacNeith so he went downstairs to the bathroom of The Northern Song for a pee he didn't need. Darian was well used to hearing his boss being deferential towards police officers, rich people, the moderately wealthy, large people, angry people and people he thought unpredictable, a trait Sholto was no fan of. There was, however, an elite level of obsequiousness he could wallow in when someone presented a particular problem, and he preferred to do his wallowing without witnesses so he could later pretend he had maintained his polished dignity throughout. Darian gave it five minutes before wandering back upstairs.

They were busy in the restaurant on the ground floor, some passing trade in the morning but mostly preparing for the lunchtime rush. There were only two doors on the landing of the first floor as he made his way back up, the Yangs' flat and the other with a nameplate for an entertainment agency, Highland Stars. No one had ever used the office, and if any money passed through the company based there Darian assumed it was part of a scam. On the second floor there were three doors, theirs closest to the top of the stairs, Challaid Data Services at the far end of the corridor and the empty office in between. He had thought he'd heard someone going into the data services office after he arrived that morning, but their door was, as always, firmly shut. Neither Darian nor Sholto had ever been inside.

As he stepped back into the office Sholto said to him, 'I've managed to sweet-talk the dragon, although it was a struggle to keep my food down at the same time. She's questioned Dent, he's going to be charged by Bakers Moor for his fight last night but he gave her nothing at all on Freya so she can't take it further. That's on the record; off the record she thought he was as honest as a Challaid councillors' manifesto, and she hinted with all the subtlety a Tyrannosaurus Rex can muster that we can keep our eyes on him if we want and she won't object because, if he's going to give anything away, now might be the time.'

'A Tyrannosaurus Rex is a dinosaur, not a dragon.'

'Aye, and they'd both bite your bloody head off given half a chance. Seeing as you're so good at identifying unpleasant threats you can go and watch him. He's out of the station so he'll either be at home or at work.'

As he drove to MacLean Street to look for Dent's car Darian realised Sholto had sent him on another full day's work on this case despite knowing Vinny almost certainly couldn't afford to pay them. That was typical of him, complaining about the unappreciated value of his hourly rate at the start but getting so wrapped up in a case that time became a worthless commodity. Darian had often wondered why Sholto had set up a private investigations company when he left the murky environs of Challaid Police and this was the answer – he grudgingly loved the work.

The car wasn't on MacLean Street so Darian drove to MacAlpin Road and went into the multi-storey car park across the street from the Sutherland Bank, circling until he spotted it. That meant Dent was in the tower, waiting for a call from the boss to say he was needed. Darian parked just close enough to watch the only door of the tower and bedded in.

Will Dent made four journeys in a company car throughout the day. The first was with Harold Sutherland, driving him to Bruaich Drive and the glass-fronted headquarters of Glendan, the massive construction company with whom the Sutherland Bank no doubt did a lot of business. Harold Sutherland was inside for forty-five minutes before he returned to the car and Dent drove him back to the bank. A little after midday Sutherland left again when Dent picked him up from the front of the building. Darian tried to follow but towards the end of MacUspaig Road he got snarled up in traffic when they turned off. He tried to catch them up, joining the daily chorus of cursing drivers, but couldn't see them after looping the area and wasting petrol, so he went back to the tower to await their return.

The third journey of the day was the one that mattered. Dent went on his own, heading west through Cnocaid and up into Barton. He stopped at a Forsyth's Supermarket and went inside. Darian waited in the car park for half an hour before Dent came out with seven or eight bags. He put them in the boot of the car and drove over to the edge of the loch.

They were on quiet roads now, and it took real effort to keep the Focus from looming big and ugly in Dent's mirrors. When the driver turned onto Geug Place, a short, single-track cul-de-sac near Ruadh Rock, Darian had to let him go. He couldn't follow and stay invisible, and this was an area where the very sight of a fourteen-year-old Focus might spook some nervy old biddy into calling the police. The few houses down the lane, a rich and tree-lined area with the mansions on one side enjoying an uninterrupted view of the loch, were all worth more millions than Darian would earn in six lifetimes. He drove around a bit and missed Dent leaving, so went back to the tower.

The last journey Dent took in a company car was driving his boss as close to home as he could. Harold

Sutherland lived on Eilean Seud, the island in Loch Eriboll towards the west bank that was so teeming with money the mainland couldn't contain it. Dent dropped his boss at the pier on Cruinn Road and Harold boarded the little ferry that would carry him and his equally wealthy neighbours across to their island. You could get four cars on the boat at a time, but Harold was on foot, perhaps a car waiting for him at the island pier. Normally anything with the whiff of the working class, like public transport, would send the mega-rich of Eilean Seud into paroxysms of anguish, but the ferry was a necessity they couldn't ignore unless they were happy swimmers.

Someone once asked Magnus Duff, the young scion of the shipping family, on Twitter why his family had never lived on the island. He said it was because if they did the ghost of Morogh Duff would rise from his eighteenth-century grave in Heilam and smite them all down. When asked why the company founder would so object to the island, Magnus said it was because it was populated by people who thought being rich people made them good instead of believing that being good people would make them rich. That, to many, seemed a fine description of a community which repeatedly blocked a bridge being built to the island because it would have granted easy access to 'ordinary' people. That meant the fire service had to keep a boat on Cruinn Road pier in case of an emergency on the island, and if there was a medical crisis the helicopter from King Robert VI Hospital in Cnocaid would have to zip up for them, all at the taxpayers' expense, of course.

Having dropped off his boss Dent drove back to the tower, changed, switched to his own car and went home to Bakers Moor. Darian watched the flat for a short while and then tried to start the car to go back to the office. It took five attempts to find rasping life in the engine and Darian was reminded of his older brother Sorley's entreaties that he buy a motorbike so he could get around the city at his own pace and with a helmet covering his face during dangerous jobs. When he did get back to Cage Street, Sholto had gone home so Darian quickly typed up a report, collected some food from downstairs and took it home to eat.

15

THE FOLLOWING MORNING Darian and Sholto met
at Glendan Station and took the train together up to
Three O'clock Station in Whisper Hill. Darian had
called Vinny and told him they needed to force another
conversation out of his ridiculously wealthy junior
colleague, Vinny texting back a few minutes later to
say Philip was happy to meet.

Sitting on the train Sholto said, 'That wee cop loves his
uncle. I could see it when we went to Castle Greyskull.'

'You think he's going to talk to us and then call up his
uncle to share the transcript.'

'Aye, and then the uncle tells Raven and we have that
army of arseholes keeping pace with us.'

'Vinny trusts him.'

'And with good reason, I'm sure. The boy will have
his back; they have the kind of relationship forged on
the wicked streets of The Hill late at night when blades

flicker under lamplight. But he's still a Sutherland, and if his uncle is after info then family comes first.'

'I'll mention Raven to him, see what his reaction is.'

Sholto nodded and said no more, believing he had imparted enough wisdom for one train journey and keeping the rest stored away for future use rather than spoil Darian with it all at once. In their working relationship each thought he was teaching the other about how the world really worked, and to some extent they were both right.

They walked out of Three O'clock Station and made their way to Bluefields Road, a short enough distance on foot. Bluefields was next along from Docklands Street, the road that ran around the huge industrial docks and was lined with large buildings that served shipping, among them the police station. The streets around it had the noise and smell of the shipping industry, and captured the spirit of the city's history in bottles of seafaring nostalgia. Darian always liked to visit, but it would have taken considerable danger money to persuade him to work at the police station there.

About halfway along Bluefields Road was the Silver Cinema, a cavernous place built in the thirties that had undergone more facelifts that anyone who appeared on its screens. It had been opened with much fanfare in 1932 by some Hollywood starlet on a flying visit to the city and had been on a crawling decline ever since. Its last makeover had been about ten years before and had been a noble attempt to recapture the style of its lost youth, dressed up to look something like it had been back in those optimistic early days. But instead of looking young again it looked old and caked in enough make-up to give it an air of desperation. No matter what it wore, the building seemed to make just enough money to keep operating and one of the reasons why was the huge café that now occupied the front of the building. Vinny and Phil, in their uniforms, were sitting under a poster of Gregory Peck and a fishy friend, a nod to the whaling past of the city, over in the far corner where the sleepy young woman behind the counter wouldn't be able to hear them.

As they sat at the small table Vinny said, 'I hope you've made more progress than we have because we've been a dog chasing its tail in a tumble dryer.'

Darian said, 'I don't know if I'd call it progress exactly, but we've got a couple of questions worth asking. DS MacNeith interviewed Dent as well and she didn't like the shape of his attitude any more than we did. I followed him yesterday, mostly just running your uncle around, Phil, but he went to one of the mansions on Geug Place with a boot full of groceries in the afternoon, I couldn't follow without being seen so I don't know who...'

Phil put up a hand to stop him. 'My cousin Simon lives on Geug Place. My uncle Harold mostly looks after him, makes sure he's all right.'

Sholto said, 'He can't look after himself?'

Phil shook his head. 'He's severely agoraphobic, never leaves the house. I heard he has severe OCD as well and I don't know what else, a shopping list of terrors. I haven't seen him for two or three years, he doesn't like visitors, but last time I went round with Uncle Harold he was, I don't know, nice but shy, nothing to say, didn't want any part of the outside world getting in.'

Sholto said, 'Is there nothing they can do for him?'

'Uncle Harold has tried, but apparently Simon doesn't want to be helped. He has his own world and it's very small and he has total control over it and that's all he wants. Uncle Harold gets his shopping delivered, has a housekeeper go round to cook his meals, makes sure he's looked after. Look, people think that because you're a Sutherland you've won life's lottery, but Simon got the short straw in the parent sweepstakes. There were three siblings. My mother was the youngest, Uncle Harold was the oldest and Uncle Beathan in the middle. He took after both of his parents, my grandparents, who were a pair of flakes by all accounts, and I'm not sure Simon's mother was a stabilising influence on that shipwreck either. I was lucky with my parents, but our family has been very rich for a very long time and that's corroded the wires that attach us to reality.'

Darian said, 'So he doesn't like visitors, huh?'

'No, they upset him, and it would upset me if you went round there. The man doesn't leave his house; he has nothing to tell you.'

'But he sees Dent regularly?'

'I don't know who delivers his food, I would assume the housekeeper. She's the only one he allows in. You guys are swinging from the wrong tree here.'

Darian nodded and said, 'Well, we seem to have shaken your family tree already. Raven have been on our heels for the last day or so, and I can't think of anyone other than your uncle who would have called them in.'

Vinny looked sharply from Darian to Phil and said, 'Why would your uncle call in Raven?'

'Shit, it's probably instinctive. They do it a lot, whenever there's any investigation going on that might affect the company in any way, cause bad PR, hurt the finances. They're obsessed with knowing what's happening and what's going to happen to them in the foreseeable future. They see it as allowing them to control the direction that future goes in. It's probably nothing, but your best bet would be to pretend you haven't realised they're there because once you acknowledge them they'll move against you. I won't mention any of this to my uncle, though; make sure he can't pass anything on to Raven.'

That was said in a way that showed obvious hope that he had won a favour from Darian, like leaving his cousin alone. Vinny and Phil got up to leave, and as they were going Vinny shot Darian the sort of urging look that told him to keep on pulling the thread he had caught a hold of. Darian and Sholto left the Silver and walked back up towards Three O'clock Station.

Sholto said, 'Not hard to picture a scene in which a lonely obsessive millionaire gets his creepy chauffer pal to lift a girl off the street, is it?'

'No, it isn't.'

'See, that's jumping to conclusions and a good investigator always keeps his feet on the ground. We have no idea if Simon Sutherland or Dent were even involved, and there are no estimates in this business. It's certainties or nothing.'

'So what do we do?'

'We go have a peek at this hideaway on Geug Place and see if it has stories to tell.'

The Blood Tree

He had planned to go to the airport and get on whatever plane would take him west, or, hell, east, it didn't make much difference. He was on the wrong side of the world and both directions led home. A concierge, or whatever they called them in Tokyo, stopped him in the lobby of the hotel and told him there was a phone call for him, said it was from England, the daft bugger. Not England, Scotland. Challaid. Home.

Harold Sutherland stepped into the small office behind the front desk and closed the door on the young woman trying to follow him in. He was twenty-six and used to paying for what his charm couldn't earn. He picked up the phone on the table.

'It's Harold,' he said.

A couple of seconds' delay and a voice said, 'Harold? At last. I didn't think that stupid girl had understood me. Don't go to the airport yet, we're getting a plane especially for you and it'll be ready in a couple of hours. How are you?'

The voice sounded far away but it was recognisable and the lack of true concern was familiar. It was Rodrick Sutherland, a first cousin and managing executive of the bank whose primary role was to put out any fires that threatened to scorch the family business. He was forty-four, a cold and unpleasant person, but he was ruthlessly effective in a crisis.

'I'm okay,' Harold said, knowing Rodrick wouldn't care about the lie. 'What about Beathan?'

Another delay. 'Beathan? They'll keep the body for a few days but we already have people on that. The report will say what it needs to say and we'll get the body back here for burial. Take longer to bury than is traditional but nothing we can do about that. No point you staying with it.'

'Shit, the meetings with Marutake.'

'Forget about that, the chairman called them an hour ago to explain everything. What time is it where you are? They told me your plane would be ready at four o'clock.'

'Ten past one.'

'Get there with time to spare. It'll just be you on board.'

They had left the airport two days before and been chauffeur-driven to the hotel. Harold and Beathan Sutherland, the two brightest young stars of the family bank, brothers here to do business with a long-standing financial partner. It was the first time they had been sent abroad alone, just twenty-six and twenty-five. They had both been determined to enjoy the trip. On the first night they went out into the city and got lost among neon and noise, drinking it in, walking into strange-looking bars and spending what might have been a lot or a little, they had no idea or care. They went into a place they thought was a bar and turned out to be a small seafood restaurant so they ate and had a tortuous conversation with a waiter about where to find one of the hostess clubs they'd heard so much innuendo about.

By the time they reached the place they were sure the taxi driver had ripped them off but didn't care much. They were here to have fun and had more than enough money to cover the cost of someone else's enterprise. The club turned out to be a real disappointment, ear-clawing music and flailing attempts at polite conversation with pretty girls who weren't interested in anything more. They did meet a man there who assured them he could provide what they really wanted, and an hour later they were back in the two-bedroom suite on the top floor in the centre of Tokyo with a young woman each.

'Do you think this is how they all do foreign trips?' Beathan asked his older brother.

'Probably. I mean, they're almost human, most of them. Even chairman grump must want to have fun now and again.'

Beathan shook his head. 'Nah, fun would kill that old bastard, he's allergic.'

★★★

The plane taking him home was luxury, but Harold barely glanced at it. The crew, Japanese, seemed to know enough to leave him alone, telling him only what food and drink was available and how quickly they would be taking off. If it was a commercial plane this one could have held over a hundred people, but instead had fewer than twenty seats. Harold sat and stared out of the window as he thought about the conversation they had had the previous morning. Thought about the letter in his pocket. He remained stony-faced.

After the girls had gone they had sat at the table in the kitchen of the suite having breakfast. Brothers with all of life's gifts, far from the constraints of home.

'Daisy wants to have another baby,' Beathan said, speaking of his wife.

Harold felt his brother had married much too soon, rushed into something he had convinced himself couldn't wait. Daisy was a striking young woman who occasionally bordered on terrifying and she had already produced one son, Simon, to guarantee their branch of the family would carry on beyond them.

'You don't want another one?'

'I didn't really want the first one,' Beathan admitted for the first time.

It wasn't a surprise to hear and Harold didn't react. 'Tell her you're not ready for another one yet, put her off, not like she can get the job done without you. I mean, she can, but she gets kicked off the gravy train if she does.'

'It should be a good thing, though,' Beathan said with that familiar faraway look. 'I should want it but I don't. That's not right.'

'Jesus, Beathan, you're a young man, that's why you don't want it yet. Don't worry, you're young and she's younger so you have plenty of time to wait and pick your moment. Your moment, not hers.'

Harold didn't eat until they were more than halfway home. As he did his mind went back to that morning, what he had seen. They'd had a first meeting with the people from Marutake Financial Group that day, an introductory thing that had lasted a couple of hours. Then some sightseeing for which Marutake provided a cheerful guide and an expensive dinner with a couple of executives. They were both in good spirits when they got back to the hotel and went to bed.

Harold had woken with a start at six o'clock in the morning. He knew. Some instinct deep inside him screamed that something was wrong and told him to get out of bed and check. He grabbed his glasses and went out of the room, across the corridor to Beathan's door, knocking on it. No answer. He tried the handle and the door wasn't locked, Harold realised later, because his brother wanted to make this as easy for him as possible. Beathan was lying on the bed, on his back, head propped up on the pillows. His eyes were shut and when Harold spoke his words seemed impossibly loud in the room. Beathan didn't stir. He shook him and there was no response. His brother was dead.

Harold knew what had happened before he switched the light on. Beathan must have brought the bottle of pills with him because he hadn't had the chance to go out and get them here. A look at the label confirmed they had come from a pharmacy in Cnocaid. There was a note on the table opposite the foot of the bed. Harold read it, folded it carefully and kept it on him at all times thereafter.

He had gone back to his room and dressed, putting the letter in his pocket, and everything else he did had been an automatic reaction. He knew what the family would want him to do, the protection he had to provide. They would all say it was to safeguard Beathan's name, and his wife and child, from the unpleasant headlines that the truth might provide. Harold knew the first priority of any Sutherland was to protect the bank. The family had always been careful to hide the struggles some of its members had.

At Challaid International Airport he stepped off the plane and into a car waiting on the tarmac. He knew the driver worked for the chairman, Nathair Sutherland, their great-uncle and the man who ran the bank and so ran the family. The driver said nothing as they went down around the loch and up the west side to Barton, stopping at Cruinn Pier where a boat took Harold across to Eilean Seud. He felt as though he hadn't slept for days and he was hungry again, but he had to do this. He had to show he had the mental strength to perform a horrifying task. The family would be judging.

There were fewer than he expected in the high-ceilinged drawing room of the chairman's mansion. Nathair and his wife, newly widowed Daisy, Harold's mother Marcail, and Rodrick, who had organised his return.

'Harold,' the chairman said, 'sit down. You look ready to drop.'

That was, he knew, an invitation to talk, to tell them everything that had happened, so he did. He omitted nothing but the girls they had picked up, telling anything that might be relevant. He told of the bottle of pills, the few he had picked off the sheets and put back in the bottle, the bottle now in his bag, unseen by anyone else. Rodrick would make sure the cause of death was put down as natural causes, the family untouched by the shame of suicide. He took the note from his pocket.

'It was lying on the table in his room. There was no envelope, so I've read it,' he said, passing it to the chairman.

Nathair didn't even glance at it, passing it instead to Daisy who read it quickly. She looked as if she had just stopped crying and was determined never to start again.

When she was finished she passed the note back to the chairman.

I have to do this. It's not that I want to, this isn't a choice, it's something forced on me. I understand the burden this will place on the family, especially Daisy and Simon who will have to carry this for the rest of their lives, and if there was another way I would take it. I have always, deep in my heart, known that father's death was what he wanted, and I think I understand why he chose it, because there were no other options. He was right. I'm sorry.

Beathan Sutherland.

16

THERE WAS NO WAY OF getting a view of 5 Geug Place without driving up and parking outside, and there was no way an ageing Fiat Punto could park on that street and not draw unwanted attention. The question was how long Darian and Sholto could sit there eyeballing the gates to Simon Sutherland's house before the presence of the working class made the locals, and their security staff, jittery.

Sholto turned onto Geug Place, its end hidden by the tall trees on either side. The foliage was intended to keep the large houses behind the tall gates hidden from the road, and they mostly served their purpose well. You had to get close to see that there were driveways behind those gates and no matter the strength of your prescription glasses you wouldn't be able to spot the houses themselves. They parked in the passing place closest to the gate of Simon Sutherland's house and sat watching it across the road.

Darian said, 'I can see half a gate and nothing else.'

'You're not looking close enough then. I can see half a gate and at least three security cameras, maybe four if that thing in the tree there isn't a bird… It flew away. Okay, three.'

'Not a surprise, is it? All the houses round here probably have a paparazzi of cameras outside for security. And someone who doesn't want to leave the house is probably paranoid about other people getting in.'

'See, for all the swings you've taken at it there you've still missed the point. Security cameras mean a security team watching the pictures, but we were told only the uncle, the driver and the housekeeper ever get into the house. If someone's seeing us and thinks we're suspicious, who comes to shoo us away?'

'They might have security staff somewhere near here, in another building.'

Sholto shook his head and said, 'All the other buildings on this street are other people's giant houses.'

'You could squeeze a few small buildings onto Sutherland's land behind that gate. He doesn't want other people in his house but surely they're allowed into other buildings nearby if he never leaves his own.'

'We'll see what shows up, but be ready to pretend you're sorry for causing alarm.'

Enough time passed for a security team to arrive from streets away but no one appeared and they sat in silence watching a closed gate. It did occur to Darian that the joke was rather on them, sitting watching nothing while security guards watched them from a comfortable office somewhere nearby. He didn't mention that to Sholto because why turn boredom into depression?

After twenty minutes the gates began to open slowly and Sholto said, 'Put on a hat and hang onto it, we've got action.'

There were long seconds as the electric gates slid back and then nothing. No car emerged. Instead, eventually, a short woman in her fifties with the black hair and tanned skin of a Caledonian walked out and marched straight for them. She had thin lips and small eyes, a round shape to her. She stepped beside the passenger window and rapped on it with her knuckles with just enough strength to suggest she was giving real thought to putting her fist through it.

Sholto cleared his throat loudly, the internationally recognised signal that he was going to do the talking, pressed the button to drop the window and leaned across Darian to smile out of the window as he said, 'Can we help you, love?'

The woman took a shocked step back from the grinning mug, scowled and said in an accent that retained only trace amounts of its original Panamanian, 'Don't call me love because I have no love for you. If you want to help me you can tell what you're doing parked out on the street like this.'

'We're looking for a young woman who's gone missing, name of Freya Dempsey, thirty-one, about your own height, shoulder-length blonde hair, pretty, wouldn't say boo to a goose if she had time to kick it in the face first. Have you seen her at all?'

'You're police?'

Having decided to be honest about their reasons for being there Sholto was compelled to stick to the risky strategy. Besides, one thing he had told Darian repeatedly they mustn't do was pretend they were policemen. Impersonating the law was a good way to piss off the police in half a nanosecond and an ingeniously stupid way to ruin your own investigation.

'No, we're not police, we're independent researchers, but we are working in conjunction with the police on this case.'

'I haven't seen this woman. Why are you looking for her here?'

'You work for Simon Sutherland, don't you? It was actually him we wanted to see, just to find out if he might have seen her, or if he might have heard anything about her.'

'Heard anything about her? Don't be so stupid, he couldn't have heard anything about this woman, you're wasting your time and mine and I am not a person who has time to sit looking at a gate all afternoon.'

Before the housekeeper could leave Sholto said, 'William Dent had contact with Freya Dempsey, and we know William Dent comes to this house, he delivers food here.'

Darian chipped in, 'Quite a lot of food for one person.'

The housekeeper, determined to win some part of the argument, said, 'Some of that was cleaning materials for me to look after the house. It's a large house to look after.'

Sholto said, 'Can I ask you your name?'

'My name is Olinda Bles. I am resident here; I have had my passport for nearly thirty years so you can't threaten me with that.'

'I certainly wasn't going to threaten you, Miss Bles, I wouldn't think of it. The last time I threatened a Panamanian lady I had to put my food through a blender for the next three or four days, and you don't want to know what that many Chinese takeaways look like blended.'

'Huh, well, maybe you deserved it.'

'Well, yeah, I probably did. Listen, Miss Bles, it's a bit silly us talking through a car window out on the street like this. Can we not come in and talk to you and Simon in the house?'

The look she gave him suggested he had just invited her to the International Space Station for a cup of tea. Before she gave what seemed like an inevitable dismissal of the idea she stopped and looked up and down the lane, thinking about things she had no intention of sharing.

'You say you're working with the police?'

Sholto nodded with the conviction of a reluctant liar and said, 'In conjunction with them. We're working... in conjunction with them.'

'Maybe it would be right for you to come in. Mr Sutherland has done nothing wrong, and this will stop you coming back because you won't be welcome back, but you must respect that he has very strict rules in his house, and it's necessary that you keep to them. You will only be allowed into one room and you must leave nothing behind, you understand?'

Having not planned on parting with anything for the privilege of entry Sholto said, 'Sure, yeah.'

They both got out of the Fiat and followed Olinda Bles through the gates and up the curved, cobbled driveway to the house. Behind them Darian heard the electric gate begin to slide shut.

17

FROM THE OUTSIDE the house didn't look like a home, rather the sort of cavernous modern steel structure a museum would build on the outskirts of town to store its less attractive artefacts out of public view. The original house was still there, a pretty mansion with a hundred years of genteel life written in every stone, but now looked like a small bird trapped in the jaws of a metal wolf, the new extensions sticking out the back and right side. They had obviously been added at different times, and although the presumably expensive architect had made every effort to design something striking, in this setting they couldn't look anything other than monstrous and threatening.

What stood out for Darian as he walked up the drive to the front door of the house, part of the original building, was how little there was to see. On either side of the driveway there were lawns and the grass was cut short but there were no flowers or shrubs whatsoever.

The only trees were those ringing the garden wall and there was no evidence of garden furniture. The windows of the building were all covered by blackout blinds so there was no chance of seeing in and there was one car on the drive, a little hatchback he assumed was the housekeeper's. Darian couldn't see a garage and assumed Simon Sutherland had no car of his own.

Olinda Bles led them into a hallway that was remarkable only for its pristine state: it was clean and bare. The floor was dark wood, as was the staircase to the right, and both looked polished enough to slide along with minimal propulsion. There was no furniture and nothing on the walls. Miss Bles turned right and along a long corridor and through to a room that was, very obviously, part of the extension. The wooden floors gave way to black tiles, the walls were plain white, and there was a huge window to their right covered entirely with a white roller blind. The high-ceilinged room was totally empty, with nowhere for them to sit, but this was where Miss Bles wanted them to wait.

She said, 'You will stay in this room and you will not go into any others. If you do I will call the security team and have them throw you out.'

Darian said, 'There's a security team?'

'There is, and if they want to keep their jobs they will do what I tell them so you will do what I tell you.'

'Are they here, the security team? In the building?'

'No, but they're close.'

As she turned to the door behind her, which led deeper into the extension, Sholto said, 'When was the last time Simon left the house?'

It took her a few seconds to decide to answer and when she did she threw it hastily at them. 'It was a few months after his mother died, so he would have been fifteen. That was nine or ten years ago. They forced him out and he didn't want to go. He didn't speak a word to anyone for months afterwards, so they didn't try again.'

'So they built the extensions around him?'

'Yes. He didn't enjoy it but he insisted they be built. He needed the room. But that is not why you're here. I'll get him, you'll have a few minutes and no more and if you say something I don't like it is over.'

Now she went through to the extension and left them in the meeting room. Alone in each other's company in the bare room, Darian said, 'What do you suppose he needs all this room for?'

Sholto shook his head. 'Normally with rich young men it would be frivolous crap that my life savings wouldn't buy a fraction of, but he doesn't seem to be the frivolous crap type.'

'He doesn't seem the any crap at all type.'

'I don't suppose there's any harm left in asking him because we're not getting a second interview no matter how we play this one. Just being here burns every bridge in Challaid that might lead us to a Sutherland, even the one across to Vinny's Dr Watson.'

There was movement behind the door Miss Bles had left through and it opened. She led in Simon Sutherland for their first look at him. He was tall and thin and pale enough to inspire Bram Stoker, and there was a clear resemblance to both Phil and Harold Sutherland, especially in the shape of the round mouth, but Darian could also see sharpness in the blue eyes that all Sutherlands near the centre of the family tree seemed to share. He had a thin face and high forehead, and his long fingers were entwined as he stood in front of them.

Sholto said, 'Thanks for talking to us, we appreciate this.'

Simon nodded and didn't say anything, remaining just inside the door so that he wasn't close enough for them to touch. Neither Darian nor Sholto made a move to shake his hand as good manners would usually dictate because he obviously didn't want that.

Sholto, convinced he was the less threatening of the two, said, 'We won't keep you long, Simon. There are just a couple of questions we wanted to ask you. Miss Bles will already have told you that we're looking for a woman called Freya Dempsey, and I wondered if that name meant anything to you.'

Simon shook his head and said quietly, 'No, it doesn't, sorry.'

'You've never seen her, met her, heard about her?'

'No, I never have.'

'You know William Dent, Simon?'

'Yes, I know Will.'

'What does he do for you?'

Sholto, bored with yes or no answers, had asked him something that required more and Simon looked annoyed by it as he replied, 'He's a driver for my uncle Harold, sometimes he brings my shopping here, that's about all.'

He had, of course, a posh end of Challaid accent, smoother than a cue ball and less obviously designed to speak Gaelic. Still, there was a hint of something in it that Darian didn't think was local, as if he was a young man who didn't hear a lot of other Challaid accents so was influenced by the housekeeper and what he saw on TV instead.

'And Will Dent never mentioned her? Because he has met her.'

'No, not to me.'

'Does anyone else come to the house, other than Miss Bles and Will?'

'My uncle Harold comes round now and then.'

'That's it?'

'Yes, just those three.'

'Okay, well, last question then, Simon. Why do you need so much space when you're living here on your own?'

Simon seemed shocked by the question, as though it were more intrusive than Sholto realised. He said, 'I like to keep things, my own things, so I need it.'

It was a halting, uncertain response, as though he felt the need to justify it, which from someone else might have seemed guilt-ridden, but from Simon Sutherland appeared no more than the words of a man not used to talking to strangers.

That was the end of the interview and Simon left through the same door he had entered from while Miss Bles led Sholto and Darian out of the house and down the driveway to the gate.

'You can see he has nothing more to say to you, he knows nothing about this woman, there's no way he could. He doesn't leave the house, he doesn't have people here and he doesn't like to touch people.'

Sholto said to her, 'Why did you let us in to talk to him?'

'To get rid of you.'

With that, Miss Bles walked back up to the house, the gates sliding shut automatically behind her. Darian and Sholto got into the Fiat and Sholto started it with his usual entreaty, 'Come on, Fiat, don't fail me now.'

Darian said, 'What did you think of that?'

'I think if you told me there were bodies piled up in that place I wouldn't call you a moron straight away. And I don't believe for a second that she let us in to get rid of us.'

'So why did she let us in?'

'That, my boy, is the next wee puzzle we have to crack.'

Diary

15/05/2018

Today was more difficult because there were visitors. I slept in W last night but woke earlier than usual today. Olinda came to the room and told me there was a car across the road with two men in it. I got up then. I laid out Tuesday's clothes and went to the bathroom to wash. I finished the bottle of shampoo in the shower so it will go to N now. I can see it there with the others. When I went out of the bathroom and through to 5 Olinda was waiting for me. She told me the two men were working with the Challaid police. They wanted to talk to me and so I met with them in the white room. That made the rest of the day much more complicated for me.

I did my best to work out how much time I spent in the white room. I tried to make sure I got times right for the other rooms throughout the day. Even now I'm not honestly sure I did. I spent less time in the white room later to try and make up for it.

After the men's unwelcome visit I went round W and touched each item that requires it. My mind was pushed sideways by these men being in my house. Olinda was right about having the white room set aside for this sort of thing though. The thought of strangers among my items makes me sweat and shiver. Just touching the items that needed touching made me realise how important it is men like them never get in. They would disturb every room and every item.

I tapped all the outdated remote controls and the old video players. I touched the old game controllers and ran my finger along the top of every book. The room settled down quickly when I did. All the disruption of me being late, of me being in the white room, was forgotten. It wasn't the same, not for the whole day, but it wasn't as bad as perhaps it could have been.

The whole day was now inevitably off balance. I knew N had been waiting for me. Every room had an atmosphere when I arrived. N never takes long to settle, light billows through it in seconds. It's the room other people would understand least. That's why I care for it so much. That's why it forgives. I opened each sealed box for a few seconds to let all the wrappers and cartons know I was there.

I went up the stairs and touched every item of clothing on the rails but one. All but the bra that scares the room. N is the boldest room because everything can still serve its purpose, just not for me. I've outgrown the clothes. I can't wear them. That's what they exist for and I can't use them at all. I spent time there to let them know they won't be forgotten.

Being in 5 felt heavier than usual today. Whenever the day is damaged being among mother's things is more difficult. The pain of struggling reminds me of how strong she always was. How hard she tried. When a person dies they leave a gap, and it doesn't shrink. It's forever there, standing broad in the very centre of your existence. You're always stepping carefully around it, trying hard not to fall in. Every sidestep you make provides another stinging reminder of what you've lost. There are days 5 can be a happy place but not today. Today it was hard and I felt painfully beaten by it by the time I left.

Tomorrow will be better. I will sleep the first half of the night in W and the second in N. I hope there will be no interruption tomorrow and time will be in the right place. When everything is done properly the world is a place of calm. I can live that. Hopefully no more visitors. To think of people from outside coming and upsetting this place is too much for me. I'll struggle to sleep tonight if I think about it any more.

18

DARIAN AND SHOLTO sat in the office, putting reports together in lieu of anything more productive, Sholto trying to write out a suitably polite but firm reminder to PINE Insurance that they still hadn't paid for the work done. People who had never hired them before were the most likely to think they had an excuse not to pay at all. Having refused his offer to chase the money to San José, Sholto was nervous the company were now planning to pretend the whole thing had never happened. He wouldn't allow that because he knew they were under pressure from past scandals and would have to cough up for silence.

They were actually waiting for a phone call while this attempt at looking busy was going on. Not one they were looking forward to, but Sholto had his excuses ready for whichever Sutherland called up and shouted in his well-prepared ear.

He said, 'It'll be Harold Sutherland first because he's the one that looks after the boy.'

Darian said, 'The boy is twenty-five years old and he's entitled to talk to whoever he wants. We were invited in.'

'Oh, aye, by the housekeeper, and don't think for a second she won't throw us under a fleet of buses if the pressure cranks up. She knew what she was doing, all that stuff about us working with the police, that was so she can pretend she thought we were the police, accuse us of misleading her, like she wasn't sharp as a tack and with better English than the two of us.'

'It was you that said we were working in conjunction with them.'

'Darian, it's very rude to throw a man's words back in his face, especially when they were as carefully chosen as mine.'

'Once the uncle finds out we'll have Phil Sutherland after us as well.'

'Your friend Vinny can hold him back if he wants us to keep on helping.'

Darian didn't ask who would hold the lawyers back. They waited all day and the two occasions on which the phone rang it was a previous client asking for another receipt after losing the last one and someone assuring them that their computer needed to be fixed. Sholto claimed that he didn't have a computer, that he'd never heard of such an invention, didn't trust modern technology and did not, in fact, own a telephone, at which point he hung up.

The clock ticked round to eight minutes to five, which Sholto decided was exactly the right time to go home.

'I've had enough of doing very little. You get in touch with Vinny and update him, and if he doesn't have anything else to offer then we pass what we know to DS MacNeith and let her take shelter from the hail of Sutherland lawyers if she goes after Simon.'

Sholto put the files into the cabinet and locked it before putting his laptop into his bag. Darian left his laptop in the office but all the files that mattered were stored only on the little memory stick he put in his pocket and took home with him. Sholto locked the office behind them and they made their way downstairs together, both with the mid-investigation blues. It happened a lot in difficult cases, the sort that more often than not went unsolved, the sense that they had reached a point where the roads all around them were blocked. There were people who seemed worthy of further inspection but there was nothing approaching the sort of proof that even the worst of Challaid's collection of erratic judges would be convinced by. It was hard not to slip into a funk.

While Sholto turned right to walk down to Dlùth Street where he parked his car, Darian turned left and walked up to Glendan Station. He had two travel cards for the train line, one for work and one for personal use. He could claim the cost of travelling the city to the client when it was for work, but this was going home. He took the train through the tunnel and across to the next stop, Bank Station. From there it was a pleasant stroll to his flat.

Darian always enjoyed that walk, especially at this time of year, going up Fàrdach Road and then cutting round the back of the building, walking along the large square of grass that served the four L-shaped buildings around it. There were washing lines and when the sun made an appearance it would be filled with kids kicking balls around. They tried to play in the rain too until someone stopped them for ruining the grass, but this day was rare in its pleasantness. There were four boys booting each other more than the ball and using a stretch of wall without windows as the goal, the three outfield players pausing their mutual assault only to try and chip the keeper in a pale imitation of the goal Arthur Samba had scored for Challaid FC against Hearts in the league the previous Sunday. The largest of the boys kept claiming his chips were dropping in despite the fact that he was endangering first-floor windows and Stretch Armstrong couldn't have caught them. None of the others argued with the bigger boy as Darian walked in through the back door.

The building was better than a man on Darian's salary should have been able to afford. The three Ross siblings had gotten an even split of the proceeds from the sale of the family home after they were done living in it, their mother dead and father in prison. As Darian walked along the corridor the place smelled of the polish the janitor used on the floors. His feet tapped out an echo as he skipped up the stairs to the first floor, round the corner and then up to the second.

Someone was on the landing already. A man in his thirties with a slack gut even his nice coat couldn't hide. He had dark hair, the puffy lips of a low-quality boxer and bags under his eyes. Darian's first thought was that he was with Challaid Police. Then he realised the man's suit was too good for that and his mind leapt from police to gangster, although he couldn't work out what he might have done to upset that lot.

'Darian Ross?'

The man had the local accent of someone raised by a Caledonian parent, which told Darian exactly nothing.

'Might be.'

'Alan Dudley. I'm with Raven Investigators.'

Like a hitman's bullet Raven staff always came in twos and were always unwelcome. The other one was presumably out front.

'What do you want?'

'I'm here with a job offer. You're wasting your time at clown college, come work at a place where you'll actually learn how to do the job.'

'I'm learning plenty.'

'Bad habits don't count.'

'I'll take my chances.'

'You only get one chance, Darian, and you're pissing yours away working for a man that can't protect you from all the wrong enemies you're making.'

Darian frowned and said, 'And what enemies would those be?'

'If you don't know that much then you have got problems. This was your one chance, Darian. I'm about to walk right past you and leave you way behind. You can stop me by saying you'll come work for us.'

Maybe it was all the very many times he had heard Sholto badmouth Raven, or the times he'd heard other more reliable witnesses disparage them just as loudly. Maybe it was because Dudley was a cretin who said work for instead of work with; even though it was factually correct it seemed like an attempt to make him feel junior. Whatever the reason, the thought of going to work at Raven ranked alongside lava-surfing on Darian's list of things to do.

He said, 'Off you go then.'

Dudley scoffed and stepped forward, shoving past Darian. Being young and full to the brim with vim, Darian shoved back. Dudley pushed hard, pressing him against the wall, getting right in his face and hissing through his small yellowed teeth, 'I'm going to enjoy bringing you down, Ross, you and the old wanker on Cage Street. Thank fuck you turned us down.'

Darian, expression unchanged, said, 'Spit on your lips after one little push? I wouldn't work for you if you were holding my balls for ransom. You're the clown, Dudley, right out of a Stephen King novel.'

Dudley scoffed again and went quickly down the stairs, his footsteps echoing behind him. He'd come with two destructive messages and had delivered them both. A job offer and then a threat. Darian went into the flat.

19

DARIAN GOT SOMETHING to eat because that was the reason he had gone home in the first place. He would have described it as dinner but the word sandwich would also be true and his definition of what constituted a meal was not widely shared. When he had finished the feast of bread and ham he called up Vinny.

The cop said, 'I'm working tonight, but it's okay, come to the Darks on Conrad Drive, meet me backstage.'

So Darian was out of the flat again, walking back down to Bank Station and taking the train, this time on his work card, up to Three O'clock Station in Whisper Hill. It took five minutes just to get off the overcrowded platform and along the concourse to the door and from there another twenty to get down to Conrad Drive, a street that ran across from Docklands Street to the train tracks. Dark, Dark, Dark was a graceful music venue with a long history and strong reputation, one of few venues in The Hill that work had never taken him to but his social life had.

At the entrance Darian asked a woman working there if she had seen Vinny and she told him to go up the stairs at the side of the foyer and follow the corridor along to the back. Darian did as he was told and found himself turning onto a walkway with an open space looking down from above the stage where a man was playing guitar and singing beautiful songs to a couple of hundred quietly happy people. Vinny was standing watching.

'So why does this gig need a police goon like you to work it?'

Vinny whispered, 'It doesn't. I know the owner, Lyall Maddock, a reformed cop, he's a mate. Every time there's a gig on I want to see but I'm working he calls up the station and asks for me to come along and keep the peace. They know it's a swizz but they let it slide, means I can't say no when they send me to police a venue populated by screaming nutjobs trying to bottle each other.'

They had been whispering low and fell silent as they listened to the song 'Stained Glass'. When it was finished and the crowd below applauded Vinny turned to Darian and said, 'So what's the news?'

'Speculative. Every avenue we've gone down has been a complete dead end except maybe Dent and Simon Sutherland, and they're both maybes at best. We went to Simon Sutherland's house and got in and he was as odd as every other number. That's probably an offensive way to describe someone with his issues but...'

'True?'

'Aye.'

'Did he know anything about Freya?'

'He said no, but there wasn't a convincing word in him. Add to that the housekeeper letting us inside in the first place. She didn't have to but she wanted to, and I don't think it was to help us. There are secrets in that barn of a house and we'd need to have a proper sweep of the place to find them.'

Vinny nodded with the expression of a man about to make a friend do something he didn't want to. He led Darian along the corridor and down the stairs, out through the front door and across the road to The Whaler's, the sort of all-night café that served you a plate of grease which, if you were one of the lucky ones, might have something solid in it. It was a good place to go if you wanted to test the mettle of your digestive system, and Phil Sutherland was already there. Vinny and Darian sat opposite him and his usually distant expression took another backward step.

Vinny said, 'Darian has a wee update on the case and you're not allowed to piss your pants about it.'

Darian said, 'I'm sorry that I went to your cousin's house.'

'You *what*? You went to Simon's house? What for?'

'You hadn't heard already?'

'No, I'm not in contact with Simon.'

'But you speak to your uncle and your uncle speaks to Simon. I would have guessed he'd have called your uncle as soon as we left and your uncle would be straight onto you. We were round there this morning.'

'Right after I specifically asked you not to go.'

'Pretty much.'

'Maybe my uncle hasn't heard yet. I don't know his exact relationship with Simon, how often they speak. I don't know what anyone's relationship with Simon is like.'

'I'd be surprised if your uncle didn't know something because when I got home this afternoon there was a Raven agent at my flat flapping his dark wings, offering me a job with them that I'm sure would have involved leaving every member of your family the hell alone. When I turned it down he all but threatened to peck my eyes out.'

Vinny said, 'Raven, that shower of pissants. At least you and Sholto are honest in your dishonesty. I can't stand people who pretend to play fair.'

Phil said, 'They tried to buy you? That does sound like it might be Uncle Harold's style. He would try to put out a fire with money before he thought about water. But that's just him trying to protect the company.'

'Not him trying to protect his driver, or his nephew?'

'You can't actually think Simon had anything to do with Freya going missing? The poor sod hasn't left the house in years. How could he do it?'

'With the help of a shifty driver who treats violence as casual amusement.'

Phil shook his head. 'I don't buy that. Simon, the way he is, he would never get involved in something as messy as this.'

'Simon the way you think he is, perhaps. Maybe there's more to him than we know, like what does he need all that space for?'

'The story I heard is that he keeps everything that comes into the house and doesn't have the ability to walk back out. Every single thing he's ever owned. If Freya had gone into the house and, worst-case scenario, wasn't able to walk back out, she would still be there, which means the housekeeper would have seen some sign of her.'

'The housekeeper who let us in, like she wanted us to see something?'

Phil didn't look at all ready to be convinced by that. He shook his head but said, 'There's a simple enough way to solve this. I go to the house tomorrow and have a look around and if I see something I'll let you know. If something happened in that house, and I think you've wandered off the edge of the map looking for a clue there by the way, then we'll know.'

Darian nodded and said, 'Maybe Simon has nothing to do with it, but Dent might and he has access to that property as well. It's a huge space, and I think you, me, Vinny and Sholto should all go.'

Phil said, 'No, no way will he let four in and I wouldn't try to force him. You and me then. Vinny, you stay out because it's too personal; I don't want you putting heat on a fractured mind. Me and you, Darian, and any link to Freya will stand out like a sore thumb in there. We go and we put an end to this one way or the other.'

'Okay, fine, just us two. I'll meet you there at nine.'

Phil stayed in the café to finish sucking mouthfuls of grease off his fork and Vinny went back across the road in less of a mood for the music. His mind, Darian knew, wasn't on Freya but on their son, Finn. What was he going to tell the boy if the worst ended up being confirmed? Darian tried not to think about it on the train home.

20

THE FOLLOWING MORNING was a Monday and the traffic was horrendous as Sholto drove Darian back up to Geug Place. When they arrived they found Vinny and Phil already there, both in street clothes. Vinny had driven them up in his car, which looked like it had finished the Dakar Rally about ten minutes earlier and had parked in the passing place across the road that Darian and Sholto had used the day before. There wasn't room for a second vehicle so Sholto had to park in front of Simon Sutherland's gates.

Vinny and Phil walked over and Phil said, 'I managed to have a difficult conversation with Simon and Olinda, the housekeeper. They've both agreed we can go in, just the two of us, but there are conditions. I'm pretty sure this has already upset him, and I think what we're doing will take him months to recover from. If it wasn't Freya we were looking for I don't think I'd let it happen.'

Standing on the road beside Sholto's car Vinny said, 'Yes you would. You're a cop. You have a cop's instincts, whether you want them or not. Whoever it was you would want to find her.'

Before Phil could think of a humble reply the gates began to slide open. The four men stood in silence and watched as Olinda Bles came into view, walking down the driveway towards them. She stood on the threshold with her arms crossed and looked out at them as though they were barbarians she had been sent to negotiate with when she'd much rather go to war with them instead.

'If you were not police you would not even get as close as you are now to the house. And you, you should know what this will do to your own cousin.'

Phil nodded slightly and said, 'I do know, and I'm sorry about it, but this is very important. It'll be me and Darian coming in and we'll be as respectful as possible.'

She made a wordless noise that dismissed utterly the value of their respect and turned to walk up the drive. Darian and Phil followed in her furious wake. As they walked Darian noticed her slip a hand into the pocket of her black trousers and suddenly the gate began to close, so that explained that little mystery. He glanced back over his shoulder to see Vinny standing on the road, looking nervously through the bars at them, Sholto sitting on the bonnet of his car.

They went in through the front door and turned right to reach the same bare room Darian had found himself in the day before. This time Simon was waiting for them. He looked like a man wishing the room was even emptier, crushed by the weight of the new arrivals.

Phil nodded and said, 'Thanks for letting us in, Simon. How are you?'

'I have been better. How are you, Philip?'

'Sorry about all this. We'll try and make it as fast as we can, and once we've ruled out what we need to rule out this will be over and you won't see us again.'

Miss Bles said, 'He shouldn't have to see you now. If you're going to be here then you're going to follow house rules.'

Both Darian and Phil said, 'Okay.'

'You will both take your shoes off and leave them in this room. Neither of you will touch anything. Nothing, okay? You don't lay a finger on anything you see in there. You will only go places I take you, so do not try to wander off on your own. If you don't like those rules you can leave now.'

Darian and Phil looked at each other and nodded their agreement.

They removed their shoes and stood by the door. Miss Bles did the leading, Darian and Phil the following, while Simon Sutherland drifted around behind them looking on the verge of tears. The first room they went into was enormous, more a warehouse than a home, and all the way along the bare floor were metal shelves packed with all manner of useless items that anyone else would have thrown out long ago. Among it were three clear plastic boxes full of neatly tied up cables, another with old telephones with their cables curled up behind them. On another shelf there was an old PlayStation 1, a controller plugged into each port and neatly laid out in front of it, a memory card in its slot and a stack of old games beside it. On the next shelf along was a PlayStation 2 with a couple of controllers and a much larger collection of games. Darian leaned in close to the PS2 games, not touching them, and saw *Final Fantasy 10* and *Sly Cooper* were at the front.

He glanced across at Simon and said, 'These aren't in alphabetical order?'

Simon looked insulted by the question, as though he thought Darian was making fun of him. 'They're all in the order I got them.'

'When was that?'

'I got those when I was about nine or ten years old.'

Darian and Phil moved around the room, taking it all in, Miss Bles always hovering within striking distance should either of them raise a hand towards the belongings. Phil looked stunned by it, his cousin's entire life laid out on display like that. He had known some of Simon's health issues, but family members speaking of it meant little until the scale was visible before you. Having completed a careful circle of the room Darian turned to Miss Bles.

She said, 'Upstairs.'

More of the same was waiting, another long, tall room running most of the length of the extension with two smaller rooms off to the side. After a circuit of looking at what any other person would politely term unsightly garbage they were shown into a bedroom and bathroom that contained the absolute least those rooms reasonably could. Every item in every room was individually displayed so nothing could be hidden in a pile somewhere.

As they walked across a corridor to the top floor of the rear extension Darian said to Simon, 'Why are all the items given so much room? Why not pile everything together?'

Simon said, 'I'm not some hoarder. I give everything room.'

In the upstairs room of the rear extension they found clothes that dated back to childhood. Some were well worn, none would have fitted Simon anymore, but all were either hung neatly on racks or had been folded and placed on shelves with the sort of care usually afforded to religious relics. Darian and Phil made their way down the aisles, Miss Bles close behind and Simon holding back near the door. Towards the end of the middle lane Darian came to underwear, pants and boxer shorts, socks and vests, and then the first thing that stood out. Among the scattered remains of a life it might seem hard for any item to catch the eye but there was a bra sitting alone on the top of a shelving unit.

Darian looked back over his shoulder at Miss Bles and said, 'All the other clothes are his. Whose is this?'

She shook her head. 'I don't know. I've never known, and I don't think he does either. It's been there for a long time, though.'

Simon came round the corner at the top of the aisle and walked towards them. He stared at the plain black bra and said, 'That's been there for more than a year, last January, I think. It just turned up. One day it wasn't there, next it was. I've never touched it.'

'You never touched it?'

'No, it's not mine. It doesn't belong here.'

'So why don't you throw it away?'

Simon looked at Darian as if he was an idiot, which, having seen the rest of the house and still asked the question, was not an unreasonable accusation. He said, 'I don't throw things out, even if I don't want them here.'

Darian and Phil both stared at it for a while. It was black, small and a bit grubby, like it had been put through the washing machine too many times and not been washed again for a couple of years since. Unlike Simon's own clothes it had been dumped in a heap instead of being laid out so it was harder to see all of it, but Phil noticed something.

He said, 'The clasp is broken. Look, it's ripped from the edge there.'

They both stared at it, thinking of a bra being forcibly removed. This one item, left to lie untouched by a man who couldn't throw it out even if he wanted to. Both Darian and Phil had heard enough stories of perpetrators keeping mementos, but Simon had known they were coming and did nothing to hide it.

Phil said, 'You don't know who left it here?'

'I've asked all the people who come here. None of them know, or will admit it.'

They toured the rest of the house. They saw his late mother's belongings, which gave them the chance to mentally compare her bra size with the one upstairs. Apart from the fact that not one of hers looked as if it had been bought at a supermarket they were also much too big to fit the owner of the mysterious one upstairs. They saw photos of the family through the years, including a group one showing a young Phil with his parents and a varied collection of aunts, uncles and cousins. Miss Bles led them through the rest of the original house, which felt like an empty home rather than the storage facility the rest of it did. There was nothing else to catch their beady eyes. When they were finished they returned to the bare white room and put their shoes back on.

Phil said, 'Thanks for letting us in, Simon.'

'Is this over now?'

'I doubt it. Don't you want to know where that bra came from?'

'Well, yes I do.'

'Okay then.'

They walked down the driveway and the gate slid open. A bored-looking Vinny and Sholto got out of the Fiat and stood expectantly.

Darian said, 'We found a bra. He says it's been there since last January, that he doesn't know where it came from. We should call DS MacNeith.'

21

'I CAN FEEL IT, YOU KNOW. It's like pinpricks in my back.'

Darian looked across the office at Sholto and said, 'What are you talking about?'

'When a rich person is angry with me and they're hunting me down. There's going to be hell to pay and I'm all out of cash.'

Vinny and Phil had gone to Cnocaid station to give details to DS MacNeith about the bra, Sholto having called already. They had known what would happen next. Simon Sutherland was arrested and taken to the station, leaving the house for the first time in a little over nine years. According to the text Vinny had sent it was the housekeeper, Miss Bles, who had put the fear of God into the arresting officers. Simon had been quiet while she had been extraordinarily loud when she found out why they were there. The police had taken the bra for tests to try and identify its owner.

Darian said, 'Perhaps Harold Sutherland won't come after us. It's his nephew he'll be most annoyed with.'

'Oh, Darian, no, that's not how these people work, has no one told you that already? I'll tell you how they operate. Behind closed doors he'll be fuming with Phil, sure he will, because that was a family betrayal, or that's how he'll see it. But people like the Sutherlands, very old money, very big money, their greatest skill is protecting what they have. It's probably genetic at this point, instinctive, like when the son of a great camanachd player turns out to be decent without trying. The last thing Harold Sutherland will do is allow anyone outside the family to think Phil is to blame. Protect the business, that's what they do. Someone else is going to have to become the enemy, and I'm willing to bet his impressively expensive lawyers will paint a large target on my sweaty back. Just thinking about it... I hope he phones rather than comes round. I can at least sound like my rectum isn't imploding underneath me but I can't look the part if he's in front of me.'

They sat and waited for the phone to ring, wondering whether they would hear from an excited cop or a fizzing lawyer first. Instead they heard footsteps on the wooden stairs, more than one person making his way up to the second floor. Sholto closed his eyes and prayed that it was two of the three men from the data services company along the corridor. Instead there was a single knock on the door, and then, having clearly decided that knocking was a courtesy they didn't deserve, the door was flung open.

The expression on Harold Sutherland's face was one that had probably never been seen in public before. This was a man who prided himself on being friendly and charming but was now in a rage so powerful that only the presence of the lawyer beside him was holding back violence. The lawyer was a tall, skinny man in his forties with the look of a referee at a boxing match who feared both fighters were wearing knuckle dusters under their gloves. It was all he could do to stop himself physically restraining his client.

In a near-trembling voice Harold said, 'How much would it cost to purchase the use of your inconsiderable talents for this case, then? Hmm? To have you conduct a proper investigation.'

Sholto chewed nervously on the question for a few seconds and said, 'One billion pounds.'

'Excuse me?'

'I intend either to die an honest man or a billionaire, Mr Sutherland. One billion pounds.'

'Good grief, the price of your virtue is going to cost you your business.'

Darian said, 'We're valuable men.'

Harold Sutherland looked back and forth between Darian and Sholto, the façade crumbling after his first, failed attempt, and said, 'You bastards. You lying little bastards. You came to me for help and so I helped you, and in response you've tried to ruin the life of an innocent boy just so you can pretend you've cracked a case. Do you understand how long it's going to take Simon to recover from this? Do you care? Years. They'll question him and my lawyers, who are there now en masse, will destroy their scattergun of stupidity and lies and Simon will be home by the end of the day but the damage will have been done. You and that bloody police force. This isn't just a bad day for Simon; this is years of his life you've ruined.'

Darian, assuming Sholto would be momentarily silenced by his phobia of the intimidatingly rich, said, 'We certainly didn't mean to do that. We're trying to find Freya Dempsey, and I'm sure you can understand our urgency.'

Harold Sutherland took a couple of steps towards Darian's desk, his teeth bared as if he was trying to decide which part of him to bite first. He said in a near hiss, 'Don't you dare try to pretend that I'm the uncaring one here. I and my family have gone out of our way to help you find this woman on the basis of a tenuous connection, while you have bulldozed your way into my nephew's life and toppled over the contentment he's spent a decade trying to build. He had to try to find a balance that made life liveable for him, and you've shoulder-charged it because you don't care about people, just the case in front of you.'

'That's unfair. You don't know us.'

'I know you're friends with PC Reno. I know he was the prime suspect before you decided to concoct this nonsense against Simon. I know you're going to suffer the heaviest blow I can throw at you, and I know I'm not going to stop swinging haymakers at you even after I've shut this place down and made you both unemployable in Challaid. I have a long memory and a long reach.'

Harold turned and marched out of the office and his lawyer, seeming to think that it had gone better than expected, nodded and went after him.

Sholto breathed out heavily and grabbed the edge of his desk, or at least the folders hanging over it, and said, 'Chee whizz.'

Darian was looking out of the window, watching the young man walking uncertainly up towards the office. William Dent, presumably having dropped off his boss and ready to pick him up again. Harold still using his favourite driver. A loyal man, Phil had said. Harold and the lawyer emerged down below on Cage Street and walked quickly down to Dlùth Street, Dent alongside them now to show where he had parked.

Sholto said, 'Oh, that was unpleasant, my guts are doing enough somersaults to win an Olympic bronze medal. Do we have any legal or semi-legal drugs that might help?'

'No. You can try downstairs. Mr Yang will have some.'

'That better not be a crack at his cooking. Even at a time like this I won't hear a word said against it.'

'I mean he has a cupboard full of that sort of stuff for the family.'

'Never mind, I'll ride it out. Have to keep riding for the rest of my life if he was serious about coming after us. The rich, Darian, they're nothing but trouble.'

It was hard to argue and better not to, so he said nothing. Instead they waited to hear how the questioning of Simon Sutherland had gone. If he was guilty they were off Harold's hook.

Blog Post

15/02/17

Ruby-Mae Short
04/08/96–12/01/17

They found my sister's body beside the train tracks in Whisper Hill a month ago and now all anyone ever talks about is her being a murder victim. There's nothing I want more than to see the police catch who killed her and I know that raising awareness of what happened to her is a part of that but someone needs to talk about who Ruby was when she was alive. She wasn't just a murder victim, she was a person.

The first flat we lived in was a small place on Mòine Road in Earmam that I mostly remember being damp and cold. I was a year and a half older than Ruby so I don't really remember her much as a baby but I do remember her as a toddler and always being on the move. Even back then she had so much energy. It's funny how the things that annoyed me most about her as kids are the things I miss the most now.

She was five when our parents divorced and a couple of years later our mum met our stepdad and we moved into a bigger, more modern flat in Bakers Moor. It was strange for us as kids, a time of upheaval, but the one constant was Ruby and her energy and happiness and loudness. She was always singing and dancing and had more space for it now. At Caisteal Secondary School she was involved in everything, dancing and acting and all sorts of clubs. She made friends easily and kept them forever. The people in her life meant everything to her, and she made time for each and every one.

As she got older she started to think about what she was going to do with her life, but she was so full of enthusiasm for so many things that she never really settled on one. I started engineering and when I got a placement with Duff she insisted we go out to celebrate. She was probably happier and more proud than I was, but that was Ruby. That was the last time we spent together and it was one of the best. Seeing her so happy, the way the energy radiated out of her and infected everyone around her, it's a memory of how special she was, how just being around her was a gift. I was on a ship that had just docked in New Edinburgh when I got the message saying she had been killed and Duff had me flown home to be with my family.

I hate having to write all that, even the good memories, because it means talking about Ruby in the past tense. Every mention of her life brings back memories of what we as a family have gone through in the last month. Hearing talk of what happened to her, newspapers and websites speculating about why a young woman was out for drinks and hinting at things I know are untrue and that I will never forgive them for suggesting. All those people want to talk about her death and the investigation into it. I want everyone to know that Ruby-Mae Short was not just a murder victim, Ruby-Mae Short lived.

Nathan Short

22

THE VISIT FROM Harold Sutherland had shaken the ground but they were still waiting for a phone call to say whether Simon had been charged or not. Waiting to hear what he had said under pressure.

Sholto was beginning to calm down to his usual mild discomfort when he said, 'We shouldn't expect much of a result out of that interview. A good lawyer can make a decent cop's day very difficult but an entire team of very expensive and determined lawyers can run the rings of Saturn around the whole legal system.'

'DS MacNeith is a good detective, she won't let this slip.'

'No, not on purpose, not out of ignorance or stupidity, but she's spent her whole career learning how to dish out justice and she'll encounter an entire squad of goons who've spent their working lives helping others sidestep it. I don't like how long it's taking either. That boy, he was already cracked, so if he was going to fall apart it would have happened by now. The legal eagles must be holding him together.'

'You really don't like lawyers, do you?'

Sholto shook his head. 'They do important work and everyone should have one, but you can say that about bowels as well and I wouldn't want to shake hands with one of them without gloves on either.'

'Would be worse without them.'

'It would, yes, but when I was a cop I saw the difference between a good lawyer and a brilliant one. A good one could get you off the hook if the evidence said you deserved to go free, a brilliant one could set you free no matter what story the evidence told. I saw too many guilty people walk free from police stations because brilliant lawyers came up against mediocre police investigations.'

Sholto didn't often hark back to his time as a detective at Cnocaid station, a period he hadn't much enjoyed. Darian thought it was partly because Sholto didn't like the job and partly because he didn't want to have to talk about Darian's father, his former colleague now in prison. Occasionally Darian was reminded that his boss just might have gone through a lot more in life than he cared to admit.

The problem with waiting for the phone to ring was that no one intended to call them. Instead they heard another set of feet making their way up the stairs and stopping outside the door, this time knocking and having the patience to wait to be let in. Sholto's desk was next to the door so he got up and opened it nervously. The woman on the other side of the threshold had dark hair and eyes and was wearing a red coat and black trousers. Her eyes were bright with mischievous laughter as she sauntered past Sholto and into the office, taking a good look around, a smirk on her wide mouth.

She said, 'So this is the famous office of Douglas Independent Research.'

Sholto closed the door before any other surprises could sneak past him and said, 'We've met?'

'Oh, no, sorry. I've met your colleague before, though, not yourself. You must be the famous Mr Douglas.'

The second to last thing Sholto wanted to be was famous. He said, 'I didn't think either me or my office were so well known. And your name is...?'

'DC Angela Vicario, it was me who interviewed Ash Lucas when Darian brought him in, and I did a little work on the Folan Corey case as well.'

Sholto's face lit up with joy at his memory's success as he said, 'Oh, yes, that's right, I remember, we have sort of met, or were in the same place at the same time anyway, Sgàil Drive, when...'

The mood in the room collapsed into misery as they remembered the last and only time the three of them had been together. Darian had called Vinny for help that desperate night and some of the aid he'd brought had been in the form of the playful but razor-sharp DC Vicario. There was nothing as happy as a smiling blade.

She said, 'I have come with what I think is good news, but not all good. I was called to Cnocaid station with a colleague because when they ran a check on the bra they found it matched one we were looking for. Do you remember the Ruby-Mae Short murder?'

Darian shook his head but Sholto said, 'Young woman found dead on the tracks behind Misgearan. They never got anyone for that, did they?'

'No, we never got close. One thing we didn't make public was that when we found her body we didn't find a bra on her. There was a possibility that she had been wearing it and her killer had kept it as a memento. We're still waiting for DNA to confirm it but the bra is from the same store where she bought most of her underwear and I'm convinced it's Ruby's, plus Simon Sutherland says it turned up in his home last January, which is when she was killed.'

Darian said, 'Why would he admit that?'

She shrugged and said, 'Perhaps it's a clever move; he knows we're going to identify the owner of the bra and he wants to set up his excuse as early as possible. Or it might be that someone is trying to make him look guilty. It's complicated, but I'm hoping to simplify it when we move him up to Whisper Hill and get him talking there.'

'Has he said anything about Freya Dempsey?'

'Nothing. There's no sign of her, unfortunately, but if he was involved in what was done to Ruby then he's very dangerous and we can't expect to have a good outcome with Freya. Look, we all like Vinny at Dockside, he's like a cool older brother to a lot of the young officers and we want to find out what happened to Freya for his son's sake as well. Have either of you heard any mention of Ruby, or anything else about 12 January last year when she was killed? Any shred of info we can get on that might help us with Freya, too.'

Both men shook their heads and Sholto said, 'No, but we've only been looking for Freya, only been asking questions about her. If her disappearance ties in with Ruby-Mae Short then we can start looking into that as well as part of the same investigation.'

'Obviously nothing that might interfere with what we're doing, but if you could check what your contacts have to say that would help. I have to go; I need to sit next to my boss while he goes jousting with the sort of lawyers a rich man can buy, which should be fun. I'll keep you updated.'

As he walked her the three steps to the door Sholto said, 'We'll hunt around our contacts and let you know if we come up with anything.'

DC Vicario stopped in the doorway and looked back into the office at Darian with a small smile before she said, 'I like your famous little office, it's unassuming.'

After closing the door behind her Sholto and Darian looked at each other with the shared expression of men who had just seen their case balloon out beyond their reach.

23

WITH THE PHONE IN the office set to divert calls to Sholto's mobile they went downstairs to The Northern Song to get something to eat. The lunchtime rush had passed so they could sit at the table at the back and Mr Yang brought their food to them, otherwise they could speak without fear of being overheard.

'You better start by telling me everything you remember about the Short case because I know nothing.'

Sholto nodded. 'I don't know a lot, to be honest, just what I read in the papers at the time. She was a twenty-year-old girl on a night out in Whisper Hill, nothing remarkable in that, drinking and the like, was spotted in Misgearan and a few hours later she was dead. They found her body the next morning; a train driver saw it from his cab so it can't have been hidden. It was dumped behind the fencing round the back of Misgearan so there was some attempt to keep it out of view.'

'Tipped over the fence?'

Sholto shook his head as he stuffed some sweet and sour into his mouth. Darian was thinking of a person trying to lift a body over the ten-foot corrugated iron fencing behind Long Walk Lane, something that couldn't be done subtly.

Sholto, chewing rapidly, said, 'No, it was over the line on the other side, I think. They didn't say that publicly, but they were looking for witnesses who might have seen anyone on Border Street, other side of the tracks, and the train driver who saw her was heading north to Three O'clock Station so I guess must have been on the left side of his cab, easier to spot her at speed. If we can get more information from the cheerful Miss Vicario we'll know for sure.'

'You think Misgearan matters?'

'Maybe, maybe not. Short was drinking there on the night, and last I heard the police hadn't identified everyone she was drinking with. Given Dockside station's relationship with that place I would guess they've gotten every slice of information possible from the staff. We can also assume old lady Docherty would rather be roasted over a spit than install any cameras in the place and the boys from Dockside would probably agree with her.'

'If the cases are linked then it rules out Vinny.'

'That's an if. Sometimes one case leads to another, or gets tangled in another, without them being directly related. I know you want them to be linked because it would make the Sutherland boy front runner. Before

Simon leapfrogged over him Vinny was prime suspect, and you want it to be anyone else, but Vinny is still number two on that list with the potential to reclaim top spot. I like Vinny, he's a nice guy, but never forget that nice people can do terrible things, too.'

For a few seconds the only sound was that of eating until Darian said, 'How do you know she's Miss?'

'Who, Short? She wasn't married, didn't have a boyfriend at the time either, they don't think.'

'No, DC Vicario, you called her Miss Vicario a wee while ago.'

'Did I? Well, she's not ringed, so I'm guessing. Is her marital status of any personal concern to you or was that question just professional interest in the accuracy of my statement?'

'Just curious about how well you know her.'

'Less well than you and not nearly as well as I'd like, and I don't mean that in a smutty way because Mrs Douglas is more than enough for a timid man like me. Vicario is smart and we know she's brave because she was willing to put herself in the middle of the Corey investigation. Just the sort of cop that would be a useful ally to have.'

'You always said to steer clear of cops. I'm getting mixed messages here.'

'Steer clear of the ones that don't like you, try and get a good relationship with the ones who do. Never personal, always professional. Simple enough.'

'She seems easy to talk to.'

Sholto said, 'Says the man hoping to talk to her a lot more. You do like the strong and playful types, don't you, Darian? I've warned you a hundred times and a hundred times again, nothing personal with cops. Forget about anything unprofessional, okay, she has far more important people to talk to right now than you and, well, maybe even me.'

'You think they'll get anything out of Sutherland?'

'They'll need to be more than smart and brave to manage. With all those lawyers around him he might be able to get out of that place in one piece, and you can be sure there's already a lot of pressure on Dockside to let the boy go. The Sutherland machine will be turning every cog at a furious pace to get the political help it needs. The bra is a heavy piece of evidence, but it might not be enough on its own to weigh down a member of that family.'

Darian said, 'He seemed vulnerable. Surely he'll fall apart if he's guilty.'

'No, think about it, if he's guilty then he isn't really vulnerable at all. If he's guilty then all that stuff about never leaving the house was invention, and the Simon Sutherland we met is just a character he's dedicated most of his adult life to playing. Why would anyone go to such freakish lengths? Maybe to cover up the despicable things they like to do when no one's watching. That's the sort of character that belongs in a dodgy thriller movie and he'll have no problem handling the police.'

Darian thought about that for a while before he said, 'The story about leaving the house might still be true, and the compulsive hoarding. He didn't throw the bra away when he knew it would be seen and implicate him. He's a rich young man who could pay for help. Simon Sutherland doesn't need to go outside because Will Dent can trawl the streets for him, pick out the girls and do the dirty work of getting them back to the house. Was Ruby-Mae murdered at the track or somewhere else?'

'Well, that's another interesting question I don't know the answer to. We'll need to find that out as well. We'll also need to find out if Dent's thirst has ever brought him as far north as Misgearan on a cold January night for a dram or three. Time for us to start poking our noses around again.'

Sholto paid for the meal before they left; no matter how often Mr Yang tried to give them a discount for their loyalty Sholto always paid full price for the things he loved.

24

As they were sitting in the traffic near The Helm roundabout in Bakers Moor, Darian got a message from Vinny. While Sholto tapped the car's steering wheel Darian read it to him.

'It's from Vinny. He's asking if we've heard anything?'

'Nothing he won't have heard already.'

A car behind them beeped its horn and Sholto nearly jumped through the roof at the sheer bad manners of it.

Darian was considering not telling Vinny they were focusing on the Ruby case right now. He had hired them, albeit with no intention of paying them, to look for Freya and this might seem like a deviation from the job description, maybe even an acceptance that if she hadn't run of her own free will then she was probably dead. In the end Darian decided his reply should embrace the naive concept of honesty being the best policy.

'I'll tell him we're going to Misgearan, that there might be a connection to Ruby. He might know a lot more about it, it's his station.'

The car inched forward until they were at the roundabout, which meant a long wait until Sholto saw a gap he considered big enough for his little car. Impatient people do not get into a car that Sholto Douglas is driving, and after more than a minute a gap appeared so large that even he was willing to drive into it. As he did Darian's phone buzzed again, another message from Vinny.

'He says he'll meet us there.'

It took longer than it should have, and Darian wished his boss had listened to his suggestion to take the train instead, but they got to Fair Road and found somewhere to park. Long Walk Lane was quiet by its standards, not the drunkening hour yet, but there were always a few people hanging around outside Misgearan. There was no sign of Vinny so Darian led Sholto to the private side entrance because it was unlikely the cop would be waiting in the main bar, not if he was there to speak to the staff. A single knock and Caillic Docherty opened it in seconds, letting them in, closing it and leading them down the corridor, round a corner and along another corridor to a room Darian had never seen before, her office.

Vinny was there, sitting large on a small couch with a bright floral pattern, Phil Sutherland alongside him. The office was small but felt like it belonged in a different building, full of very green and quite ugly plants, in tubs on the floor and pots on an old, rickety-looking desk, with faded paintings of rugged landscapes on the walls. It was a room of brightness in a building where most people preferred the dark. It was a room that didn't fit with Darian's gloomy preconception of Caillic Docherty.

He said to her, 'I didn't know you were a horticulturalist.'

In her grumpy rasp she said, 'There are eight hundred and twenty-seven interesting facts about me and I doubt you know more than two of them. Three now, if you count the plants.'

As she closed the office door Vinny said to her, 'So, Ruby-Mae Short, what can you tell us about her, Caillic?'

The look she gave him was damn near violent and would have set a herd of buffalo scurrying. Misgearan had an understanding with the cops from Dockside station and here was Vinny stomping all over it by dragging awkward questions about a serious case into her office. It was a minor and not unexpected betrayal.

She lifted the glasses that were on a string round her neck and put them on, saying, 'There's always a consequence to talking. What is it here?'

Vinny said, 'The man we're asking about works for a Sutherland. You're either pissing off me or a very rich man.'

'I bank with them.'

'Aye, but there are other banks, Caillic. We're the only police force in town.'

'You'd be a better force if you had some competition. Let me have a look at him then.'

Vinny took his phone from his pocket and got a picture of Will Dent up on it. She studied it carefully and shook her head.

'I don't know. I can't be sure. Not exactly a memorable-looking face, is he? It was January last year and it was busy the night the Short girl was in. I don't recognise him so he's not a regular, if he's been here at all. I remember telling the detective investigating it that the night she was in there were other new faces, one-off visitors. Thrill-seeking students and tourists looking for an authentic experience, a few lads off a boat I think, Caledonians. There was no trouble, though, and she wasn't draped all over anyone. The things they said about her in the papers, that's the bastards you want to be going after as well, the ones lying about some poor dead girl who can't argue back. She was no good-time girl, just a lassie on a night out.'

Vinny said, 'We'll focus on trying to catch the person who killed her first, maybe go for the ones who insulted her afterward. There's nothing else you remember?'

'Nothing I haven't told your better-dressed colleagues and I didn't hold back a word, not for something like this, a girl getting murdered like that.'

Caillic left them to use her office for a few moments and Vinny leaned forward on the couch to tell Darian and Sholto, standing by the door, what he knew of Ruby's case.

'I remember being called to it, myself and another cop, Seamus MacRae, first on scene. She had been dumped on the far side of the tracks, top of that wee hill over there, but she wasn't killed there. She'd been lying a few hours in the wet and cold, all we could do was secure the scene and hand it over to the suits. She had been placed there carefully, flat on her back, hands at her sides, not dumped. No sign of disturbance in the area so she was killed somewhere else and taken there afterwards, probably because that's around where she was picked up from. There were signs of sexual activity but that might have been after she was killed. She was conscious when she was strangled, apparently. There was alcohol in her system but less than I would have on a quiet night out, and there were no drugs. The missing bra was the big point of interest, either taken as a memento or ripped off during the attack and left behind by accident when the body was returned. I never heard of anyone becoming a meaningful suspect, certainly no mention of any Sutherland, or Dent for that matter.'

Phil said, 'I just don't believe Simon could have been involved, he's not capable.'

Darian said, 'They're certain the bra is Ruby's and not Freya's.'

Vinny said, 'It's not Freya's, it's not her size, it's for someone smaller like Short. I know Freya's size for a fact because every Valentine's Day she would send me to buy her lingerie out of spite because she knew asking the sales girl for help made me cringe myself inside out. I wouldn't have minded if she'd ever worn what I bought.'

'So it's Ruby's and it's probably been there since last January. Maybe someone put it there to set him up, but how many people ever get into that house?'

Sholto said, 'If someone did go in with it would the security cameras have picked it up? I spotted a battery of them.'

Phil said, 'I know the team questioning him have already gotten access to the security footage. If there's a story to tell from it they'll find it.'

'If someone else put it there then they'd know about the cameras, do something to stop them. But you should prepare yourself for your cousin knowing more than he's told us.'

'You know how sometimes you just know someone isn't capable of doing something?'

Sholto smiled sourly and said, 'I do, but sometimes you don't really know a person at all.'

All four of them left Misgearan that evening without having touched a drop of alcohol, a rare enough event to be worthy of mention. Sholto drove Darian home and he went up to his little flat and sat at the living-room window looking out towards Loch Eriboll and the lights of a large boat that must have just left the Whisper Hill docks and was heading out to the mouth and into the North Atlantic. Ruby-Mae Short had been a young woman looking to have a night out and enjoy herself. When she had died she was the same age Darian's sister Catriona was when he was investigating the case. That night he messaged her to ask if she was okay. She was fine.

Transcript of suspect interview

16 May 2018

40 Docklands Street, Whisper Hill, Challaid, CH9 4SS

Suspect – Simon Sutherland

Lawyer – Kellina Oriol

Interviewing officers – DI Ralph Grant, DC Angela Vicario

18:53: **DI Grant** – I'm DI Ralph Grant, with me is DC Angela Vicario, interviewing Simon Sutherland, also present is Kellina Oriol, Mr Sutherland's lawyer. Do you know why you're here, Simon?

Simon Sutherland – Because of the bra.

DI Grant – Because of the bra, the one we found in your house. Can you tell me who the bra belongs to?

Simon Sutherland – I don't know who the bra belongs to. It was left there.

DI Grant – In your house?

Simon Sutherland – Some time last January. The exact date will be in my diary. One evening it wasn't there, the next day when I went through the house it was.

DI Grant – It's a big house, easy to miss it for a few days. Could you be wrong about the day it turned up?

Simon Sutherland – I know the exact date it turned up. I go round the house every single day. If there's change I see it straight away.

DI Grant – And is there often a change?

18:54: Simon Sutherland – Never, except the bra.

DC Vicario – Did it upset you, Simon, having that bra there when you didn't put it there?

Simon Sutherland – Yes, it really did.

DI Grant – So why not get rid of it?

Simon Sutherland – I can't, I don't get rid of things.

DI Grant – You keep everything?

Simon Sutherland – Everything I can keep.

DI Grant – Mementos of your entire life, every moment collected in items and preserved in pristine condition in the safety of your house.

Simon Sutherland – I suppose so, yes.

DI Grant – So if you had a girl in the house so you could have fun with her you would want some memento of that, something to remind you of the good time you'd had together.

Simon Sutherland – That's not what happened. And it wouldn't be, because that's not how it works at all. I don't want to keep any of it, the things I keep. It's not because I want to have it, it's because I have to keep it all. I don't want anything added, any new things. They make it harder. I don't want that.

18:55: DI Grant – But you must have urges, Simon, every man does.

Kellina Oriol – Be careful, DI Grant.

DI Grant – I'm being exactly as careful as I need to be when investigating a murder, don't you worry about me. I'm right, though, aren't I, Simon? You must have some sort of sexual feelings, there are very few people that don't. You say you don't leave the house, so what happens to those feelings?

Kellina Oriol – You don't have to answer that, it's puerile. He's trying to embarrass you.

Simon Sutherland – That's okay, I'll answer. I don't go out and I don't like other people coming in. I've learned to accept the many things I can't have in life.

DI Grant – That must have been a very difficult thing to accept.

Simon Sutherland – It actually wasn't very. I don't miss things that haven't been a part of my life.

DC Vicario – So few people come into your home that you must have some idea of who could have been in last January and left the bra.

Simon Sutherland – I really don't know who brought it in. I don't know why anyone would do it.

18:56: **Kellina Oriol** – It should also be stated that Simon has willingly made all of his security information and footage, as well as his private diary, available to you in an attempt to help in any way possible.

DI Grant – Yes, he's been very helpful, up to a point. Tell me about Ruby-Mae Short.

Simon Sutherland – I don't know who that is, I'm sorry.

DI Grant – Ruby-Mae Short.

Simon Sutherland – I've never heard that name before, I'm sorry.

DI Grant – It was her bra we found in your house, torn and dirty.

Simon Sutherland – I don't know her.

DI Grant – We found her body by the railway tracks not too far from here, in the south of Whisper Hill, behind Long Walk Lane. Behind Misgearan, in fact, the bar she had been drinking in on the night she was murdered last January. Then her missing bra shows up in your house and now you claim you've never heard of her.

Simon Sutherland – That's because I haven't.

DI Grant – But her bra turned up in your house, quite possibly on the night she was killed, your diary and security footage might tell us for sure.

Simon Sutherland – I've already told you that I don't know how it got there.

DI Grant – You need to get real with me, Simon. All those security features in your house and you can't even take a guess about how the bra got in there?

18:57: Kellina Oriol – My client has already told you that he doesn't know, DI Grant, he's not going to magically learn it because you're sitting there verbally abusing him.

DI Grant – You'd be amazed how many people do.

DC Vicario – William Dent is one of the people who visits you regularly, isn't he?

Simon Sutherland – He sometimes brings the shopping, sometimes Olinda does.

DC Vicario – And do you talk with him much, discuss things?

Simon Sutherland – Not a lot, really. We talk, but not in any personal detail.

DC Vicario – When he delivers the shopping he has access to the house, though.

Simon Sutherland – Yes, he gets in.

DC Vicario – Who else has that sort of access?

Simon Sutherland – Olinda and Uncle Harold.

DC Vicario – Has William ever spoken to you about women, maybe bragged about girlfriends or offered to set you up with someone?

Simon Sutherland – He's offered to take me out to parties. He does that often. I think Uncle Harold encourages him to try to help me out. He does it to be polite and he knows I'll say no.

DC Vicario – You don't want to go out with him, party a bit?

18:58: Simon Sutherland – I do want to. I'm not able to.

DC Vicario – It must be very hard for you to be here now.

Simon Sutherland – Yes, it is, but I want to help.

DI Grant – Let me ask you something, Simon. A bra shows up in your house, dirty and ripped and even with your lack of experience you know that isn't how a bra should look, but you still don't report it to us, or to anyone else as I understand it. You just accepted it being there. If something else was dumped in your house, something that was vital to a murder investigation, would you tell us?

Simon Sutherland – Of course I would. It was just a bra, I thought someone had left it there to tease me with. I thought they were trying to force me to throw it out. My family used to do things like that. They pushed me because they thought it helped. I was just embarrassed by it being there. I really didn't see any reason to report it to the police.

Kellina Oriol – I take it from this little period of silence that you have nothing left to ask Simon. I'd say you've probably tortured him enough already.

END

25

DARIAN HAD A SIMPLE routine every morning, getting out of bed around eight, showering and then going through to the kitchen where he would look in the fridge and swear he would do some shopping really soon. For several years there may not have been a single day when that flat contained enough to feed a grown man. Faced with the desolation of a fridge that held a nearly empty tub of butter, an out-of-date carton of milk, some green and beige cheese that had started out oddly orange and a light bulb Darian had just realised didn't light, he decided to pay for breakfast at The Northern Song instead. It was an unhealthy but convenient option that both he and Sholto leaned on far too often.

He walked in the cold down to Bank Station, content with his decision to put the hire car back to JJ. Walking and taking the train to work was enjoyable for Darian and perhaps him alone in this narrow city with its clogged roads and absurd public transport. He liked the walk and making his way through the packed station, getting onto the train for the short trip through the tunnel to Glendan Station. It was the people-watching he found the pleasure in, the population of Challaid being a channel that never ran repeats and refused to commission a single dull day. He left Glendan Station and walked down to Cage Street and in through the front door of The Northern Song.

Two people were standing at the counter, waiting for an order that had already been placed. Mr Yang was there and saw Darian.

He said, 'Breakfast special, Darian?'

'Yes please, Mr Yang.'

The owner went through to the back and returned three minutes later with a warm foil tray and passed it to Darian, taking the money to pay for it with the feigned reluctance of a businessman dealing with a friend. Darian took his breakfast upstairs.

Sholto was already at his desk and when he saw the food he said, 'I can't stop myself turning into a fat old man on greasy breakfasts but it's not too late for you to save yourself.'

'Is that you trying to persuade me to give you my breakfast?'

'It would be an honourable solution to a real problem.'

'My problem is hunger and I'm holding the solution and not letting it go. Have you heard anything from Dockside?'

'No, and I can't help thinking that's probably not a good sign. They're catching up with the twenty-four-hour mark since they took him in and I don't see them going for an extension if they've made no progress, not with his lawyers waiting to pounce and claim victory if a judge refuses them more time. Better to keep their powder dry.'

'Surely the bra is enough for something.'

Darian sat and gulped down his food with the haste of a man determined to find better things to do with his time. They had no other active cases, just one that was now gripped by the police, and they needed to drum up a little business. That's what Sholto was doing with his spare time because Darian was so damn bad at it, unenthusiastic about corporate work and no good at hiding the fact.

The breakfast carton was in the bin and Sholto had the phone in his hand, about to call Glendan, the construction giants they did regular work for, when he heard footsteps on the stairs and a knock at the door. When he opened it DC Vicario walked in, looking more tired than she had the day before, many long hours in the station ago.

When the door was closed she said, 'I'm on my way to flop into bed but I thought I'd take a detour south and tell you we're releasing Simon Sutherland. Right now all we could throw at him is withholding evidence and even that would be shaky because he didn't know it was evidence.'

Darian said, 'He didn't crack?'

'We couldn't make a scratch on him. Now they'll be complaining about us mistreating a man with mental health problems, so this isn't going to get any easier.'

Sholto said, 'It was good of you to come and let us know.'

'There is a selfish motive. We're still going to pursue this, for Ruby. Simon Sutherland is at least a link to whoever killed her so we're not going to step away from him just because his lawyer's watch cost more than my monthly salary. Oh, you should see the watch, the sort of gaudy you could easily get hooked on. Anyway, we'll keep on it but we'll be under pressure, watched all the time by seniority that could hold us back.'

'And we'll have a little more freedom.'

She smiled at Darian and said, 'Exactly. You dogs of war are off the chain.'

Sholto said, 'Hang on, hang on, us mutts are all tied up in the kennels. We're a research company, and the Sutherland lawyers that can inconvenience you will shut us down before we can so much as peek in Simon's letterbox.'

'You're helping to try and find Ruby's killer and helping Cnocaid try to find Vinny's ex-wife, although I fear what you'll find by now. I can assure you, no station in the city will pursue a case against you.'

'Using private companies to chase police cases is not how it's supposed to work.'

She said, 'Maybe we won't have to, maybe we'll get Ruby's killer without your help, but I'd rather know you two were in my corner. You have a good reputation, Mr Douglas, and I'd want your skills on my side.'

Despite the transparency of the buttering-up Sholto couldn't stop himself beaming like Heilam lighthouse. He said, 'Well, of course we're in your corner, DC Vicario, that goes without saying. We'll keep looking into the Ruby killing as well as Freya's disappearance. We won't be reckless about it, no, but we will be professional.'

'That's more than enough for me. I'd better go home before I fall asleep on your floor and get rice in my hair. I'll be in touch again soon.'

As she left Darian, embarrassed at the mess, kneeled down and picked the rice off the floor that one of them had dropped in the last few days.

Sholto said, 'We're in deep enough now to feel the heat of the earth's core.'

'You do always say you want the police on our side.'

'Aye, but if they're the only ones who are on our side who the hell is going to pay us?'

26

Sholto was about to give Darian a warning about the googly eyes he was giving DC Vicario, had it all planned out in his mind, spelling out how dangerous a beautiful cop could be to a private detective, when he heard more footsteps on the stairs outside.

Sholto looked at the ceiling and, instead of his worldly warnings, said, 'Oh, bloody hell, give me strength, it's busier than Ciad Station in here today.'

It was only their second visitor of the day, but Darian didn't point that out. He was thinking instead that the new arrival must have been watching Angela Vicario, waiting for her to leave before they called in. He could only think of a short list of people who would wait for her to go before they thought it safe to enter.

The knock came on the door, an elaborate rat-a-tat. Sholto got up from his desk and opened it, looking at the new arrival. His face fell.

'Noonan. DS Noonan, I mean.'

'Sholto, you old bugger, how the hell are you? Aren't you going to invite me in?'

DS Dennis Noonan. Darian had heard the name before, heard Sholto talking about him in terms that would make an honest man's skin crawl. Noonan was, according to Sholto, corrupt to his core. He was the very worst of the bad news that floated around in Challaid Police Force. Avoid at all costs, that was the easy-to-follow advice. Couldn't avoid a man who had just walked into your office, though.

Noonan was in his late forties, stocky and with a gut, greying hair that looked like it needed a visit to the barber, blotchy skin and a fat, red boozer's nose. He had a mocking smile on his face as he sat down in the chair on the other side of Sholto's desk, glancing across at Darian.

Noonan looked at him and said, in his thick, working-class Challaid accent, 'You must be the Ross boy, eh?'

'Darian Ross.'

'Aye, aye. I remember your father, you know. Didn't work with him, probably a good thing, isn't it, given what happened to him. Not a man to be associated with.'

He was chuckling as he said it, and Sholto, who had worked closely and extensively with Darian's father, sat heavily opposite him. 'What do you want, Noonan?'

'Noonan? Dennis, it's Dennis, call me Dennis, Sholto. I wanted to come and see this place, see how you work.

Oh, I fancy this, I do, I really do, you know, when I pack in the proper job. A wee office like this, nice and easy cases, none of the shite we get in the force, get a nice wee assistant. Wouldn't have one like yours, a lad like that, oh no. I'd have a wee dolly bird with tits out to here, have her answer the phone in a short skirt, just sit here watching her. Och, it's a good wee gig you have here, Sholto, eh.'

Sholto didn't smile, didn't nod along, didn't react at all. It was unlike him, Darian was so used to seeing him try to ingratiate himself with whoever was sitting opposite him, always trying to be pally with the old cops. Not Noonan, though. Not this time.

Sholto said, 'It's no picnic. We have tough cases, and we have a lot more restrictions in how we handle them than you do. A lot more. We're working very hard here, Dennis, so don't go thinking it's an easy retirement plan.'

Noonan smiled, looking round and grinning at Darian with yellow teeth, then back at Sholto. 'Well, it's good to see you still care, eh, got some of the old passion for this job. No, I still think I'd like to do it. Getting towards the end of my run with the force, they're always dropping hints about my age, makes a man feel unloved, you know. I think something like this could be for me. And there'll be a gap in the market, won't there, eh, Sholto, because you're not going to be doing this for very long.'

'Is that right?'

'Oh, aye, aye, you'll be evacuating the office. Hey, you know, I might even rent this very office for my own, eh, if I decide to follow in your footsteps. That would be a laugh, wouldn't it, Sholto? I'll sit where you are and get my glamorous assistant sat over there by the window where the boy is, get her in a tight top with a breeze coming in the window. You'll be... Well, I don't know where you'll be. Might be in The Ganntair, but probably not. You'll get convicted, I mean, that's guaranteed, you know that, but I don't suppose they'll waste a cell on either of you two. You'll be pottering about your garden, if you have one.'

Sholto was still expressionless when he said, 'That a threat, Dennis?'

'Not a threat, oh no, come on now, I would never threaten a friend, a former copper. No, no, I'm trying to help you out here, Sholto. The force, it's watching you and it doesn't like what it sees. Let you get away with a lot of nonsense in the past, all that palaver with Corey and his mob, and now you're at it again. They're coming for you, Sholto. Coming for Douglas Independent Research. Running an unregistered private detective agency, oh, Sholto, tut, tut, they're not going to let that go on.'

Sholto glanced past Noonan to Darian, then said, 'We didn't fold when Raven tried to lean on us, tried to lure Darian away. We didn't crumble when Harold

Sutherland came in here shouting his mouth off, and we won't be intimidated now.'

Noonan smiled and said with mock shock, 'Harold Sutherland? You've been making an enemy of Harold Sutherland? Oh, Sholto, I had no idea, things must be even worse than I realised. I came here to try and warn you, help you, but I can see now it's too late. You're finished, the pair of you.'

Noonan got up and walked to the door as he was speaking, that last sentence delivered sternly enough to be a threat, whatever the cop wanted to call it. He let himself out, left Sholto and Darian sitting in the office. Darian leaned back in his chair and looked out of the window, watching Noonan stroll off down Cage Street, making sure he was gone before they spoke.

'A cop.'

Sholto nodded. 'A dirty cop. And he wasn't here representing the force, he was here on behalf of his other employers. He was here for Harold Sutherland.'

'He could shut us down, though. You've always said it, cops are the ones we have to fear the most.'

Sholto was looking unusually thoughtful, staring down at his desk. 'They are, but Noonan is a bad choice for Sutherland. He works out of Bakers station, not Bank, so this isn't his patch, and he's not loved. Other cops hate Dennis Noonan. Other *humans* hate Dennis Noonan.'

'So…?'

'So we still have a job to do and we're still going to do it. We'll, uh, keep an eye out for Noonan and his colleagues, though, maybe try and shore up a few friendly cops of our own. The police can destroy us, but they can rescue us, too.'

27

THEY WERE DIVIDING up responsibilities for the rest of the day when Darian got another message from Vinny asking if he'd heard that Simon was about to be released. When Darian gave him all the details Vinny suggested meeting up at Dio's, the arcade on Last Street. It wasn't an obvious location, but that just added to the intrigue. Sholto was hitting the phone. He wanted to try and get hold of a contact that might be able to show him Freya and Ruby's mobile phone logs for the week or so before each went missing.

He said, 'The police will already have seen them I suppose, but Challaid Police are quite capable of missing things that are obvious even to me.'

It took Darian twenty-five minutes to get down to Last Street, not that close to a railway station and he'd put the car back, which he now regretted. It took him another five minutes to find Dio's because the big sign that had been above the door had either fallen off or been sold for scrap, likely the latter. The place was still open, the machines hooked up and flashing, the building almost empty on a Tuesday morning. There were a couple of kids who should have been in school and were dressed in their uniforms to prove it, a couple of alcoholics who were sheltering from the cold and had no intention of parting with a single coin in machines that wouldn't give them a drink in exchange, and Vinny. He was at a cabinet near the door playing *Streets of Rage* with a level of concentration unbecoming in the circumstances. The arcade was long, narrow, low-ceilinged and had an outdated and dark decor that smothered the room in gloom, punctured only by the too-bright machinery.

Darian stood next to Vinny and said sarcastically, 'Gee, they must be making a killing in here.'

Vinny smiled. 'I used to come here all the time when I was a kid. Heard the place was shutting down so I thought I'd come for one last visit. Dio hasn't owned this place in twenty-five years, you know. Used to belong to the Creags, and I heard the Scalpers, the Caledonian gang the Creags are pally with, had the place last, pretended people they were hiding in the city worked here legitimately. White Hawk Drive is just round the corner. I thought we could go and interview a few of Freya's friendly neighbours.'

'You haven't spoken to them yet?'

'I was told to keep my nose out of it when Cnocaid station started their investigation so I did. I let them get on with it but they haven't gotten very far.'

'You think your nose has any place on her street now?'

Vinny groaned as Axel Stone died another death and he stepped away from the cabinet. 'I gave them plenty of time and they gave me nothing for it. Now they're getting all pumped up on Simon Sutherland and Ruby-Mae Short and there's no word of Freya, like they've given up on her when she's running out of time here.'

Darian was shocked and didn't hide it. 'Vinny, mate, she's been missing eleven days, you know what that probably means, you don't think she's still alive, do you?'

'I know the chances are skinny. Shit, I knew that from the start, there was no way she would run away from Finn and not get in touch if she could, but if there's a tiny chance we can bring her back then I'm going to push for it, and it would help to have your weight behind the effort.'

They walked round to White Hawk Drive, Vinny lighting a cigarette and vowing he would quit once the packet was finished, just like the last few hundred. Freya lived on a pleasant street, a much more suburban feel than you would expect in that area, trees lining one side, most of the houses with drives and manicured front gardens, semi-detached houses on both sides. It was the sort of place where residents would secretly compete to have the nicest garden and bitch about any that bettered theirs.

Darian said, 'She somehow managed to live well for a woman who let your good self slip through her fingers.'

'Aye, a miracle that. Her job, she's an account manager at Caledonia Advertisers, pays pretty well. She's smart, that one, knows how to get the most out of herself.'

'So how do we do this?'

'There were a couple of neighbours she absolutely hated. Actually, she didn't have much time for any of them, I think, but there were a couple in particular she talked about, one next door and the other across the road. She said one of them was always peeking out of the curtains when she was in the garden, spying on her, and the one across the road was an interfering busybody, so if anyone knows anything it'll be one of them.'

'Spying on her?'

'She said he was a dirty old man. You know what she's like; if you look at her sideways she thinks you're sizing her up for a wedding dress.'

They started with the old lady across the street who had once made the mistake of giving Freya advice on how to discipline her child. That had made her an enemy for life. They knocked on the front door and got no answer, but they both saw a curtain twitching and knew she was home. There were plenty of good reasons for an old lady to refuse to answer the door to two young men and forcing the issue could have resulted in an awkward appearance from Vinny's colleagues.

Vinny knocked on the front door of the house next to Freya's and it was opened with the undue haste of a man desperate for any conversation he could get his teeth into. He was short and had a mop of white hair and glasses so thick Darian thought he could probably see into the far reaches of space with them. He must have been watching them across the road which meant he had seen Vinny stub his cigarette out against the man's wall and flick it into the bushes.

Vinny said, 'Hello, I'm Vinny Reno, this is Darian Ross from Douglas Independent Research, we're trying to find out what happened to Miss Dempsey from next door. I know you'll have spoken to the police already, but I wondered if you could tell us anything you saw in the days or weeks before her disappearance?'

The man nodded fast and said, 'Oh, yes, yes. I told the police and I don't know what they did about it. I told them she was getting parcels nearly every day. And, as well, there was the car.'

'The crash she had?'

'No, no, not that, a new car. It was left for her in the driveway and when she came back that afternoon with the boy, Finn his name is, F I N N, she just looked at it and took him inside. Wasn't long after that someone came and took it away, a young lad he was, looked sheepish about it, too. It was a fancy car, one of them Mercedes, I looked it up, very, very expensive.'

This was information they didn't already have, gleaned from an old man who seemed to spend most of his day looking out of his windows for Freya. They thanked him and walked back out to the street.

Darian said, 'There are explanations. A mix-up with insurers sending her a loan car when she already had her own back, giving her an expensive one because it was tied to the Sutherland account.'

'Maybe, but the sort of insurers who handle the Sutherland account wouldn't make that sort of sloppy mistake. Easy to find out if they did as well.'

'The parcels could be from work. I guess she handles a lot of different companies.'

'She does, and they send anything she needs to see to the office. Why the hell didn't Cnocaid station tell me about this?'

'You know why. You're still a suspect, Vinny, whatever they might say to your ugly face. If they were presents then maybe they thought it was a motive for you, jealousy, her moving on from the marriage while you're still single.'

Vinny stopped in the middle of the street and gave him the look of a man who'd just discovered a new limb he never knew he had. 'Me? Jealous? As in, wanted her back jealous? Are you completely loopy permanently or is this just a phase you're going through?'

'I know it's daft but as long as you're a suspect you're going to have to put up with it. If it wasn't the insurers then who could have given her the car? Not William Dent, he couldn't afford a classy piece of metal like that.'

'Simon Sutherland could.'

Darian nodded and said, 'Yeah, but he's not the

gift-buying sort, is he? If she sent it back he would have to put it on a shelf in his house.'

'Unless he's faking it.'

'There is that, but if he's faking it why not ditch the bra? There's also the uncle, Harold. There's a suave piece of meat that banged into her on the road, met her in person, gave her his work contact details and could afford all the show-off gestures of love, lust and casual interest you could wish for. Maybe they had a thing going.'

Vinny puffed out his cheeks and said, 'Hitting a man with her car until he went out with her, that's her style all right. But she sent the motor back, so if it was a gift then she was about as receptive to it as she was to most attempts to be in any way impressive towards her.'

'Unwanted attention? The sort that might make a man used to hearing yes angry?'

Vinny grimaced as they got into his car back on Last Street. 'I suppose, but how does that tie in with the Short girl's bra being in Simon Sutherland's house? It has to be the boy in the billionaire's bubble, doesn't make sense otherwise.'

'It's your partner's family.'

'I don't like leaning on the boy so much, but we'll have another chat with him about his weird bloodline, see what he has to say. We'll go together.'

THE CHALLAID GAZETTE AND ADVERTISER

07 February 2018

BRIDGE PROPOSAL DROPPED

Plans for a bridge from the Barton district of the city to Eilean Seud, resubmitted in a council meeting in late October, have again been shelved after significant objections from islanders. Put forward this time by Labour Party councillor Aila Donald, the idea was for a bridge from Cruinn Pier to the south-west edge of the island with the belief it would make Eilean Seud more accessible for the rest of Challaid and emergency services, as well as making the mainland easier to reach for the citizens living on the island.

'The idea for the bridge is an old one,' Councillor Donald said, 'it's been around for more than a century and remains as relevant now as it was then. This is an opportunity to join the one detached part of Challaid with the rest of the city and make it a safer place.'

Residents on the island disagreed, with Lyle MacBeth, a representative of Eilean Protection, a campaign group set up to oppose the bridge, calling Councillor Donald's proposal 'mischief making'. Mr MacBeth told the *Gazette*, 'Ms Donald well knows that islanders don't want this and that the rest of the city won't benefit a jot from it. This new submission never had a chance of success, and Ms Donald only brought it forward to try and create divisions between people on the island and those on the mainland.'

Councillor Donald has disputed this, stating that there is a strong economic and safety argument for the bridge, but she did repeat her accusation that the people of Eilean Seud have consistently opposed the bridge on the grounds of snobbery. The value of an average house on the island, none of which have come on the open market in over twenty years, is estimated at somewhere around two and a half million pounds, with the population dominated by a select number of families considered unwelcoming of outsiders.

Eilean Protection have dismissed all of those allegations, with Mr MacBeth saying, 'This has nothing to do with property prices or stopping people from the mainland coming across to visit the island. If we wanted to keep people off Eilean Seud we would hardly be funding the regular ferry service from Cruinn Pier from our own pockets, a service which has made the island more accessible now than at any point in Challaid's long history. What we oppose is millions of pounds being spent on a needless eyesore that will increase pollution and disturb a unique way of life on the island.'

When asked if she intended to put her proposal forward again Councillor Donald was noncommittal, saying only that, 'No good idea should be entirely off the table.' Challaid council leader Morag Blake and her Liberal Party have previously stated their opposition to a bridge, but gave no statement when asked by the *Gazette* about this new submission.

NBoS RAID HUNT MOTHBALLED

Police at Dockside station in Whisper Hill and the anti-organised crime unit at Bakers Moor station last night confirmed that the investigation into the notorious theft of over six million pounds from a National Bank of Scotland security van at Challaid International Airport in 2013 is no longer classed as active, although both have stressed the investigation remains open. No one has ever been arrested in relation to the case, and what started out as a large joint investigation has gradually dwindled to now have no dedicated officers working on it, with a spokesperson for– p8

28

GETTING TO PHIL PROVED more difficult than expected. Having called Freya's insurers and found they had no record of delivering the wrong car, and then her employers who said work parcels were never sent to her house, Vinny then phoned his colleague and had a brief conversation which he recounted to Darian in the car as they made their way north.

Vinny said, 'He's at Loch Chalum, behind Dùil Hill.'

'What the hell's he doing there?'

'Fishing. It's one of his things. He's well into what he considers working-class pursuits. Fishing is one, playing darts is another. He's in a darts team in some pub league. I've heard he's pretty good.'

'A man who stands to inherit millions playing in a pub league in The Hill? Have you thought to warn him of the potential dangers of being around sharp objects in nasty hands given his wealth?'

Vinny chuckled. 'He's a cop going round pubs in Whisper Hill, doesn't matter if you're piss poor, that's a dangerous game and he knows it. I think that's part of what he enjoys. His family collects paintings and yachts and private jets so he does fishing and darts.'

The drive from Cnocaid to the closest road to the loch was a long one, with eighty per cent of the time taken up by the first forty per cent of road. From Cnocaid they had to go east through Bank into Bakers Moor and then north through Earmam and Whisper Hill. They left the city, through the narrow gap up to Heilam, going past the graveyard, the council estate and the old lighthouse. From there Vinny could put his foot down and drive with the sort of abandon that only a man who's friends with every cop that might possibly pull him over could possess. They followed the road that looped round the back of Dùil Hill and saw Phil's car parked at a passing place on their right.

Vinny looked at it and said with a sigh, 'We're going to have to plod it the rest of the way to the loch. You bring your hiking boots?'

'No. You?'

'I'm in my trainers. I don't really do countryside, too many things that can bite you in ways I wouldn't pay for.'

'You sound like Sholto, he's terrified of dogs.'

'I was thinking more of midges, ticks and gamekeepers.'

A fifteen-minute walk uphill to the dip where the small loch was hidden from the world turned into a twenty-five-minute walk on account of their footwear, both of them hopping around to try and avoid the boggy parts of the moor, which was most of it. One twisted ankle and a near-record-breaking amount of swearing later, they crested the ridge and saw Phil, a five-minute walk away at the lochside. They stumbled down to find him sitting on a large rock, a plastic tub of worms to the side and a bottle of water in his hand, watching the float from his rod lie still on the calm surface. He knew the terrain and his well-scuffed wellies proved it.

Vinny stood next to him and said, 'Why the hell can't you just take up alcoholism as a hobby like everyone else in The Hill, least then we could meet you in a pub? Even camanachd, which tends to lead to the bottle anyway.'

Phil looked out at the loch, surrounded by hills and birdsong, no sign of Challaid or any other smear of modernity, and said, 'Don't tell me this isn't beautiful.'

'It sure is beautiful, and I would have mildly enjoyed looking at a photo of it back in Challaid.'

'You need the exercise, a man your age and your size. Doesn't take much to go from barrel-chested to barrel-bellied, you know. So what dark theory about my family have you brought to my bright hideaway?'

Vinny sat on the rock beside Phil and Darian stood in front of them both. This was going to be an awkward conversation so Vinny decided he might as well be sitting awkwardly for it.

He said, 'We've been talking to some snoopers, one of them a very possible pervert, and found out that Freya was getting presents sent to the house before she went missing, including a car that a Sutherland and not many others could afford. Looks like someone sent it and she sent it right back. Freya wasn't the sort to spit out a free lunch if she liked the food, so she really didn't want whoever was throwing luxury motors at her.'

'I don't know, Vinny. My family might be famous for having money but we're not famous for throwing it around. Besides, as a theory, that the person who ki-kidnapped her sent her the gifts, it doesn't add up. Who would risk sending presents like that?'

Darian said, 'What about your uncle Harold?'

'What about him?'

'He met Freya; they talked, might he have gotten back in touch with her? Is he the sort to fall hard and make big romantic gestures?'

Phil shook his head as he thought about it and said, 'He's had a few girlfriends over the years that I know of, got engaged once but it didn't pan out. They were all just playthings for him.'

'I thought your family was supposed to take a terribly religious view of these things, the high moral standards of a churchy family.'

'That's what you're supposed to think. The business comes first. Always does with that surname. I don't know how romantic his gestures have ever been, but I do know it's not the family way. The fact we have the money to spend if we wanted to is enough. You don't have to actually go ahead with the grand gesture to get attention.'

'Is there a way of finding out what he's been sending people?'

'Well, they're obsessive about accounting for every single penny that goes in and out of the bank but he would never put it through the company accounts. It would be unforgiveable for a personal item to intrude on profit. Anything like that would be at his house on Eilean Seud.'

Vinny tutted and said, 'He's one of that lot is he, wanting to float off into the North Atlantic instead of sharing the same land mass as us scum? Probably takes a helicopter to work.'

'He doesn't. You're not allowed anything as noisy as a helicopter on the island and you couldn't land them anywhere near the bank for security reasons anyway. Listen, I want to help, and I can probably get you into his house, but I don't think it's a clever idea.'

Vinny said, 'I laugh in the face of clever ideas. What have you got?'

'He's having one of his parties at the house, he has them every month. He does it to try and improve the bank's image among other rich people. You'd be amazed how many of them hate our family.'

'I wouldn't. Rich people love their money and hate the people who control it, which is you lot.'

'Well, for a few hundred years we didn't give two craps what people thought of us but now Uncle Harold has a penchant for PR. He's good at it, nice and subtle. I remember him telling my mother that PR at its best persuades people to believe in you, to support what you're doing and even want to be a part of it. At its worst PR is a loudmouthed halfwit screeching wildly at the converted. You have to be friendly and reach out. It wouldn't be hard to get a couple of extra people in, it's pretty much an open house, but you'll be in a crowded place with a lot of security and he's hardly going to have left something incriminating lying around.'

Darian looked at Vinny and said, 'It might still be worth it, get a closer look at his life and lifestyle, see if there's anything that can educate us about him.'

Vinny nodded thoughtfully. 'True, but I can't go. I'm a suspect and a serving police officer, so if I get spotted it botches the whole investigation.'

Phil said, 'Same here, and it's not like half the guests wouldn't recognise me straight away. Uncle Harold always invites me to these things and I always say no so it would raise an eyebrow through his scalp if I turned up now. You and your boss could go, dress up in a couple of fake names and make sure you're not seen by anyone who might recognise you.'

Darian nodded slowly. Sholto would go through the roof and into the upper atmosphere but if it gave them a snapshot of Harold Sutherland at play it would be worth the horror.

29

DARIAN WAS STANDING in the office with Sholto, who was hovering somewhere between fury and giddy panic. It wasn't the prospect of sniffing around a suspect that had him turning puce; it was the thought of being at a party filled with the rich and powerful.

'Not just a room full, not just a house full but a whole bloody island of them. How are we supposed to fit in there?'

Darian said, 'I don't know about you, but I plan to lie through my teeth.'

'I used to be a detective in the Challaid Police Force, Darian, I know how to keep a lie running, but how does anyone fit in among that lot? I don't know what to wear, not a clue.'

Darian had called and told him about the party they were going to, so they had met at the office in the early evening, Sholto dressed in a suit that was a little tight but smarter than usual after Darian told him to tuck his shirt in at the back. Darian had on his one good suit with a blue shirt and no tie.

He said, 'The dress code is smart casual.'

'What does that mean, Darian? Those two words cancel each other out and any sensible person knows it. I have a tie in one pocket and a bow tie in the other. Do I wear one or the other or neither or both?'

'Neither, and if we get there and everyone's in ties you can slip it on.'

'It's brown and yellow.'

'*Brown and yellow?* Why the hell do you have a brown and yellow tie?'

'It's the only one I've got. Well, I have a black tie as well, for funerals, obviously, but this is the only one I've got for the living. If I wear the black one they'll think I'm a waiter and I won't have the confidence to correct them. I don't want to be serving drinks all night.'

'What happened to all the ties you had when you were a cop?'

'Burned them in a wee metal bin in the back garden the day I retired, my way of celebrating. In hindsight it was a rash move, but the thing about hindsight is that you can only have it after the event.'

They left the office and drove up to Cruinn Pier in Sholto's Fiat. The small car park on the pier was almost full with cars whose heated seats were worth more than Sholto's entire vehicle. They parked at the back and walked towards the dock where the ferry would arrive in a few minutes. There were a handful of people waiting with them, most going to the party and all in good spirits. Someone made a joke about financial speculations and Sholto laughed much too hard, the way people do when they really wish they'd understood the punchline. Nobody asked who they were or what they did for a living so the lies they'd prepared could stay in their thin wrappers a little longer.

A loud man was defending the honour of the Sutherland Bank to a bored-looking woman. 'I know a lot of people view us as some cynical company that seeks to hold back the progress of others but that isn't at all the case. We're as committed to social progress and equality as anyone, but we've always insisted that these things have to be sustainable, that we spend only what we have and go at a pace that ensures nothing is rushed and the foundations are well set. I would argue that this is the very opposite of the anti-progress attitude you're accusing us of, wouldn't you? We don't just want progress, we want it to last. Isn't that what you want, too?'

From where they stood they could see with relief the ferry pull away from the pier on the southern point of Eilean Seud and make the five-minute run across to join them. It was small and white but the deck they stood on was well covered and had hot air blasting from one end. It was well scrubbed and any seagull that even thought of taking a shit on it would probably have been blasted out of the sky before it could take aim. The ferry brought them quickly across the cold water and the island came more starkly into view, lit up and laden with hundred-and-fifty-year-old mansions of understated elegance and trees older still. Darian and Sholto hung back and made sure they were the last off the boat so they could walk to Harold's house alone.

There was one narrow, cobbled road on Eilean Seud that ran from the pier in the south and curved up to the north of the long and thin island, each step carrying them further back in time to a fantasy land of old money. The Challaid rich had built mansions from banking money and merchant money and pirate money and slave ship money and whaling money, in a time when the city belonged to them and the outside world didn't get a say, a time they wished had never passed and one they were trying to re-create in miniature.

There were houses on either side, thirty-two on the island, and each was pristine. Living on the island brought with it a responsibility to maintain aesthetic standards. Even the lampposts along the street looked like they would be powered by gas and lit every evening by a man with a thick moustache and wearing a hat. Alders stretched across from both sides of the tree-lined lane to touch in the middle in places, providing a picturesque canopy for the sunlight to filter through on good days and on bad ones a flimsy cover from the worst of the rain, which, when it did get through, fell in large, heavy blobs of collected water. It would have been fairytale pretty in the fading light of a Challaid night if it hadn't been trying so desperately hard.

As they walked along the road Sholto said, 'And to think, I used to be jealous of people who lived in Barton. I thought that was the pinnacle. How naive I was.'

'I don't know, has a whiff of the gilded cage about it.'

'No, Simon Sutherland's house reeked of it, but this is just gilded. Not everything attractive is a trap, Darian.'

At the gates to Harold Sutherland's mansion a couple of smiling young women were asking people for their names and checking them against their list. Darian noticed that a pair who had been on the boat with them, who must have been regulars at these shindigs, had been allowed straight through without a check. Now it was time to test the false IDs in the face of a brief check.

Sholto smiled and said, 'I'm Corvun Reed, this is Gito Conin.'

The young woman, dressed in a trouser suit and with her dark hair tied back, looked at the list on her tablet. 'Yes, McCourt Securities. Go straight in, the house is just ahead at the end of the drive. Drinks and food are in the main study and also the garden at the back. Enjoy the evening.'

'Thank you.'

It was always a strange thing to watch, the casual lies Sholto could tell when he was getting into a performance and his nerves settled. It was as fragile as a butterfly's wings. One gust could blow him miles off course, but his acting was still, at its best, pretty good.

The drive was cobbled like the road and the long front garden was a colourful beauty parade that looked as if it had been lifted from a painting. The house was, as expected, large and imposing, and the main study the woman had mentioned was staring straight at them. It was two storeys high and had large French doors and cathedral windows which flooded it with light. Even before they stepped inside they could see it stretched back to the rear of the building, with the same design to give a spectacular view of the loch at the end of the back garden. The room had plenty of couches and chairs and sitting in them were people well used to the luxury around them. The view didn't awe them, nor did the paintings on the wall or the cost of the wine they were gulping down and would be pissing away in a few hours.

As they stood at the open French doors Sholto said, 'We'll sniff around but not too loudly. If you see the man himself, duck behind a millionaire, we don't want to get kicked out. Even a classy pair like ourselves might struggle to restore our standing in elite society if we get rumbled here.'

Sholto hiked over to the side of the room where several waiters were milling around with trays, food always a relaxant for him. Darian walked slowly through the scenery, picking up snatches of conversations that sounded as though they were competing with each other in the world championship of sleep inducement. Politics and business were the prime subjects and the subtext of both was money. As Darian reached the end of the room he turned back and saw that Sholto was deep in conversation with a smiling woman who appeared to be trying to explain what all the available nibbles were.

Darian, with hands in pockets, stepped out into the back garden, stopped, and took a step back inside, out of view. Harold Sutherland was just outside, holding court before a gaggle of sycophants.

'Don't get me wrong, I love Challaid FC, but only for what it can do for the city. There's a poisonous pall over the sport in this country, so bitter and parochial, and the people underneath it are so busy looking down on others all the time that they haven't noticed it up there. I was at the Motherwell game a few Fridays ago and the crowd loved Friday night football, but because it inconvenienced a small travelling support from the central belt it's being shelved. No mention of what's better for our fans, or that we had a Champions League match on the Tuesday, representing our country. People are more interested in establishing moral superiority than improving the actual football. Honestly, the only thing more tedious than actual politics is football politics. That's why I'd like to do something in camanachd as well, if I could find a club in this city that knew how to listen to reason. Such a great sport and yet they're proud of their amateurism. It's absurd. I may have to set up a club of my own and get them into the league; if I do they'll show the rest just what professionalism looks like.'

When he had finished his spiel there was some muttering of agreement from men pretending to be interested and some flirtatious cooing from the one woman whose husband was standing with his arm round her. Harold Sutherland was a charismatic man who found controlling a conversation easy and it was the simplest thing in the world to make a powerfully good impression on people. That, Darian thought bitterly, was something that could easily be abused and perhaps its rare failures could provoke a stern response. At the same time, though, this did not seem like a man who would need to throw a car at a woman in a crass attempt to win her over.

When Sutherland moved away from the patio outside the door and across to the side of the garden to speak to people there Darian stepped outside. He took a glass of wine from a passing waitress just so that he wouldn't stand out so much and headed towards the end of the garden to check the view.

'Quite something, isn't it?'

Darian turned to find a woman in her thirties with short hair, high cheekbones and skin dark enough to shine under the lights in the trees.

'It's extraordinary, yes.'

'I'm Asteria Hobnil, everyone calls me Asti. I work for Duff Shipping. I handle our Asian accounts. I don't think I've seen you here before.'

'Gito Conin, McCourt Securities, first-time visitor, long-time wisher I could afford to live here. I thought the Sutherlands and the Duffs didn't get along.'

'Hate each other with a passion. If they didn't love being rich so much they would have burned the city to the ground fighting one another centuries ago. The Sutherlands still think all the Duffs are boorish and the Duffs still think all the Sutherlands are stuck up and they might both be right, but at least the Duffs have fun and do some good. Harold keeps inviting people from the company because he's trying to build bridges, metaphorically speaking of course, and Duff keeps sending us along to pretend we're all pals now but really to spy on him.'

Darian chuckled unconvincingly at the mention of spying and said, 'So what's he like, Harold Sutherland? I've only met him once through work.'

'He's determinedly likeable, which is impressive at first, but I have a deep distrust of people who only behave one way, only have one setting. He never switches off.'

'Oh, I've seen him angry.'

'Really? The one time you met him and you managed to make him crack. You'll have to tell me your secret. Every Duff in the city would love to know... Is that man looking for you?'

Darian turned to follow Asti's gaze and saw Sholto, sweat glistening on his face under fairy lights, walking through the garden, staring to left and right. It looked very much like time to leave.

The Descent of Poison

A man lay between white sheets, the full-length window open and the wind blowing salt air into the room. Beside him lay a woman of twenty-six, as beautiful as any he had ever met, naked, the mother of his children. Life was the idyll he had been told throughout his youth it would become.

Out on the air he heard the low drone, moving closer and flitting in and out of view, the small white plane sweeping across Loch Eriboll and over the hills to the east, beyond the horizon. He smiled to see it and think of the endless sky, the truest freedom he had ever known, the only one that brought him joy.

Joseph Sutherland leaned across and kissed the perfect bare shoulder of his wife Marcail, listening to the sweet sound of her sleeping mumble as he slipped out from under the sheet. He put on the trousers and blue T-shirt lying on the wicker chair in the corner, the clothes he had worn the day before, his shoes at the foot of the bed. He made his way down to the garage in silence.

It was early morning, the staff awake and working but the three children still asleep. He slid open the garage door, pulled on his helmet and started one of his classics, the Matchless Silver Hawk, riding it along the single street of Eilean Seud to the pier. The boatman was already in place and smiled a good morning as he always did when

Joseph rode the motorcycle up the ramp and onto the small deck. Without instruction they sailed across to Cruinn Pier and the boatman let the ramp down.

The ride north along the lochside was at first slow but then, beyond the edge of the city where the road was always empty, gloriously fast, revitalising. The ride to Portnancon Airfield offered a taste of freedom, dressed in its speed and danger but limited by the road below him.

At the Second World War airfield he stopped at the gate at the end of the narrow road and opened it with his personal key, riding up to the three green hangars with curved roofs and the one at the end that belonged to his family. His twin-engine plane was ready for him, as always, kept so for the whims Joseph's staff were paid to serve. That was his good fortune.

It took minutes to start and get the plane out of the hangar and then he took off, roaring fast from the strip, one of his favourite places and almost abandoned now because of the monstrosity on Whisper Hill. He would never follow the others to the other side of the loch.

Challaid was below and from the sky it seemed so small, a narrow horseshoe of grey looping round cold dark blue, not the suffocating mass of people and expectation that it seemed on the ground but a toy he could fit in his hand and crush when it bored or frustrated him. The buildings were specks and the hills at its back no longer a cage, but a bump easily scaled, far away and irrelevant as he soared above.

He had spoken many times with Marcail about how pointless it was, how all of his achievements could never add up to more than a sentence in the book of his family's existence. He was twenty-eight and all his life had understood that the only journey he could make was in other people's footsteps. It was a path rich and beautiful and perfect and empty.

Marcail would be down there, probably with the children, Harold, Beathan and Nina, perhaps eating breakfast out on the lawn by the loch as she liked to do on warm mornings. There were so few of those in a city built on coldness, but this summer had been more generous than most and children could believe that made up for past failures. One day they would understand.

Joseph flew over Stac Voror and north towards Whisper Hill, the sight of the scar on its top he wasn't allowed to fly over souring the view. Much of Challaid was ugly from on high, grey and brown stone and concrete, cars and lorries and dirt, while a glimpse beyond the hills showed the unspoiled, the world before people chose to ruin it.

He brought the plane left and pointed it towards Eilean Seud, the slip of land that had always been home. He had never had an excuse to be unhappy with the life it gave. He thought of his family and he smiled. A glimpse of the horizon, of what might be and what he knew would be, his mind finding rest.

Far below they would be watching him, enjoying breakfast and laughing at the obsession that sent him into the sky. They would watch the white bird-like speck, turning back to face them. They would see it dive suddenly and hit the water, and they would know that he was dead.

30

SHOLTO SPOTTED DARIAN at the end of the garden and came towards him at a sort of trot, a man trying not to run because that would draw unwanted attention but unable to walk because urgency shoved him forward. He paused when he saw Asti, unsure of her before he decided that caution had to be thrown into the storm that was brewing.

'I just saw Bran Kennedy, the head of Raven, and I think he saw me.'

Darian frowned. 'You think?'

'He gave that little shudder he always gives when he sees me. Even from across the long room I'm sure of it. He'll be coming after us and he won't be alone.'

They both looked up towards the French doors and it wasn't the head of Raven Investigators in Challaid they saw but Alan Dudley, his thuggish junior, doing a terrible job of standing in the doorway and searching the garden while trying to look like he wasn't. That told them Kennedy wasn't at the party to enjoy himself. He was providing security and had help with him.

Sholto said, 'How do we get out of here without them seeing us?'

Darian looked over his shoulder at the loch and said, 'How's your swimming?'

Asti Hobnil, who had been listening, said, 'I don't think you need to get your nice threads wet. See those bushes over there? Go round behind them in the gap at the bottom and you'll end up on a path that runs along the side of the house, keeps you as far from the party room as possible. If they haven't alerted the front gate you can make a run for the ferry. If they come down this way I'll stall them. Shouldn't be hard, last thing Harold Sutherland would want is a scene.'

Darian and Sholto both stared at her and Darian said, 'Uh... thank you.'

She smiled. 'I told you, I'm a spy, it's my duty to help fellow rogues, Mr Incognito.'

Dudley had left the doorway and was walking slowly through the garden, which meant there was no time left for conversation. They turned and walked with conspicuous speed across to their left and behind a tall hedge that ran up towards the house and hid the large greenhouse and tool shed from view of the main lawn. They moved quick, Darian striding and Sholto shuffling, until they found themselves on the narrow path Asti had promised would appear.

At the front corner of the house they stopped and peered round, checking for Ravens. All they could see was the idle rich making their way in and out of the doors to the party room on the other side of the building so they stepped out. There was a long, curving path that led to the drive and then the gate. From now on it was walking only because innocent men didn't run. The innocent probably didn't walk as quickly as Darian and Sholto did either, but they were trying their best. There was no way to look anything other than odd as they strolled past the two girls at the gate on their way out just twenty minutes after going in. One of them gave Darian a curious look as he passed them and he tried to respond with the most adorably innocent smile he could muster, not breaking stride in the process.

On the walk along the lane to the pier they were the only people leaving and passed a few stragglers heading the other way. They both looked back over their shoulders and saw no one pursuing them. The only people at the boat were the two sailors working it and timing was perfect because they were just about to leave. Darian and Sholto stood nervously under the canopy on deck as they inched away from the pier and into the dark water between the island and the mainland.

The older of the two sailors, a man in his forties with the sort of beard and thick jumper combination that seemed designed to announce his occupation to the world, joined them at the railing. 'Nothing wrong is there, lads, leaving so soon?'

Even though the man was smiling Sholto shook his head vigorously and said, 'No, not at all, not at all, absolutely not.'

The sailor laughed, and leaning back on his heels he said, 'Would I lose my shirt if I put a bet on you two being nervous about security waiting for you at Cruinn Pier?'

Darian judged the man perfectly when he said, 'You can probably hang onto your clothing.'

'Thought so. Come into the cabin so they don't see you. If they're there we can hide you below until they bugger off. You wouldn't be the first.'

They went inside where it was a little warmer and a little quieter and where they could see anyone on the pier before anyone on the pier saw them.

Sholto said, 'How did you know?'

The sailor said, 'The only people at these parties who get their suits at Polla Clothing are either working the event or not supposed to be there and the waiters don't get to leave this early. I managed to live forty-three years without being able to tell the difference between something off the rack and a tailored suit. It's only in the last three since I started working this route that I've seen enough of the latter to get it.'

'You haven't fallen in love with the posh hard enough to turn us in?'

'Ha, some of them are all right, but I'm a man of the sea, not a man of the bank. So what did you lads nick?'

'Nothing, we just didn't have an invite.'

'Ah, okay. We see that often enough, people running from the security, most of them manage to grab a keepsake on the way out, a candlestick that turns out to be worth six hundred quid, something like that.'

'You can get candlesticks worth six hundred quid?'

'Oh, aye, a lot of these rich folk, they're full of...'

Sholto said, 'Shit?'

'I was going to say creativity, but I suppose that, too.'

As the boat edged towards Cruinn Pier a radio crackled and a garbled message came through that the sailor leaned in to listen to. He turned to Darian and Sholto. 'That's them telling us to look out for you. Of course, we haven't seen you.'

As his crewmate steered the boat into dock the older man went out and stepped onto the pier to secure the vessel. From the cabin Darian and Sholto could see a handful of people waiting for the ramp to be let down for them, but they all looked dressed to thrill, not kill.

The sailor came back inside and said, 'No one dressed cheaply enough to be security; you two can make a run for it.'

They thanked him, even though he seemed to consider helping people get one over Harold Sutherland's security team a privilege, and got off the ferry. They practically sprinted to the Fiat at the far corner of the small car park.

Sholto mumbled under his breath as the car started and they pulled away. They both remained silent, scanning the mirrors, until they were out of Barton and down into Cnocaid, which felt just far enough to relax. Now that Sholto was heading steadily east towards Bank and Darian's flat they could talk.

He said to Darian, 'So what did we learn tonight, apart from the fact that I was right about rich people being more trouble than even they are worth, that we should wear trainers to their parties and that this city would be nothing without its sailors?'

Darian said, 'I learned that on the evening Freya went missing Harold Sutherland was at Challaid's match with Motherwell, so all the way across the city from where she was last seen.'

'Okay, but you would expect him to have concocted a neat wee alibi for the time it happened, because he was hardly going to do it himself, was he?'

'No, I suppose not, but the more I see him the less I can picture him showering Freya with expensive gifts. It would be far too desperate for someone like him, women cooing in his ear at the party the whole time we were there. He would see buying her a car as crass. A man like that would be smart enough to know what a woman like Freya would want from him. He'd know her pride wouldn't let her be bought.'

'Or maybe the charm is all part of the act and when it failed with Freya he lost the plot. Maybe it failed with Ruby as well and that's why he targeted her.'

'We seem to be accusing a lot of Sutherlands of acting. Do you believe Harold is performing?'

'Not really. He doesn't strike me as the sort, but you'd be amazed how often I've said that before and very quickly been proven wrong.'

Darian said, 'I still think tonight was worth the effort, just to learn a little more about that family.'

Sholto muttered noncommittally and then pointed out they were on Havurn Road and coming up to Darian's flat on the corner. He found a spot and parked.

31

DARIAN WAS ABOUT TO say goodnight to Sholto, who we'll be honest and say wasn't the last face he wanted to see before he went to sleep – that honour belonged to Angela Vicario – when Sholto's phone rang. It took an almost indecent struggle with his hand reaching into his pocket before he pulled the phone out, leaning back and wrestling with his seat belt as he did. God knows what anyone walking past outside would have thought was going on.

Sholto frowned at the number and answered. 'Hello, Sholto Douglas.'

Darian sat and listened but only because he knew from Sholto's formal response that it was work and might have been about the party. If he had thought it was Mrs Douglas he would have given his boss some privacy. This was someone Sholto wasn't sure of and the pacey mumbling on the other end told Darian the subject was something someone found exciting.

Sholto said, 'I'm in the car with Darian, we'll come straight round.'

He hung up and Darian said, 'What's this?'

'That was Warren Corvo.'

'Who or what the hell is a Warren Corvo?'

'You know him, one of the three lads from Challaid Data Services along the corridor, I can't remember which one of them, they're all the same to me. He called to say that someone's breaking into our office and that we need to get round there sharpish if we want to stop them.'

As he was talking Sholto was putting the car into gear and pulling out from the side of Havurn Road, heading east to try and get to the office on Cage Street. Darian was thinking about the phone call and sticking his brain in the holes he found.

'If they know we're being broken into why aren't they stopping the burglar? They're twenty feet along the corridor.'

'They're not at their office. He was calling from home.'

'Then how the hell does he know we're being broken into? Does he sleep under his desk?'

'I didn't exactly have time to interrogate him, Darian, I was a little too concerned about getting off the phone and onto the road. Now stop talking to me, you know I can't drive quickly when I'm distracted.'

The problem with that statement was the crucial point it left out. Indeed Sholto couldn't drive quickly when he was distracted, but that was principally because he couldn't drive quickly at all. This was the painfully annoying part for Darian, having to sit in the passenger seat knowing that if they stopped and switched places they would spend thirty seconds stationary but get there minutes quicker. He couldn't suggest it because Sholto would call that a distraction and his pride would never accept it anyway. If he was going faster than usual then to him it meant they were already going remarkably fast.

Darian knew all these streets, could recognise them even in the false light of urban night-time when the city was clothed so differently and the familiar tried to look strange. They were on Raghnall Road, or Rag Road to locals who mostly don't remember the sketchy story of the eleventh century hero it's named after. There were the two sets of gates to the dock on the south bank of the loch on their left, once the entrances for working men who powered the city and now a monument to the gentrification that had slain the soul but kept the wallet of the area. That meant they were about five minutes of Sholto's driving away from Cage Street, three if Darian had been behind the wheel.

Stuck at traffic lights, watching two cars go past and knowing that neither could possibly be in as much of a hurry as they were, then they were pulling away again, minus the screech of tyres Darian would have aimed for and going past the Glendan HQ building on Bruaich

Drive with its glass frontage, and Darian knew they were two minutes from Cage Street, a minute and a half of his driving, so beyond the point where switching roles would help.

He had been thinking on the journey that this couldn't be a coincidence. They were on Eilean Seud when someone decided now was a good time to try and break into their office. Oddly perfect timing. So who would know? Raven Investigators because their boss Bran Kennedy had eyeballed Sholto at the party? One call to an underling and they could have had someone forcing the door, believing that Sholto and Darian were hiding on the island and bound to be caught there. They were the most likely candidates but that brought questions.

Darian said, 'How are you going to handle this?'

'We're going to go in and try to stop our place from being turned over.'

'But how do we stop them? There might be three or four of them and they might be armed. Do we attack? Do we hold back and box them in?'

'Oh, chee whizz, I didn't think of that. Maybe we should hold back. I do like my office, but not enough to give it my last breath.'

'We'll get closer and play it by ear.'

'I do wish my hearing was better.'

Sholto found a spot on a double yellow on Greenshank Drive and they got out, heading round the corner and onto Cage Street.

32

THEY RAN DOWN CAGE STREET with no view of the office from that direction. What they saw as they got closer was Mr Yang, Mrs Yang and the three junior Yangs standing out on the street looking back at the building.

As they stopped beside them Sholto said, 'Mr Yang, what's driven you out of your bed?'

'We got a call, one of the Data people. There's someone in there, breaking in. I don't want my girls in there with someone breaking in, they could be dangerous.'

His son Michael, the eldest child and probably big enough to look after himself at that point anyway, gave his father a sulky look but said nothing. Mrs Yang looked much more annoyed than frightened, a woman usually full of fire and mischief that their two daughters had inherited.

Darian said, 'Has anyone called the police?'

Mr Yang said, 'Of course we did, someone is breaking into the building where we live. The man called and said you were coming but we called the police, too, as many as possible.'

Sholto said, 'Any sign of them?'

'The police? The Challaid Police? Even if the man had thrown me out of the window and my blood ran down to the corner they wouldn't be here until three weeks next Tuesday. I would be better calling my school friend who's a policeman in China. He would be here faster.'

His wife whispered something in Chinese and Mr Yang grabbed her hand, holding it firmly. Darian and Sholto, on this occasion, considered the reliably lackadaisical police response to be no bad thing. They wanted to know who was breaking into their office before the cops turned up and spoiled the surprise.

They looked at each other and nodded, Darian assuming his boss was thinking the same as him. So he was, but with a lot less enthusiasm. They knew they were going to have to go in and at least try to identify the intruder and their intentions, because waiting out on Cage Street with the Yang family was only offering the person an easy escape. Sholto grimaced, sighed once, then a second time and nodded again at Darian.

Darian said to Mr Yang, 'We're going in. Get yourselves off the street and away from the doors in case he comes out this way. He might be armed.'

Mr Yang said, 'I'll wait, and if he comes out this way I'll tackle him.'

'No, seriously, he could be very dangerous; we don't know what we're dealing with here.'

'I'll get one of my cleavers, one that can stop any animal smaller than a cow and slower than a rabbit.'

Sholto said, 'No, Mr Yang, really, that lad in there could be any sort of dangerous if he's daft enough to spend this long robbing the place. Never hit a crazy person with anything smaller than a bus, not even a cleaver. You get the family somewhere safe. I couldn't stand the thought of you getting hurt and me not getting fed because of it.'

The nod Mr Yang gave was stiff enough to pass for a short head-butt but it was agreement and that was enough for now. They had wasted too much time getting to Cage Street and speaking out on the street in hissed urgency. Whatever the intruder was looking for he was bound to have found it in the one-room office by now. Unless, Darian realised, he wasn't very good at this. That shifted suspicion away from a well-prepared Raven employee and onto someone else. Darian just didn't know who that someone else would be.

They went in through the side door, the one they always took. It gave them access to the stairs that would take them straight up to the office. Even opening the side door was a risk; if the intruder had an unseen accomplice that's where they were likely to be. If there was a backup then he wasn't lurking in the stairwell, which was empty when they went in. They closed the door behind them, Sholto holding the handle and pushing it softly to avoid any noise.

This was all about stealth now, not a strong suit of either man. They walked up the wooden stairs, looking up into the darkness as they went and neither spotting danger. They could have been walking into a trap, bubbling with treacherous danger, and they wouldn't have had a clue. It only occurred to them later how this break-in had exposed their inability to properly handle this kind of threat. Two men walking into an unknown but probably dangerous situation by going up two flights of stairs in the dark towards a threat that may have been waiting for them, watching their every movement. Not for the first time, Darian would later wonder how he ever managed to make it from one end of the day to the other unscathed.

On the first floor they could see the closed doors of the Yangs' flat and the Highland Stars Entertainment Agency. There was no sign of disturbance. They turned the corner and sneaked slowly up to the second floor. Two steps from the top and leading the way Darian stopped. He could see their office door ajar, and he waited for Sholto to get alongside and see for himself. Through the slit they could see feeble light moving, someone with a dim torch. Before Sholto could think of a convincing way to articulate retreat Darian moved forward.

They stood either side of the door and gave each other the sort of look that vaguely competent gunslingers in movies give each other because they didn't know what else was expected of them in the circumstances. They were working this out on the hoof.

Darian pushed the door open and called out, 'Okay, you're blocked, so stay right there.'

He ducked his head round the door to look inside and saw the mess, paper from Sholto's desk all over the floor, and a single person by the filing cabinet at the back of the room. He was trying to force the locked drawer and struggling pathetically because he hadn't brought the right equipment. With the torch in his hand he spun round to face the door and Darian recognised Will Dent.

'Come on, Will, what the hell are you doing?'

The Sutherland driver stared at the doorway and made a calculation. He could only see Darian and Sholto which meant it was two against one and he wasn't scared of either of them. Suddenly he made a sprint for the door, head down and shoulder-charging into both men. All three fell out into the corridor, Will crashing into the bannister. Sholto rolled over and swore vividly while Darian tried to grab Will by the ankle and got a kick in the neck instead. Will was the first to his feet and bolted down the stairs.

On Rails

Every evening, at eight o'clock, Mungo Alason would get out of bed in his flat in Whisper Hill and have a shower. He would then walk through to the kitchen and from the yellow cabinet take a bowl and a packet of cornflakes and sit down to eat. It was silent, but for the rumble of his fridge that he had long intended to replace. He was forty-one and some variation of this had been his life for twenty years. It never occurred to Mungo that he deserved better or that he could have more. This was so normal to him and any change in routine would have been frightening. Having finished eating, he washed the bowl and spoon and returned them to their places before he left the flat and went down the stairs to Garbh Street. It wasn't an attractive place, the tall and ugly flats on either side of the narrow road, and it wasn't a fun four-minute walk to Three O'clock Station, but he was so used to it in the dark and rain that he barely looked up as he went, automatically sidestepping people on the crowded streets around the station building. They were all coming in and out of the main doors, the large front all lit up, but Mungo was going in a different way, as ever. He hardly needed to break stride, taking his security card from his pocket and swiping it into the slot on the door and quickly punching in his passcode as he put the card back in his pocket with his free hand. The red light on the panel turned green and he pulled the door open and entered. He was in the back corridor and made his way along to the changing room, opening his locker and putting on his overalls with the Duff Shipping Company logo on the breast like a football shirt. A second man walked into the room, older and smaller than Mungo. 'All right, Mungo?' he said as he began to open his own locker and pull on the overall that exactly matched Mungo's in everything but size. That was the other driver, there were always two of them for security reasons, and they would exchange no more than a handful of words in the next eight and a half hours, providing nothing went wrong. Mungo went out of the changing room and along a corridor, using his card again to get out onto the platform and along to the train. It was platform number seven, right at the back and only ever used for the freight trains that Mungo drove. The company manager was already walking along the platform with clipboard in hand, marking something on every page of the wad he had, each page representing the cargo of each car. There were eight and Mungo could see that two were the red tanks that meant chemicals; they would have been collected at the docks and taken here. The manager met him by the engine and flipped to the last page for Mungo to sign, which he did. 'Good night and good luck,' the manager said as he always did, probably thinking it was clever, and walked away. Mungo went up into the cab and made a few checks before he stepped back onto the platform. 'Here,' a voice said quietly behind him, and Mungo turned expecting to find the other driver. Instead there was a man in his thirties, dressed like a station cleaner but with the look of someone who had never suffered manual labour in his life. He was holding out a small but thick envelope for Mungo to take. 'What?' Mungo said. 'Take it,' the man told him, 'give it to their guy at the other end, he'll be in the staff toilet, he'll give you your five grand. Take it.' He pressed the envelope into Mungo's hand and made off down the platform. Mungo stood and looked down at what he'd been given. The man had spoken as though Mungo was supposed to expect this, but it had never happened before, there had been no warning. It felt light and insubstantial. It wasn't drugs because surely an envelope full wasn't worth this much effort or five thousand pounds of anyone's money, and it was too flat to be the precious stones they said passed through the docks routinely. It was something someone wanted to sneak out of Challaid by unpredictable means, and he couldn't imagine what that might be. He heard the thick security door to the platform open and, without thinking, stuffed the envelope inside his overalls and began to climb back into the cabin as the other driver emerged to join him. Could it have been for the other driver the man had the envelope? As he stepped into the cabin beside Mungo his companion looked his usual self, not like someone expecting a delivery that hadn't arrived. 'Right, we got clearance, call it in and let's go. Sooner we go the sooner we get back,' the man said, all the conversation they would have in the loud cab. The other driver started them up while Mungo radioed in to get final permission to depart, and they pulled slowly away from the freight platform, past the passenger platforms and out from under the protection of Three O'clock Station, the lights of the built-up area around the station puncturing the view ahead. Mungo sat on his too-narrow seat with the envelope pressed against his chest, feeling it when he moved, wondering what he had done. He should have refused to take it and then he should have reported it to someone. Having failed to do those things he should throw it out of the window when they got clear of the city so he couldn't be caught with it at the other end. It could have been a trap, a test he had already failed. They took security seriously, the company, their ships bringing cargo in from all over the world as they had done for hundreds of years and shifting them by rail to the central belt, and that included many sensitive items. They moved slowly through Bank and up to Ciad Station, slowing to a halt as they were switched onto the tracks heading south through Gleann Fuilteach and into the mountains. As they crawled forward Mungo leaned a little more on his seat than usual, looking out for anyone in a policeman's uniform, or the Duff Shipping security officer. No one tried to stop them. The journey was the same as all the others, as it had been since the national rail line came through the mountains to connect with the city in 1907, leaving the lights of Challaid behind and swooping into the dark beauty of the empty Highlands, few named places, nothing touched by man's spoiling hand for so many miles but the line beneath them. It was four hours and twenty minutes south through the blackest hours of the night and there was nothing but the noise of the train and very occasional radio messages. They reached Glasgow and slowed again, rattling into Queen Street Station and stopping at the given platform, both getting out. Few people were there in the dead hours, and some wore security uniforms, but it was the same collection of sleepy faces that always met them. Mungo signed for them as he always did, confirming the delivery and time, and then told them he needed the toilet. He was pouring with sweat when he went in. There was a man in a suit with stylish hair and a gold watch standing by the sinks, dark eyes and a dimpled chin, showing his too-white teeth when he smiled at Mungo. 'You have it?' he asked in what sounded like an English accent. Mungo reached into his overalls and took out the envelope, passing it to the man and looking sideways to the cubicles to make sure no one was there. 'Good work, I appreciate it,' the man said, taking another envelope from his pocket and passing it to Mungo. 'I'll see you next month,' the man in the suit said and walked out of the bathroom. Mungo took the new envelope and unzipped his overalls, reaching down to put it into the pocket of his trousers and zipping back up again. He walked back out to join the other driver, nervous again, and they walked together across the station to get into a different cab. There were three cars attached to it and he signed for them. The train they had delivered would be moved out of this station by a driver already getting into it, taken to be unloaded elsewhere. They would return this one in the night with whatever small cargo it carried and be finished their shift as the sun came back around. They were given clearance to leave, slowly and quietly at this hour as they moved through the edges of the southern city, and it felt excruciating to Mungo. The long journey north in silence, moonlight rolling silver down the sides of the mountains and showing snow on the peaks, sometimes smothered in the clouds and nothing but the blackness, then into Gleann Fuilteach and the lights of Challaid. They switched tracks again at Ciad Station, moving through Cnocaid, Bank, Bakers Moor and Earmam before reaching Whisper Hill, the long straight run north in the dip with the backs of the buildings on either side looking so tall. Back where they had started as they rolled slowly into Three O'clock Station. Mungo signed the return slip and went into the changing room, taking off his overalls and hanging them in his locker. 'See you tomorrow,' the other driver said as Mungo left. He used his security card at the door and stepped outside. No alarms went off and no one was waiting to grab him. He walked through the cold hours of early morning, his breath jumping out ahead of him, trying to get away, and he reached Garbh Street and home. His checked shirt was sticking to him and he could smell the sweat as he sat at the kitchen table and carefully cut open the envelope with a knife. There was exactly five thousand pounds inside in fifty crisp one hundred pound notes, the roguish face of King Alex looking back at him from every green one. Mungo didn't know what he'd done and didn't know what to do with what he'd been given for it, but he knew he'd do it again. A month later the same man handed him another envelope, this time in the corridor just inside the security door. It was the same size and feel as the first, the same reward given by the same man in Glasgow. It happened again the following month, and again after that, and after the eighth month Mungo was no longer nervous about it. He never looked in the envelopes. He was getting sixty thousand pounds a year for almost no extra work, and as long as there were no disasters no one would ever find out.

33

DARIAN WAS ON HIS FEET before Sholto, and after a glance confirmed his boss was okay he was off down the stairs after Dent. He could hear footsteps ahead of him, hitting each step at pace. This was where Darian could catch up because even in the dark the stairs were familiar to him but not to Dent. Darian could use instinct to move faster than his quarry. He felt he was getting closer and Dent felt it too because he started to gamble on the first-floor stairs, going down two at a time and risking breaking the only neck he had. Dent jumped the last five steps and landed hard. It must have jarred his ankles, but desperation can persuade you to ignore any pain that might try to slow you, so he bounded to the side door and out into the night, ahead of Darian.

As he came down the last of the steps Darian heard a noise outside, the sound of a person who had been hit by something they wished they had avoided, a wobbly shout smothered by the noise of the door banging shut.

Darian pushed it open and ran out into Cage Street, nearly tripping over Mr Yang. The restaurant owner was sprawled on his back like an upended turtle, waving his hands around as he tried to remember how to get up.

Darian shouted, 'Are you okay?'

As Mr Yang rolled over and raised himself onto his knees Darian saw the glint of a meat cleaver big enough to halve a horse lying in the street. Mr Yang, in a tone of self-disgust, said, 'I missed him. I swung and I missed him.'

Darian, who had stopped the chase to check on his friend, asked, 'Did he hit you, are you hurt?'

'Shouldered me, that's all, I'm fine. Go after him, Darian, go after him. He went up to Greenshank Drive, go.'

Before Darian could start to run the door behind him burst open and a red-faced Sholto wheezed out onto Cage Street. Under the streetlights he saw Mr Yang on his knees, gasped and said, 'Mr Yang, he got you too, are you okay?'

'I'm fine. Don't waste time with me, get after him.'

They began to run up the street, Sholto struggling to keep up. At the corner with Greenshank Drive Darian stopped to look for Dent and Sholto caught up with him, saying, 'That Mr Yang is a hardy old bugger, shame he won't do what he's told.'

Darian was ignoring him, looking up and down the road and catching a glimpse of a man who might have been Dent going round the corner with Morhen Road, the route you would take if you were aiming for Glendan Station and a train that could put meaningful distance between you and your crime.

Darian said, 'There, Morhen Road. I'll chase, you take the car. If he gets on a train I'll call you and tell you where to go. If you corner him…'

'Don't worry, I don't corner bigger people than me without shouting for help first.'

Darian set off at a sprint towards the corner with Morhen Road, hoping to close the gap. By the time he reached it, Dent was nearly up at the opposite corner with Gallows View, the street on which the railway station stood. Darian wasn't the natural athlete of the Ross siblings; that honour went to his older brother Sorley, an exceedingly good camanachd player who wouldn't only have caught Dent by now, he would have battered every ounce of useful information out of him. Darian's reaction to falling behind was to run with longer strides, right on the edge of his balance, which felt faster but perhaps only because of how close he was to falling over.

Up to the corner and onto Gallows View, the long curving road with the station to his right and more people around. He couldn't see Dent, but that was because he was looking in the wrong place. When he looked away from the station entrance he saw a man running down a gap between two buildings, a travel agency on the ground floor on one side and an estate agent's on the other. Behind the buildings was a large corrugated fence to block access to the railway lines, and Dent was going for it.

Getting across the busy road took thirty seconds, too many taxis threatening to run him over, and then he had to get down the alley and over the high fence. He quickly reached the conclusion that Dent had toes more pointed than his because Darian struggled to get a foothold, pulling himself up and feeling the metal at the top dig into his fingers. It hurt, but not as much as Dent getting away would, and he forced himself up and over, trying to lower himself carefully on the other side but eventually having to let go and drop into the long grass, the fence higher on the rail side.

The grass was tall and the embankment before him was a steep drop into darkness, a wide valley with the twin tracks leading into the tunnel on one side and the station lit bright on the other, the backs of buildings opposite visible as silhouettes. Darian moved to the edge of the drop, almost falling as his dress shoes had no grip. The only pair of nice black shoes he owed, cheap but presentable, were no better for stalking through wet grass than they were for sprinting, but he had to do all this in an outfit designed for a rich man's party.

There was something there, a shadow that didn't quite fit with its surroundings, and Darian crept closer.

It was towards the tunnel mouth: Dent crouching in the grass at the top of the hill, hoping Darian would go the other way. Stealth suited Dent because he had darkness behind him but Darian was framed by the lights of the station and as soon as he started to walk towards him the driver made his move. He began sliding down the embankment on his backside, looking for more distance and taking risks to get it.

Darian shouted, 'Come on, Will, we know it's you, you can't outrun this.'

Darian was about to slide down after him when he saw movement on the other side: Sholto at the top of the embankment opposite.

Sholto called out, 'You're surrounded, Will, just climb up and give up.'

Dent was down on the line now, standing in the middle of the westbound tracks, and a sense of terrifying inevitability grabbed Darian's stomach and squeezed it hard. He shouted, 'Come on, Will, come back up, we can help you. Come up.'

Dent was a shadow, standing looking back and forth between Darian and Sholto, and then his face became clear. Someone had shone a light on him and Darian could see the fury and desperation in his face. It wasn't the light but the sound that made Darian turn and look, seeing the large freight train clear of the station and moving towards them, a blocky cabin and bright yellow front to make it unmissable. Dent saw it and stared, jerking as though he was about to take a step but then not moving.

Sholto screamed, 'Will, please. Will.'

Darian screamed too but when he thought about it later he couldn't remember what he had said and it was unlikely to have been anything more than a terrified shout. The train was close. There was a wail of brakes and a deep horn but it was too late to stop. Darian and Will Dent were looking each other in the eye, the driver not moving. The tension went out of him and his shoulders dropped. Darian forced himself not to turn away when the train hit him.

34

THE WORLD STOPPED FOR what seemed like hours but was only seconds. Darian stood on the top of the embankment and looked down at the train, now still on the tracks, no sign of Will Dent. The two men in the cab of the train sat where they were and didn't move, stunned by what had happened. Sholto was across on the other side, and although Darian didn't notice it at the time he too was rooted to the spot. In the seconds after another man's death a moment of respectful silence was forced upon them by shock. Dent was under the train. Darian couldn't see him because the massive metal beast had moved forward another seventy or eighty feet before stopping at the mouth of the tunnel.

Everyone seemed to move at the same time. Darian tried to run, skidding down the slope as Dent had done, trying to kneel and slide on his feet but slipping and going on his backside instead. By the time he was at the bottom two men in overalls were getting down out of the cab of the train, a man in his forties and a smaller, older one. The three of them stumbled towards the section of track where Dent had last been seen. Darian caught movement from the corner of his eye as he passed the link between two carriages and turned his head sharply to see Sholto struggling to make his way down to them.

The taller of the two drivers got down on his belly and looked under. He said, 'Oh Jesus.'

Darian looked to see for himself the grim scene below. A description isn't necessary because no one needs or deserves to have the details darken their mind. No one's family should have to read about what became of their loved one in a book like this. They knew at a glance that Will Dent was dead.

The older train driver said, 'I'll call it in.'

He climbed back into the cab as Sholto finally reached them. He looked at Darian and said, 'He's dead.'

'Yeah, he's dead. Don't look.'

It took only a couple of minutes from that point for the police to arrive. The first on the scene were a couple of constables who had been at the station and came running down the track with torches. The line had been shut, bringing an unsympathetic city even closer to a grinding halt than usual. They checked the body and asked a few basic questions, not getting too far above their pay grade. A still-breathless Sholto handled the talking.

He said to them, 'There was a break-in at our office, Douglas Independent Research on Cage Street. It was William Dent, that's the deceased. We chased him and he climbed the fence on this side. My colleague, Darian Ross here, he went on foot, I took the car because we thought he was going for the station. As I drove past I saw Darian climb the fence on Gallows View so I went round to Cladach Road thinking I could intercept him, cut off his escape. He stood on the train tracks in between us. He just stood there and let the train hit him.'

One of the officers said, 'He must have done more than break into an office to take that way out.'

Whatever that may have been they never found out because the officer chose not to follow up his speculation. A couple of minutes later more cops arrived, and then a couple of ambulances. Within five minutes the area between the station and the mouth of the tunnel was crawling with people and shifting light. One of the train drivers was with them and Darian asked if he was okay.

The man touched the place on his chest where his shirt pocket would be, a nervous twitch Darian had seen him do a few times, and said, 'Yes, aye, I'm okay. I'm... okay.'

He sounded like he was trying to convince himself, but at that point they all were. There was no way to be okay in the wake of what they had seen, what they had been a part of. It was horrifying and they were all shattered by it, but the need to focus on what Dent had been doing forced Darian and Sholto to turn their minds away from the death and back to the break-in, and that helped.

A detective from Bank Station appeared beside them. 'Sholto, fucking hell, I thought this sort of thing was behind you, bodies and mayhem.'

'I hoped they were, but it seems where there's life there's death, Conall.'

'Very profound, Sholto, very profound. So what's the God's honest reason for this life turning to death? More to it than a burglary gone wrong?'

This was when they had to share everything they knew. Darian had hoped they might get away from the scene without spilling it all, give them time to talk to Vinny and DC Vicario before the nasty truth shocked everyone. Once Dent's motives were out in the open word would filter instantly back to Harold Sutherland, and on to his nephew, and that was going to give them time to distance themselves from their employee, set up defences. Darian's first instinct was that Dent was obviously involved in Ruby-Mae Short's killing and Freya's disappearance, but his second thought told him it didn't mean he was working alone. He had known they were at Harold's party, that's why he had attacked the office that night. Someone had told him. Raven or Harold or perhaps even the Sutherland who had gotten them on the guest list, Philip.

Sholto said to DS Conall Archer, 'When you dig around you're going to find out that William Dent was working for Harold Sutherland as his personal driver, and you're going to find out that he's being investigated both for the murder of Ruby-Mae Short from last January that Dockside are looking at and the disappearance of Freya Dempsey that Cnocaid are handling.'

'Sutherland? Wait, Freya Dempsey? Is that Vinny Reno's missing ex? Oh, shite.'

He moved away quickly to make what looked, under the arc lights now set up alongside the train, like a series of frantic phone calls. DS MacNeith arrived and addressed Darian and Sholto only to tell them she would speak to them properly the following day, and it didn't seem like she was planning on offering any good wishes. DC Vicario showed up with a colleague a few minutes later.

She told them, 'I'll make my pitch for information, but we'll be at the back of the queue. Bank will handle the scene and Cnocaid are working an active search for a missing person so that'll get priority. You really should have called us about the burglary instead of handling it yourself.'

Sholto said, 'The police were called, they just weren't arriving. We went to our office and found he was still there. There wasn't much else we could do.'

Vicario nodded and said, 'That might be enough to keep you out of trouble if it's accepted he was going to flee before the police got there. I know you've given your witness statements twice already, so you should go home. There'll be a lot of people wanting to talk to you tomorrow. If I can hold back some of the wolves I will.'

Darian said, 'Thanks, Angela.'

He didn't notice her smile at the mention of her first name; he had been familiar without thinking. If he had thought about it, he would have realised he hadn't earned that yet. Angela patted Darian gently on the shoulder as he and Sholto turned away from the train and the lights and the teams of people in white forensic suits and made their way through the long grass and up to the fence on the far side. A panel had been cut away from it, the whole section would have to be replaced, and people were coming in and out. They got into the Fiat and Sholto picked an exceedingly careful path out between police cars, an ambulance, a large black van and, just coming up the street, what looked like a large crane on the back of a lorry.

35

THE FIAT PULLED INTO the parking place on Dlùth Street at the bottom of Cage Street that Sholto always used when at the office. Neither of them had said a word on the short drive from the station. Tiredness had hit them both in a heavy wave and was making smart choices difficult. They should have gone straight to their beds, but the night wasn't done with them yet. They had to check on the office and they had to check on Mr Yang. As they turned the corner they could see the whole Yang family out on the street, talking to cops. Challaid Police had finally turned up, but only because someone getting hit by a train had forced them to accelerate a process that typically moved at the speed of coastal erosion.

Sholto walked up to Mr Yang and said, 'You okay, pal?'

'I am, yes, we all are. We heard what happened; the police are here because of it. Are you okay too?'

'We're all right. Saw some things our eyeballs would rather have avoided, but these pictures get placed in front of you in life now and then.'

A young detective from Bank Station came over and introduced herself as DC Sarah Lowell. She said, 'I know we already have statements from you, but it would help us if you could check your office to see if anything was taken.'

They walked past the spot where Mr Yang had been knocked over and Darian noted there was no sign of the meat cleaver now. Had the police seen it they would no doubt have wanted to talk sternly about Mr Yang's intentions, so Darian guessed that either he or his eminently more sensible wife had returned it to the kitchen where it belonged. No need to make the Yangs' night any more awkward than it had already been.

As they were walking up the stairs to the second floor an only slightly familiar face appeared above them, waiting. He nodded when he saw them and said, 'Mr Douglas, Mr Ross, I'm Warren from Challaid Data Services. I called you earlier on.'

He was a dashing man in his late thirties, sweeping black hair and large eyes, an expensive black coat and silver wedding ring. His local accent tilted towards the posh side of the loch, which typically meant it sounded a little more Anglo and a little less Gaelic, not so much spit in the pronunciation.

Sholto said, 'We appreciated that, thank you, Warren.'

Warren ran his hand through his hair nervously and said, 'What a night. I was talking to one of the cops when I got here, they told me what happened with the guy and the train. A hellish thing to be a part of, but I'm glad you're both okay.'

He sounded like he meant it too, this man they hardly knew, which was unexpectedly nice of him. People were treating them was as though they had been the ones hit by the train, and nobody seemed to have a lot of pity for Will Dent.

Warren continued, 'I told the cop I wanted to come up and make sure our office was safe, but I figured it would be, it was yours he was targeting. I'm glad I bumped into you. We'll need to talk about security for the building at some point, maybe try and get a meeting with the owner about it if we can find the guy.'

Darian nodded and said, 'I didn't know we had any security as it was.'

Standing in the dim light of the landing Warren said, 'We put some in a few months ago. We got a contract with the council, handling some data for them, and part of the agreement was that we had to make sure everything was extremely secure because they're paranoid about information being stolen or leaked, so we upped the security from non-existent to minor. There's a camera up there so we've got the landing covered and it sends alerts to my phone if there's movement registered outside of working hours. I checked the feed and here was some guy making a hard job out of forcing your door.'

Darian and Sholto both looked up at the white plastic circle on the ceiling that he had pointed to as a camera. Sholto said, 'I thought that was a smoke alarm.'

'No, no, that's a camera.'

'So we still don't have a smoke alarm.'

'I put a letter into your mail box telling you about it when it was being put in, I thought you knew it was there. I got in touch with the owner, eventually. He said he was on holiday in Mexico, so I emailed him the details and he agreed to it. No one else in the building objected, although I never managed to make contact with the talent agency downstairs, if there's anyone there to make contact with. I should have made the effort to come along the corridor and talk to you about it.'

'I don't remember seeing that letter.'

Darian glanced through the open office door. The light was on now and he could see the piles of paper that had smothered Sholto's desk now carpeting the floor. There could have been a letter from the king in there and it would have had a fifty-fifty chance of ever being read. Darian had always suspected that a lot of worthwhile offers and information got lost in those piles.

Darian said, 'Well, thanks for the call.'

The two of them went into the office. It wasn't hard to work out that Dent hadn't taken anything with him because the only things of importance or value were still locked up in the now slightly damaged filing cabinet. They stood in the middle of a room that had never looked or felt smaller and scanned the damage he'd done trying to find something that in the end would have done him no good.

Sholto said, 'What the hell did he think he was going to find in here?'

'I don't know. He must have known where we were so he took his chance, but for what?'

'Unless he thought we were sitting on the evidence that proved his guilt and didn't realise it.'

'Then how would he know we had it?'

'That I can't tell you.'

They left the office in the hands of the police, no point giving them a key because the lock was broken on the door. Sholto drove Darian home for the second time that long night.

BAKERS MOOR STATION – SEARCH REPORT

16 May 18

Name of suspect: William Dent
Case No.: BM06-160518
Address searched:

40 MacLean Street,

Bakers Moor,

Challaid, CH5 1NI

Search of domestic premises

Catalogue of items of interest found –

Samsung tablet – Found on tablet were deleted searches relating to murder investigation of Ruby-Mae Short (Case no. WH22-120117)

Searches dated: Jan 13th 2017, Jan 14th 2017, Jan 19th 2017, Feb 16th 2017, May 11th 2018, May 14th 2018

Terms searched –

Jan 13th 2017 –

- *Ruby Short*
- *Ruby-May Short*
- *Ruby-Mae Short*
- *Ruby-Mae Short murder*
- *Ruby-Mae Short Misgearan*
    Jan 14th 2017 –
- *Ruby-Mae Short murder investigation*
- *DI Ralph Grant*
- *Detective Inspector Ralph Grant*
- *DC Angela Vicario*
    Jan 19th 2017 –
- *Ruby-Mae Short*
- *Ruby-Mae Short witness's*
- *Ruby-Mae Short witnesses*
- *Ruby-Mae Short Misgearan*
    Feb 16th 2017 –
- *Nathan Short*
- *Ruby-Mae Short family*
- *Ruby-Mae Short pictures*
- *Ruby-Mae Short murder investigation*
- *Dockside police station Challaid*
    May 11th 2018 –
- *Ruby-Mae Short murder investigation*
- *Douglas Independent Research*
- *Ruby-Mae Short Douglas Independent Research*
- *Sholto Douglas*
- *Darian Ross*

- *Ruby-Mae Short Sholto Douglas*
- *Freya Dempsey*
    May 14th 2018 –
- *Ruby-Mae Short William Dent*
- *Ruby-Mae Short Sutherland*
- *Ruby-Mae Short murder*
- *Freya Dempsey*

Single page with Raven Investigators logo relating to on-going investigation. Page listed as page 2 of 2, not clear who it was addressed to, page 1 not found.

Quote: ... *Ross and Philip Sutherland gained access to the house and searched the property. The evidence they found was presented to the police and our belief is that they are convinced of the involvement of William Dent. It's likely they've gained additional evidence from following Mr Dent, and that evidence would be held securely at their office, 21 Cage Street, Bank. We will continue our investigations, as instructed.*

Sincerely,
Bran Kennedy

Cash totalling £2,560 was found in a plastic bag hidden in a basket of potatoes in the kitchen cupboard. Request has been made to access details of Mr Dent's account with Sutherland Bank. No bank slips found on premises.

Holdall in wardrobe containing several changes of clothing and Mr Dent's passport in a side pocket.

Possibly left from previous holiday but clothes unworn and possible exit bag.

All relevant information passed on to Dockside station in relation to Ruby-Mae Short murder investigation (case no. WH22-120117) and Cnocaid station in relation to Freya Dempsey missing person investigation (case no. CN35-070517).

Deep search of premises to be carried out afternoon of 16/05/18, will be attached to this file.

36

DARIAN WOKE WITH THE sort of sore muscles and dull headache that overexertion caused. Sleep had been fitful and he was up early, the scenes behind his eyelids grimmer than anything he was likely to see in daylight. He shaved and forced himself to eat a bowl of cereal with milk as suspicious as anyone he had met in the last few days. Normally he would have ditched it and gotten his breakfast from The Northern Song, but he wasn't sure Mr Yang would be open this morning.

The trip to Cage Street was bleaker than before, Darian looking at the floor of the train instead of at the people, not interested in how the good and more often bad of Challaid were conducting themselves that morning. The line was open again, the disruption now behind everyone else. As he walked through Glendan Station he looked around for any sign that something tragic had happened, that a man had lost his life just a few hundred yards down the track, but there was none.

The death of Will Dent had caused only temporary inconvenience.

Walking down Cage Street he could see a strand of blue and white police tape tied to a drainpipe on the Superdrug store opposite that had presumably stretched across to the other side of the street but had been ripped away hours ago. That was the only admission this had been a crime scene. How quickly a place moved on from the events that occurred there. To his surprise, The Northern Song was open as usual and people were going in to collect their food. Darian went in the side door and up to the office, surprised to find Sholto ahead of him.

Sholto said, 'You sleep as badly as I did?'

'Yeah, sleep didn't want me to begin with and when it came around I didn't much like the look of it.'

'Bad pictures playing?'

'The same one, over and over. I just don't understand why he didn't step out of the way.'

'We'll never know. Maybe a person gets to the point that they realise the game is up, that their guilt is about to be proven, and the choice between a lifetime in prison and a quick death is a decision we wouldn't all agree on. People like to say the survival instinct keeps them fighting, but that's not always true.'

Sholto was trying to convince them both that Will Dent was guilty of killing Ruby-Mae Short and possibly Freya Dempsey as well, because believing he had been evil was the one thing that extracted some of the poison from the trauma that surrounded them. He had to be guilty.

Neither of them got any work done. They sat at their desks and stared into space, unsure what they were supposed to do now anyway. They were looking for Freya but if Dent was guilty then the police were likely to find some trace of her before they could. Darian kept checking his phone to see if there had been a message he had missed, but no one was calling. It was a strange relief to hear footsteps on the stairs and a knock on the door because it meant something was about to happen to break the chilly grip of nothingness.

Sholto let DC Vicario in and she looked at them both sympathetically. 'Well, you two have a habit of keeping me up all night with nothing happy to show for it.'

Sholto said, 'Nothing to show? What did you find out about Dent?'

'A few things, but not enough. We know he showed a lot of interest in Ruby's murder right after it happened, but we haven't found anything that clearly says he was involved and nothing to say he had ever heard of her before her death was reported in the media. We still have to check his phone, it was in his pocket and it's… broken. That might have more on it, more web searches; we're hoping it'll help.'

Darian said, 'It says something that he had any interest in it.'

'It says he had an interest, it doesn't say why and we can't just guess.'

'What about Freya?'

'Nothing. The only indication he had ever heard of her came from searches made after you questioned him the first time, which is a reasonable time for him to get interested in her case. There were other things, though. He had cash and a bag packed to run with, so there was either guilt or fear there. There was one particularly interesting thing. When Bakers Moor raided his flat they found the second page of a two-page note from Raven Investigators that mentioned you and your work, suggested that you thought Dent was involved in Freya's case and might have evidence to prove it. It had your address on it. We've talked to Raven and they say it was days old and part of a security update to the Sutherland Bank, not even to Harold Sutherland specifically, just the security department.'

Darian looked at her and said, 'Do you believe that?'

'I don't know, it looked like it was written to point someone in your direction. I hear Bran Kennedy is a good liar. We couldn't get any more out of him but maybe someone else could. Would help to know how Dent got his hands on a letter sent to the security department of the bank. If he stole it then he looks like a desperate man trying to cover his tracks. If someone gave it to him...'

Having rolled her grenade into their morning DC Vicario announced she was going home to get some sleep and left the office. Darian and Sholto both grabbed their coats and left the office just a minute behind her, down to Dlùth Street and the Fiat. They drove straight to Alexander Street in the south of Bank and the Challaid office of Raven Investigators.

The building, on a pleasant curved street, was four storeys of brick with plenty of tall windows to let in the little light that beat its way through the clouds and the shadow of Stac Voror. They had to park a way down the road and walk back up. In the reception area inside the front door they saw that Raven had the top floor, so they trudged up the stairs and found themselves in a hallway where a secretary behind her desk was the only person in view. To get to the Raven offices they had to get through the double doors beyond the smiling woman looking up at them.

She said, 'Hello, welcome to Raven Investigators, how can I help?'

Sholto said, 'We'd like to speak with Bran Kennedy.'

'Do you have an appointment?'

'We've got something better than that. We've got boiling hot pan of trouble to throw over him.'

'Eh, can I ask who you are?'

'I'm Sholto Douglas, this is Darian Ross.'

'Oh, well, I'm afraid Mr Kennedy isn't in his office at the moment...'

Sholto laughed and said, 'Isn't it funny how the mention of our names reminded you of that. You're a good secretary; we could use someone like you. Couldn't afford you, though.'

Sholto, in a rare moment of damned bad manners, turned and pulled open the double doors, wandering into the offices uninvited, Darian scurrying to keep up. There was an open floor, maybe seven or eight desks, only three of them currently occupied and Darian recognised Alan Dudley at one. At the back of the large room was an office on its own, and Sholto was already moving towards it with the certainty of a man who had complained here before. He pushed open the door, ignoring the staff closing in on them from behind, and found the man he was looking for.

Bran Kennedy stood up from behind his desk and said, 'Douglas, what the hell are you doing in a proper investigator's office?'

'I've come to ask you a series of very awkward questions.'

Sholto and Kennedy stood opposite each other and glared waves of wary hate across the room, like a washed-up bullfighter who'd forgotten to bring his sword and a malnourished bull with no heart, facing off in the arena after the crowd had gone home and the lights had been turned off.

The three employees who had been at their desks, two men and a woman, surrounded Darian in the doorway, one of them grabbing his arm before Kennedy said, 'Leave him, lads; let's hear what Oopsy the clown and the boy blunder have to say before we chuck them out. Go on, Sholto, tell the nice people what's gotten your blood pressure all riled up? I never saw you this red in the face when you were a cop except out of embarrassment.'

'I'm just here to tell you what you already know.'

'Well, that is a huge surprise, I'd better sit down before I faint.'

One of the men behind Darian sniggered but Sholto ignored him and said, 'You know that a letter you wrote was found in the possession of William Dent, and that it provided him with the reason, no, the advice, to target us, which in turn led him to his death. I know you've claimed it was a general update to the security department of the bank, but you also know as well as I do that the police aren't buying that. A case like this, Sutherland's being questioned about it, no way your updates just went to the security chief. The police are coming after you Bran. Me and Darian, we'll be after you too and I suppose you think you can handle us, but the police, Bran, the whole vicious, seething lot of them, you know what it means when they smell blood. That letter painted a bloody great big target on your back, and a lot of people with good aim are ready to take a shot. I hope you've got a good shield to hide behind. So, who did you deliver the letter to?'

Kennedy had grown angrier the longer Sholto went on, but he took his time before he answered. In a voice that seemed too small for his large, ugly, totally bald head he said, 'I gave it to the security officer, as I always do. I would never lie to the police about something like that. Now, lads, if you'd like to escort these trespassers out of the building.'

The three employees shoved them all the way down to the front door and out into the street with practised precision and glee. They walked back to the car and Sholto said, 'He's nervous about the police, which means he'll run for the cover of whichever Sutherland is paying him the big bucks. Let's see which one moves first.'

37

IN THE OFFICE DARIAN had several messages from Vinny, telling him what he'd heard at the station, which was nothing more than DC Vicario had already told them. The sense underlay each conversation that Will Dent was the guilty party and he had worked alone, the guilty man gone and nothing left to do but find Freya so Vinny could organise a funeral. It wasn't a positive thought, but it was an inevitability they were prepared for.

The phone call they had been waiting for was to Darian's mobile and it came from Phil. Darian answered and said, 'Hello?'

'It's Phil Sutherland. Listen, I've had a call from my cousin, Simon, and he wants to talk to you and your boss, wants to talk to me as well. Can you get round to his house straight away?'

'Yeah, we can.'

'Me and Vinny are already on our way, we'll see you there.'

Darian hung up and looked across the room at Sholto. He said, 'That was Phil, Simon Sutherland wants to see us at his house right away.'

Sholto raised his eyebrows and then raised the rest of himself from his chair. They drove up to Geug Place, Sholto viewing this first step by Simon as a sign of his guilt, a man worried he was about to be rumbled so making defensive manoeuvres. Darian couldn't quite find a way to disagree with that, whatever his gut said. They parked behind Vinny's car outside the gate and the four of them congregated.

Sholto said to Phil, 'How did he sound when he spoke to you, your cousin?'

'Scared. The police have been here to talk to him early this morning and I don't think he's handling it well. They haven't got anything against him but he's not used to having all these people rummaging through his life.'

Sholto said, 'No, he's not. Might be a good thing that it's changing now.'

The gate began to open and the four of them walked in and up the drive. Olinda Bles was waiting at the front door. She looked as if she'd been crying and her expression said she blamed them for it. They approached and Vinny offered his condolences for the group.

She said, 'Never mind your sympathy. Simon will see you, come in.'

Olinda held the door open for them and they hiked in, Phil going first and heading straight to his right without being told, along the corridor and through the door to the empty room. He walked with the confidence of a man who belonged in the mansions of the quirky rich. Simon was waiting, standing back towards the door that led to one of the wings filled with the junk that had at various times passed through his life. The four men came in and stood facing him, lined along the wall opposite.

He said, 'Thank you for coming, I'm sure you're busy.'

While the other three nodded politely, Darian took the opportunity to speak first. 'Can you tell us what you know of William Dent?'

Simon looked to the floor, hurt. 'I couldn't believe it when I found out that he was dead. And how it happened, I couldn't believe it. He was doing what he did for me. I didn't tell him to, I didn't know why but he thought he was helping me.'

'Row back a length. What was he doing for you?'

'Breaking into your office. It wasn't just himself he was trying to find any information about, it was me, too. He was convinced we were both being framed. Someone put the bra here to make it look like I was involved, and you might know something about it.'

'Why did he think that?'

'He said you had been following him around and investigating the case. I said it was good because you'd find who did it, but he said you would help set us up. He said someone else had brought that bra here and you were going to help them get away with it. You'd blame us for the Short woman and Dempsey, even when you knew we were innocent.'

'Why on earth would we do that?'

'Because he killed his ex and you want to protect your friend.'

He was looking at Vinny, and so was everyone else now. Vinny scowled at him and said, 'Are you off your fucking head? I mean, obviously you are, but this is really pushing it, pal.'

Phil said, 'Simon, Vinny didn't kill Freya, that's absurd.'

Sholto said, 'And if he had we would never cover it up, not a chance.'

'Then you'll accept my offer to work for me now to find the person who did. I have money, I want to hire you.'

Sholto shook his head. 'We're already working the case for Vinny, who admittedly has much less chance of ever paying us but still, it's first come first served. If you care about us finding the truth then you have nothing to worry about, we're looking hard. It would help if you told us everything you knew about Dent.'

'He was a friend. I don't have many, you know that already. He cared about doing the right thing, but, I don't know, he just couldn't trust people. I struggle with trusting people, too, I suppose, but I don't have to live among them. He was a better man than you think.'

Darian said, 'After Ruby-Mae Short was killed Dent repeatedly searched for information about the case on his tablet. If he had no interest in it then why would he do that?'

Simon stared blankly and said, 'I don't know why he would do that. Maybe it was all over the news, I don't know why else.'

Sholto said, 'Simon, if it turns out you're lying to us about any of this you'll end up in court and you could even end up in prison.'

Darian reached into his pocket and, stepping forward, he said to Simon, 'This card has my number on it. If you remember anything, if you find something out, call me, any hour of the day or night, doesn't matter. William Dent has too many connections to bad things to be the man you're trying to tell us he was. If you think of something that would explain that gap then call me.'

Simon Sutherland took the card and Darian could at least be certain he was one person who wouldn't throw it straight in the bin as soon as they left. As they started to file out Darian noticed Phil give a small nod to his cousin, as if he was trying to reassure him. They walked out and left Simon in the empty room.

On the way down the drive Vinny said, 'This isn't moving us forward. I need to find out what the hell happened to Freya and this is nothing to do with that.

Much as I want to catch who killed Short, Freya is my priority.'

Sholto said, 'Someone bought Freya expensive gifts before she disappeared. Then William Dent decides to play with a train rather than be caught by us. Calling us here, accusing you to your face, that's not a dumb ploy.'

Phil shook his head and said, 'He was being genuine, surely you could see that.'

'I'm older than you lads, I've met more liars than you have, this city is overflowing with them. I'm not saying he's one, but the best actors are so good you don't even realise they're doing it. Sometimes they're so damn good even *they* don't realise they're doing it.'

'He's not acting. He's not.'

Phil and Vinny left because they had to get back to Whisper Hill while Sholto drove them down to the corner of Geug Place.

Adopting the tone he used when he wanted you to think he was just goofing around but he was actually making a serious point, Sholto said, 'There is another person who could have bought Freya expensive presents, and who definitely met her more than once. And he had potential access to Simon's house to plant evidence. And he knew we'd be away from the office last night. Wee Phil's been right by our side all the way, helping us get at his vulnerable cousin and flashy uncle, but how innocent is he?'

'Shit, Sholto, you're not serious. First you accuse Vinny and now Phil.'

'I'm not accusing him, I'm pointing out that he fits the profile, nothing more. He's not even the person I'm most interested in right now.'

'Who is?'

'Olinda Bles.'

FROM THE NEW WORLD TO THE OLD CITY

A LOOK AT THE ABUSE OF CALEDONIAN IMMIGRANTS IN CHALLAID

It's a testament to the sensitivity of the issue that when I met the first immigrant I interviewed for this piece it was in private and they agreed only on the assurance that their identity would not be revealed. That, says Leonor Daza from the charity Caledonians in Challaid who help people moving here for the first time, is not uncommon. Too many people, she says, are coming across the ocean for a better life and to get it they must first spend a year living in fear and suffering exploitation.

'I couldn't say anything,' the young woman tells me. She's twenty and nervous, speaking to me in the Earmam office of Caledonians in Challaid. She's been in the country for eleven months and one more month of employment will entitle her to the dual passport she came for. It hasn't been an easy first eleven. 'I know I get paid a lot less than the minimum but I can't say it. I have to work long, long hours and I can't complain because I know I will lose my job. They always say that, if you are trouble you lose your job and then you won't get another, no passport.'

This is a story repeated by many mouths. With twelve months of employment required for a dual passport the threat of losing a job is the threat of losing the opportunity to become not just a citizen of Scotland but Europe.

Many feel they are being held hostage by unscrupulous employers who see them as cheap and disposable labour, easy to mistreat and, when they leave after twelve months, easy to replace with more young people arriving in the city from the Caledonian countries.

'It's a fairly even split between people from Panama and those from Costa Rica,' Leonor Daza tells me in the same CIC office, a small place that receives no government or council funding. 'Even though there are more people in Costa Rica, Panama has longer and more ingrained links here so it balances out. Very few come from Nicaragua because the passport laws are so much more restrictive for them. The people who come are mostly young, in their late teens or twenties, and they have their whole lives ahead of them.

They take jobs paying criminally low wages, often the jobs no one from Challaid would do, and they're forced to work in unacceptable, dangerous conditions. Most will share a flat in Earmam or Whisper Hill with six or seven other people, a one- or two-bedroom flat, and they say they're willing because it's only twelve months and at the end they can leave.'

The young woman I've come to interview doesn't want to tell me where she lives, but she does admit she shares with five other people. 'It's not great. It has one bedroom and three of us sleep there, three in the living room. The landlord knows there are six, he charges for six.'

That too is a breach of the law, both housing and safety regulations, but landlords also see 'twelve monthers' as a chance to make easy money.

Knowing that this is happening, what are Challaid council doing about it? Eunan O'Brien, Liberal Party, is the council spokesman on immigration. 'We have clear policies already in place to make sure that all people coming here, wherever from, are treated with the respect they deserve, and are protected by the same laws that we would expect all citizens of Challaid to enjoy.' When I point out that these laws don't appear to be enough to protect the twelve monthers he half shrugs. 'It's a problem, not of powers but of enforcement. If people don't report criminal activity then there's not a lot that can be done. We're committed to making sure people feel able to report these things, and we've always said that if immigrants have themselves done nothing wrong then they have nothing to fear from police contact.'

It's a familiar promise with exasperating wording to Leonor Daza. 'The council have been committed to improving the lives of Caledonians in Challaid since the CIC was founded nearly thirty years ago, what they haven't actually gotten round to doing yet is improving the situation for anyone from Caledonia. And the language has never changed either, always the hint that an immigrant might have done something wrong, that they must be scared of the police rather than an abuser.'

Due to a delay in completing interviews this piece didn't appear in last month's issue as planned, so I realised that the young woman I'd interviewed at the CIC would have completed her twelve months. I managed to get back in touch with her. She told me that on the day she got her dual passport she quit her job, left her flat and got on a train that took her all the way down to London, despite the uncertainty of her status there as the British leave Europe. She already has a new job and a better life. Although she still doesn't want her name to be used in the article, she did give me the name of her employer in Challaid, Highland Specialist Plastics.

HSP have a factory making tailored plastic parts for export in Bakers Moor, using part of an old warehouse building that was once one of many belonging to the famed Challaid Whaling Company. I asked HSP for a comment and they stated that they were 'committed to the best working practices and to ensuring that all employees from Caledonia were treated fairly and given the best chance to gain their passport.' When I visited their factory security wouldn't allow me to enter and none of their employees were willing to speak to me. HSP, it seems, are one of many for whom commitment to rhetoric on the twelve-month question is not matched in reality by a commitment to the people at the heart of it.

38

Olinda Bles left Geug Place at one thirty-two, and Sholto started the car thirty seconds later. It was an awkward drive because of her competence relative to Sholto's. While she was aggressive and quick on the road, as you have to be if you want to get anywhere in this city, Sholto still couldn't bring himself to put his foot down for fear of hurting the accelerator. Darian gave him a couple of looks but chose silence over arguments.

Bles drove south through Barton and into Cnocaid, heading down towards Gleann Fuilteach, the valley that leads out of the city. She had almost reached down to the university but turned instead into a quiet residential street. She pulled into a narrow driveway and went into a neat semi-detached home, the sort that in Cnocaid would set you back a couple of hundred grand.

Sholto said, 'Well, that's the nicest home I've ever seen a housekeeper call her own.'

'I'm not sure looking after Simon Sutherland counts as normal housekeeping. I'd bet the family pay her very well for her babysitting.'

'Maybe he pays her well for her silence as well.'

With that they made their way to the front door and rang the bell. Olinda Bles opened it and, with the least possible surprise in her voice, said, 'I don't know why you had to follow me all the way from Simon's house like this is a spy story. Come in, I'll talk to you.'

Sholto did his best to look sheepish because it's what she wanted to see but he didn't really care. They were getting to talk to her away from the Sutherland house and that was the aim of all this. Olinda led them through to the kitchen at the back of the house, a large and bright room. She started making three cups of tea while they sat at the table and waited politely, guests in another person's house and that meant conducting themselves with a certain decorum. They weren't cops, they couldn't assume a right to be there so they had to keep themselves welcome for as long as possible. They didn't start talking until she put their cups and a plate with chocolate digestives on the table in front of them. Darian took one and Sholto took three so Darian spoke first.

'How well did you know William Dent?'

She sighed and there was true sadness in it. 'I didn't know him well. He was a friend of Simon's, so he was at the house now and again. I spoke with him, not that much. At first, you know, Will would come to the house and I don't think he wanted to be there. It was Harold's idea, to have someone else at the house, a man of around Simon's own age. I could get the shopping every time but his uncle wants him to see more people, to make the isolation less. I agree with that. We have to be careful not to make it too obvious to Simon, but getting him to interact with more people is important. It wasn't easy at first but eventually they would speak and then they would have proper conversations and then they were friends. Not friends in the way that a young man like you has friends, Mr Ross, but in the only way that Simon can have friends, where every word he says to a person counts. For Will, I suppose, it was a way of doing work that involved no work, if you understand, so he liked hanging around the house.'

'It doesn't look good for Will. The evidence the police have found suggests an interest in Ruby-Mae Short.'

'I heard. I don't know what to say. Will, I think he was the sort of man who would do things in the moment, without thinking. He was reckless, he teased, he liked to play games, I think. Murder? It would be cruel to think that of him.'

'But he was breaking into our office.'

'And you chased him onto the railway tracks. I don't know why he tried to steal things from you, he was an unpredictable boy, I suppose. He must have had his reasons.'

Sholto took a loud slurp from his cup and asked, 'How did you end up working for Simon Sutherland?'

'I've been in Challaid since I was eighteen. Nearly thirty-five years since I came over. I was one of the lucky few because I had older family that had come before me, a brother and a cousin, and they were able to help me get a job looking after children. I was a childminder for a family in Barton for a while because I was cheap and rich people often pick the cheapest option, even to care for their own children. That's how they get rich and stay rich. After Simon's mother died his uncle Harold wanted someone to keep the house, but mostly to look after Simon. He was vulnerable, struggling a lot at the time, much worse even than now, so I cared for him. The family I had been working for knew Harold, their child was older by then, so they recommended me to him.'

'He didn't just take Simon to live with him and his staff?'

'I do believe that Mr Sutherland cares very deeply for Simon. I know that he was very close to Simon's father, his brother Beathan. He cared for him, but he didn't want a son of his own, not with the responsibilities he has at the bank. That came first. It always does for them.'

Darian said, 'You've been with them a long time. You must feel a lot of loyalty towards the Sutherland family.'

'I am close to them and I care for them because while a lot of people see only the money I see the people. They have suffered like all God's children do, they have lost people and things that mattered very much to them, they have struggled like we all do in this life. All of this, it is more suffering, and it needs to come to an end. I hope that the police will find a way. Not you because you are not real police. I know how much use you will be.'

Sholto smiled a little but Darian couldn't help his defiance when he said, 'You know well enough the influence the family have over the police. The family will get what they want there. We might not be much use to you, but we're just trying to find Freya Dempsey.'

'And I hope very much that you do find her.'

Sholto grabbed the last biscuit off the plate and they got up to leave. He thanked Olinda at the door and her look told him exactly how much that was worth.

Back in the car Sholto said, 'That was a funny one, that. She picked her words carefully. I don't know, something's troubling her good little Christian soul, but I don't think there's any way in hell she's going to tell us about it.'

39

BEING IN THE OFFICE when you wanted to be out in
Challaid getting things done felt grim, but if there was
nothing left to do then there was nowhere left to go. It
seemed no progress could be made until the police came
up with more information regarding Will Dent. If they
could prove that he and he alone was guilty of killing
Ruby-Mae Short and that he alone was behind Freya's
disappearance then it was over. If they found evidence
of others being involved then there might still be work
to do. For now all Darian and Sholto could do was sit
around and wait, maybe make a couple of phone calls
along the way to pass some time.

Darian messaged Vinny to ask if he had heard
anything just as Vinny was messaging him with the
same question. Having six different police districts in
the city with more history of competing with each other
than working together meant information tended to
flow more slowly between them than impatient people

could stand, and those caught in the vice of a criminal investigation tended to be reasonably impatient. Sholto, having lived inside the machine, was used to the drag of waiting for another station to remember the existence of the telephone.

There used to be a lot more police stations in the city, local knowledge covering smaller patches. About fifteen years ago they reduced it to six, one in each major district, but that's misleading. Dockside in Whisper Hill and Second Station in Earmam just deal with local policing because there's plenty hot stuff there to handle. Bakers Moor station handles its local patch plus the anti-organised crime unit, which operates city-wide. The other three stations, Bank, Cnocaid and Piper Station up in Barton, all have multiple city-wide units working out of them, there being fewer local issues to occupy their time.

Sholto said, 'There are four stations involved in this, so that's going to turn it into a crawl. Bank where Dent died, Bakers Moor because Dent's flat is there, Dockside leading the Short investigation, Cnocaid hunting Freya. If they start sniffing at Simon Sutherland again that'll bring Piper Station into it. We have to wait for them all to talk to each other before they talk to us and half the occupants of those places operate with their mouths sewn shut. The fact it concerns Vinny, one of their own, that might speed it up.'

Darian nodded noncommittally, both because he couldn't believe any force could be so slow in this day and age and because he wasn't convinced even Vinny's involvement would quicken the pace. That was Sholto trying to throw the hangdog a bone.

The knock on the door caught them both by surprise. The one good thing about the heavy wooden stairs was that no one, or almost no one, could sneak up on them because the office door was right at the top and every step echoed off the bare walls. They both jumped in their chairs and Sholto got out of his and opened it, hoping to find someone as likeable and helpful as DC Vicario and instead being confronted by the sight of Bran Kennedy. The chief officer of Raven Investigators had not come alone, because Daniel doesn't wander into the lions' den by himself if there are others he can force to go with him. There were two young men tucked in behind him, ready to throw their bulked-up muscle around should tempers be roused. He had taken two with him because he knew Sholto would only have Darian by his side and Kennedy liked the comfort that superior numbers brought.

Sholto said, 'What do you want? Here to try and bully us or buy our silence? I'd be more receptive to buying than bullying but you can stick your money up your fat nose as well.'

Kennedy smiled and said, 'Oh, Sholto, don't leave someone who brings good news standing out on the doorstep. Invite me in.'

'You a vampire that needs an invite to cross the threshold? All the stories of ghouls at the standing stones and a monster at the mouth of the loch but you're one I would believe in.'

Kennedy chuckled as Sholto stepped aside to let him in but Darian could see and hear the stiff acting behind the mirth. 'I've come to share some news with you. I do this as an investigator, because I believe in doing what needs to be done to get to the truth of the matter.'

Darian was on high alert for a lie to follow as Sholto said, 'What the hell yarn are you spinning now?'

'The Sutherland case. It's not our case anymore. I've stopped working for Harold Sutherland, stopped reporting to him, stopped gathering information on his behalf. The bank still has its own security department but they're far more concerned about financial goings-on than life or death. That whole place isn't concerned about personal or personnel issues, just political and financial stuff. When Britain voted out of the EU they were having kittens because their value took a big dip being right next door, but some little dead girl doesn't rock them one way or the other. I don't like that. We were the ones Sutherland had poking around in all this and we're done with it.'

Sholto looked at Darian and the frown they shared showed neither was willing to believe in this sudden outburst of moral standards. Sholto said, 'Raven Investigators ended their relationship with the Sutherland Bank.'

Kennedy smiled and said, 'It's more complicated than that, Sholto my boy, you know it always is. I'm sure the big chief on his throne down at Edinburgh HQ has already been on the blower to some chinless wonder on East Sutherland Square making sure the bank knows there's still a lot we can do for them. Just won't be working with Harold Sutherland anymore, that's all.'

Sholto said, 'Don't bring me a red rose and not kiss me at the end of the night. Tell me why you walked out on Harold Sutherland. It must be significant.'

'I already told you, Sholto, I'm an investigator. Just because you're a tin-pot operation in this little hovel with one childlike acolyte and we're a professional outfit with a real office and staff doesn't mean you have some sort of moral high ground. Honesty matters to the successful as much as it does to you. If we're working with someone who would rather protect family interests than do what's right then I'm not willing to work for them, and the bosses down south, who have an even nicer office than I do so you'll hate them even more, agree. Now, that's all I'm going to say because I have no more words that would stand up in front of any of our city's talented and logical judges. I've already said more than I should and I'm leaving now. Good luck, Sholto, and believe it or not I really do mean that. What happened to the Short girl, and maybe the other one, no one at Raven takes that lightly.'

Kennedy turned and left, and his silent companions, looking disappointed at the lack of violence that had been waiting for them on Cage Street, followed. The door closed and the men who had ghosted up the stairs clattered their way back down, the game over. Sholto looked at Darian with neither sure how to react.

Sholto went first, saying, 'He walked out on Harold Sutherland. Bloody hell, what reason could he have for shooting himself in the wallet like that?'

'He said Sutherland was protecting family interests rather than doing the right thing.'

'He did, aye. Family interests.'

SCOTTISH DAILY NEWS

WHERE THE MONEY CAME FROM

AN ASSESSMENT OF THE ORIGINS
AND EVOLUTION OF SCOTLAND'S
BIGGEST COMPANY

The Sutherland Bank wants you to think it's always been here, which, given that it was founded in 1632, is a very easy thing to believe. The Sutherland Bank wants you to believe that it only ever does the sensible thing, and its dour and steady approach to everything it does in public helps make a persuasive case. More than anything else the Sutherland Bank wants you to believe they'll always be around, and that that's a good thing, and they've carefully crafted a sense of inevitability to that effect. Despite their seeming omnipresence, the Sutherland Bank is a business like any other, and when you treat it that way its vulnerabilities come further into the light. Just as there are challenges in its future there are stories in its past, some that they have spent centuries keeping to themselves. In this two-part essay we will seek to bring just some of them into the open.

The power of the Sutherland family in Challaid stretches far back beyond the bank they would eventually found, with the clan involved in the twelfth-century wars of independence that would bring Scotland its nationhood and the family its first taste of real power. The Sutherland clan was given extensions to its existing land holdings on the north coast as reward for their role which included Challaid, then a port town with a reputation as wild and unpleasant, less than a century removed from bloody slaughter over its control that ended with the ragtag army of Raghnall MacGill saving it. It was in this moment that we witness the first example of the Sutherlands' brilliant instinct for politics. Rather than attempt to impose control over his new domain Dand Sutherland indulged the unruliness of its people, and so won them over, a stepfather who turned a blind eye.

For generations thereafter the Sutherland name pops up only occasionally, rulers of a large swathe of the northern Highlands that they didn't really control, obviously wealthy and politically influential but never at the forefront. It's always been assumed this was simply a family trait, a genetic quirk in a clan that loved power and money but loathed the attention it brought. Instead we should look at the Sutherland attitude of secrecy, of being the power behind the throne and never sitting on it, as a product of their environment. The family didn't become who they are in a vacuum; they were shaped by Challaid, a city that has, since its very beginning, cherished its isolation from the south, its separateness. The family have lived for centuries in a culture which stubbornly clings to the Gaelic language to be different from the rest of Scotland, that has its own poetry and storytelling and songs and sports so that it can look in the mirror each morning and see nothing of the rest of the nation. The Sutherlands, like almost all the people of Challaid, don't want to be like us. They have always looked at anywhere south as bad and suspicious, the Gaelic word for southern, deasach, being appropriated for use there as a mild insult. Those from what we call the central belt, and they refer to sniffily as 'the south', have always been seen not as countrymen or friends but as rivals or obstacles. Even Inverness, barely ninety miles of rail line south through the glens, is viewed as being suspiciously Anglo these days. Challaid has always looked north and west for allies. North to the northern isles and Scandinavia, west to the Western Isles and Ireland. It has, as a quirk of its early involvement, been an enthusiastic home for large numbers of Caledonians. Anywhere but south.

The key to their current influence lies in the century and a half between the arrival in Challaid of Queen Iona, The Gaelic Queen, in 1545 and the first Caledonian expedition in 1698. The additional power gained by the family's support of the queen's bloody power grab made them rich to the point that, in 1632, Lord Cruim Sutherland formed the bank we know today. The official story, as told in the subtle and sometimes rather dull advertising the bank engages in that's supposed to foster that sense of reliability, no bright colours or whacky taglines for them, is that Cruim wanted to help several local people in Challaid to set up businesses trading with the rest of Scotland and other North Atlantic nations and so set up the bank as a temporary measure to help them out. What a noble, gracious and friendly chap that makes him sound. The story tends to stop there, simply a man fortunate enough to be able to help some friends and nothing more to see, the bank's subsequent success presumably an unrequested reward for his goodness. Taking a closer look at the few companies he initially bankrolled and what they meant is difficult because the Sutherland Bank doesn't share that sort of information from their extensive archives and extracting any secret from Challaid is virtually impossible. What we can see is what people in the south thought those deals were by accessing the previously private Buchanan collection, a collection of letters and files from the desk of the long-serving seventeenth-century leader of the house in the parliament, Lord Buchanan of Stirling.

In his letter to Prince Robert, Lord Buchanan speculates that the Sutherland Bank derived much of its income in its first ten years from four deals, one with Brochan Campbell, one with the Portnancon Shipping Company, one with Einar Asbjornson in Iceland and another with the Purcell family in Ireland. Brochan Campbell was, to put it generously, a notorious swindler and crook based in Challaid, the Portnancon Shipping Company made its fortune shipping slaves, Asbjornson was at the time a wanted man in both his own country and ours for murder and theft and Gerard Purcell was a pirate turned land grabber. These people may well have been friends of Cruim Sutherland, PSC and Campbell were based in Challaid, Asbjornson lived there for at least two years when on the run and Purcell docked there often in his seafaring days, but it's easy to guess why the story of the bank's early clients doesn't go into any detail about who they were.

The first fifty to sixty years of the bank's existence can be separated from the rest because of a reasonable difference in attitude. In those first two generations almost everything they did seemed to be full of risk, while almost everything since has been centred on the steady consolidation of those successes. Having created a bank that quickly came to dominate Challaid commerce, in the 1650s it expanded south in a brazen attempt to place its wealth close to the throne and parliament in Edinburgh. Priorities and policies began to evolve again as the bank's influence grew, and it's almost possible to see the strings of history being pulled when we look back through the records of laws passed in that era. A law in 1662 to place a tariff on money loaned from outside of Scotland of sixteen per cent. A law in 1664 to limit any financial institutions lending in relation to its holdings. A law in 1669 stating that no financial institution should be given lending power in Scotland without parliamentary permission. That last one was crucial, meaning that no new bank or institution could be formed without all of the Lords in parliament being given full details of it, which meant the then Lord Sutherland knew what everyone else was going to try to do before they could do it. It was said these laws were passed to protect investors from a series of banking collapses that happened in the central belt in the decade previously. Letters in the Buchanan collection suggest at least two of those banks collapsed because of aggressive moves of the Sutherlands, costing many small investors and businesses in Glasgow and Edinburgh their livelihood. Buchanan's letters also suggest that the family had been making significant donations to the crown since the days of The Gaelic Queen and had never stopped.

It was in 1698 that the bank pulled off the last of its great gambles. An expedition to Panama had been proposed to create a passage from the Atlantic to the Pacific and was viewed in Challaid as a risky investment that the government, who backed it, could scarcely afford. Many thought they were playing with the nation's future, the economy already close to ruin, and records suggest Lord Niall Sutherland was one of the doubters. Two debates were held on what became the Caledonian expedition and Lord Sutherland spoke against it in the first and didn't attend the second. Not long before the mission was set to depart the Sutherland Bank, at remarkably short notice, stepped in and funded a massive expansion to the numbers sailing, assigning its own people. As we know, those people included the likes of Alexander Barton and Gregor Kidd, brutal former pirates, or privateers if you prefer the official version, who would lead the ships to their violent and ultimately successful conclusion, earning themselves knighthoods and legitimacy and the bank untold fortunes.

The Sutherland Bank was set. Political power was guaranteed, and a constant flow of income merely needed to be protected by keeping up with the times, the need to gamble on the future now behind them. In part two we'll look at the bank's more recent history, including the power it continues to wield over what is supposed to be an independent parliament. While their political influence has been somewhat curtailed by the abolition of the Lords in 1952 and its replacement with an elected second chamber in Edinburgh, other routes to influence have been found. We'll also examine how the Sutherland family themselves have changed in the modern world, but how in many ways they, and the city they still call home, have hardly changed at all.

40

'YOU NEED TO GO HOME. Go and get some sleep and we'll take another crack at this in the morning when we might know more than the nothing we know now.'

Darian said, 'That's more hours we're wasting. We should be out there...'

'Where, Darian? There's nowhere out there for us two to go. Do we go to Geug Place or Eilean Seud? To do what? Do we go to the police and if we do, what do we tell them? They're the ones with access to the Sutherlands and their legal team, so we wait for them. Rushing just gets us to the wrong location faster.'

'Rushing? Freya Dempsey is out there somewhere and we're going home to get some sleep because we're a bit stuck. That can't feel right to you.'

Sholto wasn't programmed for confrontation, least of all with people he liked. When faced with this sort of conversation with Darian he liked to treat it as an opportunity to educate. He assumed his most scholarly expression and leaned back in his seat, the desk in front of him once again covered in piles of papers that seemed to have somehow found their own way back to their original places.

Sholto said, 'When Vinny brought this to us she had been gone for, what, five days. At that time she was missing and there was a chance, however slim, that she had left of her own accord. We were looking for someone who might have run, so we were hurrying because the more of a head start a person has the less likely we are to catch up. Then we found the connection to Ruby-Mae. It was chasing Freya that brought us to that, and if they're connected then I think we have to assume that the urgency has gone from our investigation. It's likely that the only difference between Freya and Ruby-Mae is that we haven't found Freya's body yet. It's likely to be the same killer and the same outcome. We have to recognise that the best speed to go at is the one that will deliver the correct result, not the fastest result. I want to catch this bastard, Darian, just as much as you do, and that's going to mean us both being awake and alert enough to pounce when he passes in front of us, if he's still alive enough to do so. I know you're young and full of enough fire to burn the city down, but you're also smart enough to know that rest matters.'

There were moments in his speech when Sholto was so certain of his accuracy he began to sound smug, but Darian couldn't disagree with him. It was hard to admit but there was every chance they had been too late to save Freya before they even started.

'It's just rotten, you know. The fact she's probably dead, that Finn will never see his own ma again. Doesn't seem right that we weren't able to do anything to help her.'

Sholto nodded. 'Powerlessness is a horrible and cruel thing when you realise it applies to you, too. When I was a young cop I thought I was going to be able to help so many people, but the truth was that I was mostly just cleaning up after other people's horrors. There are four hundred and seventy-nine thousand people in Challaid, if you believe the census, which I don't, and we have no influence over the behaviour of any one of them. If they choose to do something appalling all we can do is react to it, and that makes us feel weak. Thing is, Darian, cleaning up after the bad guys, it still matters. It's how we stop them from doing it again. We want the power to stop them the first time but as that's not possible this is the next best thing.'

Darian thought about that a lot on the way home. He picked up a meal from The Northern Song and got the train through the tunnel. It was crowded but he got a seat opposite a couple arguing loudly, in Gaelic so it sounded like they were spitting on the floor half the time, about a gas bill. Darian was still lurching towards maturity. For example, he was immature enough to feel resentment towards the people on the train because none of them were acknowledging the traumas happening in the city around them. On the other hand he had recently acquired the maturity to understand how childish that resentment was, demanding a person recognise the pains of strangers as well as their own, a burden no one should be asked to carry.

He walked with his bag of food to the flat. It was in these moments of quiet misery that he wished he had a girlfriend, as bad as his taste had proven to be, or a close circle of friends away from his work. He could have picked up the phone to his sister Catriona or his brother Sorley but he didn't feel comfortable with that. Instead he took a plate from the kitchen through to the table by the window in the living room and sat looking out at the loch, eating slowly.

His mind returned to Bran Kennedy, a greedy person walking away from good money. He had said Sutherland was trying to protect the family. Any Sutherland had the money to give Freya expensive gifts she didn't want. Simon couldn't have met her outside his house unless he was lying about who he was, and for that to be the case he would have had to fool a lot of very clever people. If he was lying then why leave the bra to be found? It was unlikely, but it wasn't impossible. Harold had met her but there was nothing to suggest he had any wish to meet her again and nothing to link him to Ruby-Mae. If Simon didn't leave the house then he would need Dent to do a lot of the work for him. Harold had been at a

Challaid FC match at the time Freya went missing, so he too would have needed Dent to do the dirty work. There was a third Sutherland. Sholto had mentioned Phil and Darian drifted mentally back to him, the quiet young man of money who had met Freya several times and who could command the same undue protection from his uncle and uncle's driver that Simon did.

As he watched a small yacht make its way to the south harbour in the early evening light Darian picked up his phone and made a call.

DC Vicario answered and said, 'Hello?'

'Hi, DC Vicario, it's Darian Ross, from Douglas Independent Research. Listen, uh, we've hit a bit of a dead end on this, but we've collected a few interesting pieces of information along the way. I wondered if we could talk, compare notes.'

'Tonight?'

'Are you free?'

There was a laugh in her voice when she said, 'I am. You can buy me a drink. You know MacCoy's, on Wodan Road?'

He smiled at the thought of a cop wanting to drink in a pub named after an infamous bank robber. 'I know it, I'll see you there in, uh, three-quarters of an hour.'

41

DARIAN TOOK THE TRAIN to Mormaer Station in Earmam and from there a Challaid Cabs taxi up to Wodan Road, a curving street named after a possibly fictional mercenary said to have helped The Gaelic Queen. DC Vicario had picked an amusing drinking spot. She worked The Hill, so it made sense that she would want to live somewhere nearby, so this might have been her local.

A long narrow building, the back of it looking out onto the loch, a view of the docks: the kindest thing you could say about MacCoy's was that it tried its best. Maybe thirty years ago, when it was built, it might have been pretty nice, fashionable, raising the tone of the grotty neighbourhood. The surroundings had since dragged it down to their level, and it looked scruffy, only hints now of what the owners had once aimed for and given up on.

Inside the decor was dated and gloomy, not many patrons to liven it up. That would have been another reason she had picked the place. The bar ran along part of the wall on the right as you went in the door; the few drinkers in the place were either lined up at it or at the tables way down the back where the large windows gave you a view of the water. All except one, sitting on her own at a table against the wall on the left, out of earshot for everyone else.

Darian walked across and said, 'Hi, DC Vicario, thanks for meeting me.'

She said, 'Angela. These are drinking hours, not working hours. I got you a pint; there isn't a hell of a lot of variety round here. I had the choice of two wines, the red or the white.'

He sat down opposite her. Her black hair was curlier than before, as if she hadn't had time to straighten it with all that was going on. There was a smile on the edges of her dark eyes when she said, 'So what's the big news that you had to get me to buy you a drink for?'

'Not news, questions. Did you know that Raven have stopped working for Harold Sutherland?'

Now she was interested. 'What? They're giving up Sutherland money? Why?'

Darian took a swig of his pint, horrible it was, as if the barman had reached out of the window to dip the glass in the loch, and said, 'We don't know. Seems to have been a falling-out. Could Harold have been the one sending Freya gifts? Maybe Raven found proof.'

'Well, if they did they're a step ahead of us, because we have nothing.'

'I, uh, I don't want to piss you off here, because I know that you're doing everything you can in this case, everything...'

'But...'

'We had a visit from a colleague of yours to the office, DS Noonan, you know him.'

She grimaced and said, 'Yeah, I know of him.'

'He was dropping hints like they were hot, telling us we're going to get shut down, all smug and jokey about it but, you know, he's dangerous. The Sutherlands are involved in a criminal case and everyone, I mean, absolutely everyone, knows that they have connections in the police force. We both know they have cops in their pocket, senior ones, high enough up the chain that they can shut down areas of investigation, make evidence go walkabout if they don't like the look of it. Noonan's the weapon they sent to shut us down when we wouldn't be bullied or bought.'

Angela didn't look annoyed. Instead she nodded and said, 'Yeah, they have connections. Clever about it, too, the way they do it. I've seen it. The security department of the bank, they're the ones that come and create the contacts, help out cops so they can get favours, build a relationship with you, give it a year or two and they have you wrapped round their middle finger, sticking it up at the rest of the city. They're bloody good, but, no, they're not going to stop us this time. No one's told us to back off. Noonan's an ugly piece of human garbage;

I'll make sure he doesn't get too close to you again. Evidence going missing, I don't know about that.'

Darian gave her a look that cut her off and she smiled her wide smile.

'Okay, yeah, I know it does happen, I'm not saying no, we're still a force with… problems…'

'Ha, that's a hell of a polite way of putting it. I heard things were getting worse, not better. The Anti-Corruption Unit in chaos as it gets rebuilt and the inmates running the asylum.'

Now she looked a little annoyed, but covered it well. 'No, you're getting carried away. Things aren't worse, they're just about the same. You're believing the worst of us, and, frankly, I'm a little offended.'

Her smile took the sting out of what might have become an argument. Darian said, 'I just worry about the dead ends we keep running down. It shouldn't be this hard to find the truth.'

'It's been tough. Is that what you wanted to see me about, to break the news that you think some of my colleagues are still corrupt and that neither of us has a clue what we're doing with this case?'

He laughed. 'No, not just that. It would help us to have Noonan held back. Plus, I feel like I need to talk it through with someone, get a fresh perspective. And, uh, I kinda wanted to see you again.'

'Oh, you kinda did, did you kinda?'

Darian was beginning to turn a fetching shade of red

at this point and said, 'Okay, I'm not good at this sort of thing, but, yeah, I did.'

'You're right, you're not good at this. Look, I do like you, but right now we're both tangled up in the same net and we need to get out of that first. When this is over, soon, I hope, I think, then you can try and bowl me over with your sparkling seductive conversation. I think when this is done I'll be interested in being bowled over.'

They walked out together onto Wodan Road, an ugly place that looked menacing in the dark.

Angela turned to face him and said, 'I'm walking home from here, you have a car?'

'I'm not driving after taking a drink, officer. I'll walk up to the ferry terminal at the docks and get a taxi to the station from there.'

She smiled and said, 'Good answer. And don't worry, Darian, I won't count this as a first date. We'll have another one of those later when you can raise your game.'

She reached up and kissed him briefly on the lips, a soft peck that was full of promise, and he wished his breath didn't smell of the crappy beer he'd just had. He smiled as he watched her walking off down the street. His record with women had been, to be polite about it, shite, and he knew it was foolishness to fall for a cop, but she was the good kind of trouble. She was the best kind.

42

WHEN DARIAN WOKE it was to a distant noise and a certain sense that he hadn't had enough sleep. He rolled over and opened his eyes. What had it been? Something familiar, he thought, and through the fog of his half-sleeping brain came the memory. His phone.

He reached across and picked it up from the bedside table. None of his furniture had cost anything. The Ross siblings had kept very little of what had been in their parents' house and what hadn't been worth selling had been shared between the three of them, which didn't leave much each. Most of the rest of Darian's belongings had come from charity shops and second-hand places, some of it not built to last much longer.

It was three fifty, according to his phone when he looked at it, confirming the reason for his tiredness. The number was new, no name to identify it, and his mind raced ahead of the finger reaching out to drag the answer icon. It could have been anyone, including some time waster with a scam to run. More likely it was someone from the police or from Raven or Sutherland Bank's security department. The timing was more important than the number because that told him it was an emergency. Only the drunk and the urgent call you at three fifty in the morning.

He answered and said, 'Hello.'

'You have to come to my house, please. Someone is in here.'

It was said in a whisper, a desperate hiss from a man filled with so much fear he couldn't stop it snaking out his mouth when he opened it. Two seconds into the plea Darian realised he was talking to Simon Sutherland, panicked and alone with a stranger in his house.

'Call the police, Simon, and I'll be right round.'

'I will, I will. You have to hurry.'

There was a second after hanging up during which Darian paused and tried to understand the feeling creeping up on him. There was some excitement there, the feeling that this could be it, the vital moment. Someone had broken into the house before to plant Ruby-Mae's bra and implicate Simon and now the same person was trying again. This could have been an attempt to repeat the trick and implicate him in Freya's disappearance. A person who thought they could get in and out unseen and unheard, or a person who didn't care because they were sure Simon had no one to call for help. A person who didn't know he had Darian's number and perhaps didn't understand that the last few days had changed Simon, just a little. People had been in his house, strangers he had allowed in and spoken to, and he had been dragged out to the police station. He had Darian's number and was willing to call it, to call the police, too.

Darian scrambled out of bed and began to pull on clothes that should have gone into the wash basket ahead of the next time he was close enough to running out of clothing that he was compelled to switch the washing machine on.

A thought pricked at him, the underlying part of that feeling he hadn't been able to identify before. If Simon Sutherland had killed Ruby-Mae and Freya then this could be part of his plan. He feared that Darian and Sholto were getting too close so he lured Darian to the house to get rid of him. If Dent had been working for him then he died trying to find out just how close they were and that had sent Simon into a panic. It made only a fraction of sense, which was a little more than most alternatives.

Darian called Sholto, waiting a frustratingly long time for an answer. Sholto typically woke up in stages and the first two were long and groggy and usually a few hours away. Eventually the phone was answered with a croaky, 'Sholto Douglas.'

'It's me, Darian. I just got a call from Simon Sutherland saying someone is in his house and he wants me to go up there. He said he'll call the police as well. I'm going to go up in a taxi and see what's going on.'

In a split second Sholto skipped to the wide-awake phase and said, 'No, you will not. That could be a trap; you don't know what's going on here, Simon calling you up in the dying hours. Stay at the flat and I'll pick you up, we'll go up together and we'll tip off our friends in the police before we go anywhere as well.'

He hung up before Darian could argue back. The risk of a trap was low because Simon was smart enough to understand that Darian would call for backup, and the police, himself. If it was a genuine emergency then he couldn't wait for Sholto to trundle his way through the city to get there.

He pulled on his shoes and tied his laces and on the way to the door of the flat he called Vinny. Through to voicemail. Vinny would either be fast asleep or out on a shift, so Darian left a message.

'Vinny, it's Darian. I just got a call from Simon Sutherland saying that someone's in his house and me and Sholto are on our way up there. You might want to swing up and join us if you get the chance.'

Darian slipped the phone into his pocket and went downstairs to the front door of the building. He stood out on the street, shivering in the cold, waiting for what he knew would be an interminable length of time for Sholto to get there. These hours, so late or so early depending on which way round you look at a clock, are the moments when Challaid is at its most beautiful, the sun threatening to take the world back and the grey of the moon across the still loch, clinging to the surface. It's quiet, and it feels like a city with no evil, just a place any person would want to live their life. Those are the least honest hours of the day. Darian waited, edgy.

CHALLAID CITY COUNCIL PLANNING DEPARTMENT – PRIVATE FILES

PLANNING APPLICATION

11/10/12

Address: 5 Geug Place, Barton, Challaid, CH1 2LS

Owner: Simon Sutherland

Application: Application for extension to existing property. Two-storey, north facing, ground floor approximate floor space 1,150 square feet. Design submitted separately.

Comments: Extension to be built on existing property in large, private garden. Walled and tree-lined, will hide construction from all view. Concern about noise in area, large new build in traditionally maintained area, large vehicles using narrow lane for access.

Update: Challaid City Council planning committee pass application 5 votes to 0.

PLANNING APPLICATION

19/0614

Address: 5 Geug Place, Barton, Challaid, CH1 2LS

Owner: Simon Sutherland

Application: Application for extension to existing property. Two-storey, west-facing to rear of existing property, ground floor approximate floor space 2,000 square feet. Design submitted separately.

Comments: Extension to be built in large private garden. Walled and tree lined will hide construction from public view. 4 existing complaints from neighbours regarding noise while project is underway and objecting to design of exterior, considered out of place in traditional area, and to heavy vehicles using narrow lane to access property. During previous extension build, road was damaged, trees damaged with several cleared for vehicle access, road blocked on multiple occasions for residents.

Update: Challaid City Council planning committee <u>pass application 4 votes to 1</u>.

PLANNING APPLICATION

16/08/15

Address: Auri (14 Geug Place), Barton, Challaid, CH1 2LS

Owner: Simon Sutherland

Application: Application to add basement to existing property. Approximate floor space 210 square feet, accessed from within property. Design submitted separately.

Comments: Low risk of disruption for popular form of extension. 4 properties on same street have had similar applications approved in last 3 years, no objections formally raised for any. Some risk of heavy vehicles using lane but recent road upgrade makes that acceptable.

Update: Challaid City Council planning committee <u>pass application 5 votes to 0</u>.

43

SHOLTO ARRIVED ON Havurn Road quicker than expected, which left Darian with the image of his boss hunched over the steering wheel, knuckles white, eyes bulging as he watched the road ahead, pushing the car as fast as forty miles per hour. It stopped at the side of the road and instead of getting into the passenger seat Darian walked onto the road and round to the driver's side.

He opened the door and said, 'I'll drive.'

They had made this mistake before and weren't going to repeat it. Sholto unclipped his seat belt and got out, stumbling into the road and running round to the passenger side. Darian noticed how rumpled his boss looked, even by his standards, shirt hanging down at the back, hair all over the place so it almost covered the baldness on top. This was Sholto in a state of rush Darian hadn't seen from him before.

He got into the driver's seat and as soon as Sholto pulled the passenger door shut behind him Darian accelerated away with a screech, the momentum forcing them back in their seats.

Sholto said, 'Whoa, Nelly, calm it down and put your seat belt on as well, we're no use to anyone if we're wrapped around a lamppost.'

Darian pulled the seat belt round in between changing gear and trying to work out the quickest route from Bank to Simon's house. In the daytime it wouldn't be the obvious one, using the main streets that looked the quickest route on a map but would be clogged, but at this hour of the morning when the roads were much clearer it made sense that the shortest route should indeed be the fastest.

Sholto, with one hand on the door and the other gripping the side of his seat, said, 'What did Sutherland say to you, exactly?'

'He said someone was in the house and he wanted me to come round. He was talking in a whisper and he sounded terrified.'

'I suppose we're about to find out if he's as good an actor as I think he might be. What did you say to him?'

'I told him I was on my way round and to phone the police.'

Sholto mumbled something under his breath and said, 'Well, if he did call them I wouldn't rely on him to get the message across, and if you don't nail the point with that lot you'll be lucky if they show up at all. Who else did you call?'

'I left a message with Vinny but I haven't gotten an answer yet.'

'Not your girlfriend?'

'My…? Vicario? I wish she was and, no, I haven't.'

The conversation was annoying Darian because he was busy reminding the car that thirty miles an hour was a legal limit but not a technological one. They were in Cnocaid already with the yellow light of lampposts flashing past outside, occasional bursts of white from twenty-four-hour shops standing out among the darkly sleeping buildings. It was disorientating but Darian could find his way on instinct.

Sholto mumbled something like a prayer under his breath and then said, 'A message won't do it, I'll make a few calls. I don't want us being at the house alone, getting caught with our pants down. We need some honest backup.'

Darian focused on the road while Sholto wriggled unpleasantly and pulled his phone from his pocket. He held it in one hand as he scrolled unsteadily through the numbers. Darian had caught a glimpse of the list in Sholto's contacts before and it was Tolstoyan in length, seemingly everyone who had ever committed, investigated, witnessed or heard a rumour about a crime in Challaid in the last twenty-five years and owned a phone. It was the benefit of experience that

Sholto liked to point out: if you stick around long enough you'll learn who to talk to.

He pressed dial and Darian heard one side of a short conversation, Sholto saying, 'DS MacNeith, it's Sholto Douglas here, sorry to wake you. We've just had a call from Simon Sutherland to say that someone's breaking into his house, you'll want to get your people there... Yes, of course we are. Goodbye.'

Darian said, 'That sounded like you hung up before she could tell you not to do something.'

'Aye, well, I have other people to call and not a lot of time to call them, the speed you're going at.'

The next person he phoned was DC Vicario, a call containing the same information but in a friendlier tone.

That ended when he hung up and, in his grumpiest voice, Sholto said, 'She told me she would come straight round, and to say hello to you. There isn't something going on between you two is there, Darian? Tell me there isn't, not you and a cop.'

'Concentrate on your calls.'

A third call went through to Sholto's contact at Piper Station in Barton, the nearest to Simon's house and the ones who would handle any investigation into a crime there. That was a confused conversation, Sholto having to try and explain that it was a Sutherland, that he never left the house and that he might have been involved in two murders, or might not have done anything wrong and could be a victim himself. That the cop Sholto was talking to didn't know who Simon was and what he had recently been accused of showed how little communication there was in the force.

He hung up on the last call and said, 'Right, at least when we go in there'll be a battalion of nice uniforms on our heels, although I'd prefer a few of them to be in front of us.'

They passed shops and restaurants far too expensive for either of them ever to frequent and turned onto King Robert Street, a few businesses and a couple of blocks of very expensive flats and a triangle of grass at the corner with black railings that acted as a private park for the people living hereabouts. It was small but it was flat and that gave them a view down towards the loch and the back of Geug Place. Reaching out of the dark sky a finger of black cloud seemed to have stretched down to the ground, touching a glow at the bottom.

'Is that smoke? Chee whizz, that's smoke.'

Darian nodded. A column of thick black smoke and, as they headed for the corner with Geug Place, they didn't have to guess where it was coming from. They were driving straight towards it.

44

THE CAR SPED DOWN Geug Place and stopped with a shudder that left them almost sideways outside the gate. They both got out, seeing the flickers of orange through the trees and the billows of smoke carrying the souls of every item Simon Sutherland had ever owned into the night.

Darian ran to the gate and gave it a hard shoulder barge, but it didn't move even a fraction. He shouted, 'We have to get in. How do we get in?'

Sholto said, 'We have to get in and open the gate from the inside so the fire brigade can get in. And I have to move the car out of their way.'

Sholto ran round to the driver's side of his car to move it clear of the gates. Darian was still holding them, trying to shift something he already knew he didn't have the strength to budge.

He shouted, 'Simon, Simon, are you there?'

There was no reply, no movement but the dancing shadows. He looked quickly up and down the street, hoped to see a part of the tall railings and wall around the garden that might be more accessible than the rest, but there was none. What he did notice was that none of the neighbours had come to try and help, and, given the smell of burning that had settled over the street, the growl of the fire and smudge against the sky, there was no way they could all be ignorant of the emergency unfolding. Darian cursed the lot of them, unaware that many of the people who lived there were ageing or positively elderly and could do nothing more than call the emergency services, which, telephone records would show later, three already had. Darian had no obvious route into the front garden.

Sholto slammed the door of the car as he got out and stood back, staring at the gates and the railings and trying to come up with a plan.

'We need a ladder. You won't be able to climb that and I'd have a heart attack just watching you fail.'

There was no time, given that it was possibly already too late. Darian moved down towards Sholto and kept going right past him to the car. That dainty little thing couldn't hope to smash its way through the gates. It would have been sliced to bits trying, but Sholto had parked it right up against the railings to keep as much of the lane and house entrance as possible clear for more important people. Instead Darian walked round to the back and put his hands on it, pulling himself up so that he was on his knees on the roof, and then standing.

Sholto shouted, 'Here, what are you doing? You'll break your neck and my car.'

Darian ignored him, stepping back carefully and taking a one-step run-up. One stride and a jump and he was grabbing on and pulling himself up to the pointed tip of the railings.

He said, 'I'll try and get the gate open for you.'

Sholto was looking up at him and shaking his head. It was high at the top of the railings and he could see a terrified bald-headed man in the street on one side, the blackness of the garden below and the undulating light from the house on the other. Darian swung his leg over and lowered his weight, feeling the flaking paint dig into his fingers before he let go. There was a swoosh and a feeling of weightlessness that gave a tempting sense that everything was bliss, and then he hit the ground. It was enough of a thud to provoke a shout from him and an echoing one from Sholto on the other side.

Darian shouted, 'I'm okay.'

That was a guess when he said it, but confirmed when he stood up. He had landed on his feet, fallen backwards and rolled onto his side and now that he was standing again the only pain was in his ankles and neither was badly damaged. He picked his way past branches outstretched as if to block him and onto the drive, running up towards the house.

It was not, at that point, a home any longer because a home envelops a person and their existence. It was now an incubator for a fire desperate to burst out and engulf the garden it could see beyond the cracked windows. The heat was fierce, as if it were a hand pressed hard to his face to try and stop him from getting any closer, and the house and light made the scene difficult to process, an attack on his senses. Darian stopped and took a step backwards, not out of fear but because instinct told him not to step beyond that range and because he hoped to find Simon without burning to death in the search.

He saw a figure move. Black against the building but it turned to see him, to look at him. Not Simon, but Harold. The older Sutherland stood closer to the house, looking back over his shoulder at Darian, a look of shock, eyes half-shut against the heat. He was breathing heavily, there was a black smudge on his face and two buttons had been ripped from his coat.

Darian stood beside him and said, 'Simon?'

'He's still inside. I tried to get him out, I tried. He's still in there. He called me, he was scared, but he won't come out.'

Darian put his hands to his mouth and shouted, 'Simon, where are you? Simon, can you hear me?'

His phone. He reached into his pocket and found Simon's number in the call log, calling him back. There was no tone, no voicemail and no answer, the phone dead. Darian was about to shout again when he caught movement out of the corner of his eye and saw Sholto coming up the drive, limping heavily and red in the face. The drop from the top of the railings had not been so kind to him, and there were tears in his eyes as he joined Darian and Harold.

'Bloody hell, this whole place is murder. We can't get in there, but we can still help, we can get that gate open for the fire engines. They'll be coming; we have to get the gate open.'

He was right, of course, because if the fire engines were delayed then Simon's already tiny chance of survival would be wiped out. Darian was close to agreeing when he looked up at the house and saw it, movement this time more solid than the swaying fire. In a window on the first floor of the new wing he could see the black figure of a person silhouetted in the glow. A man stood and looked down at them, not shouting or trying to escape. A man who would rather stay and burn.

Darian shouted, 'Simon, open the window. *Simon.*'

Harold screamed, 'Simon, come down, please, for God's sake.'

The figure stood motionless, and then moved away out of sight. They paused, silent among crackling chaos, expecting him to return to the window, but he didn't. Simon Sutherland had walked into the fire and he hadn't come back.

Darian looked at Sholto and opened his mouth to speak but before he could Sholto said, 'No, Darian, no. I will not let you go in there. We will do all we can to help him but that does not include dying by his side.'

Darian didn't want to defy his boss, and he knew Sholto was almost certainly right, but he couldn't stop himself.

Darian nodded to Harold and said, 'Don't let him leave, Sholto. The gate was locked. It was locked with him on the inside.'

'What?'

'It was locked and he was here. Just don't let him go.'

Darian bolted away from him and ran for the front door of Simon Sutherland's burning house.

Sholto shouted, 'Darian, don't, Darian.'

By then Darian was kicking in the front door and ducking his way inside as flames and smoke drawn by the draught from the new opening swept past him.

Diary

16/05/18

With all the hard times there have been I find myself thinking of mother a lot. So many of the things she warned me about have now happened. All she said makes sense to me now. There were so many that I didn't take seriously but should have. The more time passes the more I realise how wise she was. I wish I had realised at the time. I wish I could have told her she was right about it. No one should have to wait so long to understand the cleverness of a loved one. We should know instantly. We should be able to recognise and benefit from that great wisdom. Sometimes I feel ashamed when I think of how I used to believe mother was overreacting. I thought maybe she was hysterical and I had inherited whatever's wrong with me from her. That was stupidly unfair. She understood this family. She warned me well.

When a person takes the long walk up the road they leave parts of themselves behind. You'll carry those parts with you for the rest of your journey, so you have to hope that they aren't heavily weighted with bitterness or anger, making your path harder to walk. Instead you want them to be light, to illuminate and add a skip to your step. For the first few weeks and months you won't understand what you've been left, and that's when the confusion of grief can overwhelm you. Time goes past me in ways I can't ever comprehend or control. A big lump of it is in my hands and then falling through my fingers as I flail about to try and catch it. The harder I squeeze the more pops out, and then it's gone.

This family is poisoned. Time is no antidote. Those were her words. She understood them all. Even the ones you think you can trust. The ones that seem so honest and normal. Every one of them. No one is untouched. The Sutherland clan can't be saved from itself. It will all come crashing down some day. I hope it's soon. The longer it stretches the worse it'll get. It's the money's fault. The lesson that a lifetime of wealth teaches you is a lie. It tells you that, because you have it, you must be superior. It says you can do what you want. There are different rules. You can test them. Push the boundaries hard. What other people say can't be done becomes a fun new challenge. No wonder our large family tree has been filled with thrill seekers. So many died young.

Mother warned me something like this might happen. She told me to be ready for it. Told me what to do when it started. I was always ready. It didn't surprise me. That was why I bought number fourteen, Auri. It's why I had the basement put in. I know I managed to keep it secret because if I hadn't they'd have come to question me about it. The police don't know. The family don't know. I bought it with the money that mother left me from the secret account she had. Father set that up. He didn't want all his money being held in the family bank. He wanted his secrets. He left detailed instructions for her about how to use it safely. She passed it on to me in turn. I did only what needed to be done. It's cost so much. Maybe doing the right thing is always expensive. I think that both my parents understood that. There's no cheap goodness.

It's so much pressure. Uncle Harold and Phil. Ross and Douglas, the two pretend private detectives. Detective Sergeant MacNeith and the other cops that have come after me. I've done nothing wrong. Perhaps none of them will understand that fact. I'll show them all. I'll make it clear to them, I hope. Hopefully it'll be safe. I hope it's soon. I want things to go back to normal. My life is stretched. I can feel it. The strain of everything just waiting to snap. Nobody else really understands. They still think it can somehow help me to leave the house. Soon I'll tell them. I'll have to, whether I choose or not. It feels like things are ready to fall. It's about time too.

I think I heard someone in the house. It must be him.

45

THE HEAT HIT DARIAN hard, a stifling punch that had him gasping and made him want to turn around and do the sensible thing. Instead he gulped in some air and pushed ahead, into the hall of what had been the original house.

He shouted, 'Simon, where are you?'

He had hoped that Simon had left the window and made his way to the stairs, trying for the front door, but there was no sign of him. Instead there was smoke and, pushing out through a door at the top of the old stairs that led towards the new extension at the back, fire. He had to move fast because the exit was seconds away from being closed off to him. Darian had been in the house before and that gave him a chance. He went right through the door to the empty room, little chance of fire in there because there was nothing to burn except Darian. He ran through to the extension and saw the beast waiting for him.

The huge room was full of it, rich in fuel with the collection of a life lined up on shelves just waiting for their chance to burn. The smell was of plastic and something else, something chemical he couldn't identify, and the smoke seemed to be running back and forth across the ceiling in rippling waves. This was a room a smart person would stay in for seconds, a minute if they were brave and two if they were stupid, only staying longer than that if they wanted to share the fate of the crackling items that filled the place.

Darian chose the less sensible of the two options and ran towards the stairs when the smart choice would have been to turn around. He ran through smoke trying to choke him and found himself in a section of the room where the items seemed to be mostly metal and little of it burning, just wavering under the heat. Darian inhaled deeply there and instantly regretted it as his lungs filled with a sharp taste he wanted rid of but would have to live with. He ran on and up the stairs.

It was worse on the first floor, thicker smoke and more fire. This wasn't the growing crackle that downstairs had been but a full-on roar, a fire that had as much control as it could want and was ready to make hay with it. Here there were clothes and magazines and bits of cardboard, a selection of items that almost seemed to have been picked with flammability in mind.

There had already been times in his life when Darian had felt very afraid, had been threatened, but he'd happily admit that to that point the fire was the scariest thing he had ever witnessed. Something about fire separates it from other threats. Perhaps it's the relentless and thorough nature of it, but to Darian it was the slowness that scared him most. A bullet or a knife are evils either to be dodged or which provide very brief suffering, but fire likes to take its time, to make the experience as agonising as possible, as if it's revelling in the power it holds, drowning you in heat. Flames were climbing from the top of the shelves to the ceiling, tendrils jumping out from the sides and trying to get at anything it hadn't yet cornered, always looking to spread, to claim more. In the middle of it all stood Simon Sutherland, eyes wide with terror, motionless.

Darian half shouted and half coughed, 'Simon, come on, we have to go. Simon.'

He ran to him, a hand over the side of his own face to try and protect it from the ferocity of the heat, feeling the back of his hand burn red as he went. He reached Simon and stopped, putting his hands on the young man's shoulders.

He said, 'Simon, *move*, you have to move.'

Simon Sutherland was tearful as he said, 'I do want to.'

This was more than just the memories of his life, this was his whole world burning around him, every part of who he was and who he intended to be turning to ash, and the same instinct that made him collect it all was convincing him to stay and turn to ash with it.

He wanted out, but on his own he wouldn't have been strong enough to fight for the exit.

Darian said, 'We're leaving.'

He moved behind Simon and shoved him, not so hard that he might knock him over but enough to force him to take the first step. Darian kept his hands on Simon's back but it was hardly necessary now, Simon moving freely when he felt the choice was no longer his to take. He had needed someone to break the spell.

They could both feel their clothes begin to melt into their skin as they got to the top of the stairs and the rage followed them down. Darian was struggling to hold his breath and he could hear Simon cough and gasp, but they didn't slow down, not until they were across the floor and into the empty room. There was smoke there now but still no fire. Darian could feel his shoes sticking to the tiles as the soles melted, and through the door he could see the corridor ablaze.

Simon, his voice a wheeze, said, 'We can't get out.'

The fire blocked the front door, carpets and wallpaper and bannisters helping it along. They were going to have to run through it, which would certainly cause them pain, but it would be a few seconds and Darian felt sure he could make it. Simon didn't seem convinced. Darian was about to try and talk him into running when he heard the noise outside and noticed the flash of blue coming in through the front door and windows, puncturing the orange and greys. The fire engine was at the front door and people were shouting, getting themselves into position.

There was a lull, and above the fire and the movement, through the burst window closest to them, Darian heard Sholto's voice straining at its highest as he screamed, 'Don't just wave it around, get in there and get them out.'

Darian was about to shout back, to let them know they were close, but then a strange thing happened. It started to rain in the house. Out in the hall water started to fall into the fire, the hose shooting in through windows burst to pieces by the heat and in through the front door. This was the moment to move.

Darian shouted, 'Now.'

He grabbed Simon by the arm and held particularly tight as he pulled him out and across the hall to the exit. As they reached the door two figures in sand-yellow outfits and with breathing apparatus covering their faces came in and they all but crashed into each other. The firemen grabbed them and helped them out, beyond the smoke and the fire and back into the world of air and life.

Darian and Simon stumbled out, coughing and retching, Sholto running to Darian and holding him by the shoulders until he got his breath back, both of them relieved.

A fireman ran up to them shouting, 'Is there anyone else in the house?'

They all looked at Simon and he said, 'No, no one else.'

Darian was breathing in lungfuls of cold air like a man dying of thirst diving into a pool of water, so it was only at the last moment that he saw the figures running up the drive towards them. Vinny and Phil were in uniform and both looked panicked. Phil ran to his cousin to check on him while Vinny stopped at Darian.

Above the roar of the fire he shouted, 'Someone get a bottle of water, he needs water.'

Darian nodded and Phil shuffled away to find something for them to drink. Darian said, 'Thanks.'

Vinny said, 'Thank Christ you're all right. Do you know what happened, how it started?'

Darian looked at Simon and then across to the figure of Harold, still standing on the grass, looking uncertain, moving slowly towards them. Darian said, 'I don't.'

Vinny looked at Simon too and said, 'Do you know who did this?'

Simon nodded sadly. 'I do, I know. And Freya Dempsey, I know where she is.'

46

THERE WAS A SECOND when Darian thought Vinny was going to swing for Simon, staring at him and reaching out a hand to a terrified man with lungfuls of smoke. Simon pulled back but Vinny only put a hand on his shoulder. From a distance it might look like a friendly gesture, but Vinny Reno had been a cop in Whisper Hill long enough to know how to make things look like something they weren't. Vinny was a barrel-chested bruiser and the hard grip of the shoulder was a reminder of how close the big hand was to Simon's throat.

Vinny looked him in the eye and said, 'Where is she? What happened?'

'Nothing happened to her. Nothing happened because Will and I weren't willing to let it happen.'

He was shaking his head and looking scared, a man with an answer to a question that hadn't yet been asked. Simon Sutherland wanted to explain everything despite

Freya being unaccounted for. Vinny wanted his ex before the story.

'Where is she?'

'I own number fourteen. She's in number fourteen, Auri, just down the street on the other side of the road. It's smaller, but it's, I suppose, reasonably okay. I've never been in. I own it, though. She's in the basement.'

Vinny looked at him and then at Darian and Sholto.

Darian said, 'We'll go, come on, we'll go.'

Simon said, 'Wait, there's a lock, it's a security thing. I had it put in on the basement. You'll need the code. Three, zero, zero, one. That's to the basement. There are keys for the gate and doors but they're in there.'

They all followed his watering eyes back to the only place he had called home, the only place he had ever accepted and ever wanted to be, now turning to charred steel and ash in front of him.

Sholto said, 'Go, you two, go, I can't handle falling over any more fences. Go, and I'll keep an eye on...'

He trailed off. His eyes flitted across to Harold Sutherland, to Phil Sutherland standing near his uncle with an uncertain look.

Darian and Vinny set off running down the drive and Darian was, within ten yards, reminded that he had just breathed in a lot of smoke and been burned and was exhausted. He coughed when his legs tried to go up through the gears and he had to slow down and spit some dark and ominous-looking phlegm onto the drive.

He turned to see Sholto stopping Phil from trying to join them: no Sutherland welcome. Vinny didn't have enough sympathy to slow down but thundered on past the fire engines and down to the gate. Darian picked up the pace and turned left to head down Geug Place, narrow and with high trees and bushes on either side. In the daylight it was a picturesque way to make it feel rural, the walls shrouded in greenery, but at night it made identifying the numbers on the gates difficult. Darian saw Vinny ahead, slowing to check the number on one of them, then running on to the next.

They had turned the slight curve in the road and were towards the bottom of the lane when Vinny stopped and said to Darian as he caught up, 'This one. This is it. Give me a leg up and I'll pull you up after me.'

'What? I can't get you up that high.'

'Aye, you can, stand against the gate, back straight, knees bent. Hurry up, Darian.'

He cursed under his breath, but he did as he was told. Darian did his best, which wasn't easy because he was weakened and Vinny was a heavy old beast. It hurt like hell, Darian could feel his legs begin to buckle. Vinny stepped up onto Darian's shoulder, Darian wincing in pain. Then nothing. Vinny was up and grabbing the spikes at the top and pulling himself up.

Now for the reason that Vinny had gone first. He reached a hand down for Darian, who had to take a run-up to grab it but when he did it was as if he was weightless. Vinny lifted him up in one swinging movement and then Darian was grabbing the spikes and pulling himself over. They both lowered their weight and had to drop the rest of the way, hitting the cobbled ground and falling over.

They ran up a short drive to a house smaller than Simon's. This one was two storeys of traditional gneiss, a little smaller than the original Sutherland home would have been before the extensions. The size mattered nothing to them, but they both noticed the darkness and emptiness of it.

Simon Sutherland had said he owned it and that he had never been in it, and it didn't look like anyone else had either. High walls surrounded the garden and that was just enough to hide the jungle it had become from the neighbours. The grass was thigh-high and the weeds taller, and even in the moonlight Darian could see the clumps of moss sticking out of the drainpipes and clinging to the roof, more weeds reaching out between the cobbles beneath them. They went to the wooden front door and Vinny looked in the small window before trying the handle to find it was locked.

He said, 'What do you think?'

'I think you're a cop and you put doors in all the time. Add another to your list.'

Vinny had never lived his life waiting for second invites, so he put his shoulder to the door and hammered into it. It didn't budge an inch, didn't even rattle.

He grunted. 'That's not a normal door. Reinforced, I think.'

'We need something to smash it with, force our way in.'

If there was anything useable in the front garden it was buried under the grass and in the darkness they couldn't go feeling for it. They ran around the side of the house. Nothing there. Then to the back, a long garden running down towards the edge of the loch, a mesh fence around a large flat stone at the water's edge, a piece of history few understood and they had no time to look at.

'There. Birdbath.'

Darian had spotted it, the top peeking out over the long grass around it, a stone circle that looked weighty. Vinny went across and grabbed it, tried to lift it but struggled. Darian helping, they shoved it, rocked it back and forth until it came loose and Vinny picked it up. With it on his shoulder he started running, straight to the back door of the house and charged it, assuming it was as secure as the front. The first time it buckled but it didn't open. It needed a second run-up, all of Vinny's weight and the impact of the birdbath to smash the door around the multiple heavy locks and get them in.

The second the door burst open an alarm started screaming, loud enough to wake the dead in Heilam cemetery across the loch. Vinny tossed the heavy birdbath onto the pavement running around the side of the house. Ignoring the alarm, they carried on into the house. Vinny was a cop and they were doing the right thing so neither feared the law.

They found themselves in a long, empty, dark corridor with a hard wooden floor that seemed to stretch the length of the house with a staircase at the head and doors on either side as you went along it. In a horror movie it would be the scene where a door would suddenly open and something awful would leap out, and Darian wasn't ruling out that happening here. The whole house had the atmosphere of a trap. With the pulsing screech paining their ears they walked halfway down the corridor until they saw a small light: a security box on a door that surely led to the basement.

They stood beside it and Vinny pressed three, zero, zero, one and then enter, and everything changed. The alarm shut its damn mouth and the door clicked open a fraction, enough to show them a line of light. Vinny pulled the door open and they were standing at the top of a flight of stairs leading to another door. They walked down and found it was heavy, metal, but the same code that had unlocked the one at the top of the stairs had opened this one, too. They pulled it open and they found her.

The basement was large and well furnished; they could see a sofa and a TV, a table and a bed, and a small kitchen, all in the one open space. There was an open door through which they could see a shower, and they could guess a toilet, too. A light was on and a woman was standing in the middle of the room looking nervous.

She recognised Vinny and said, 'Oh, thank God.'

Freya ran across to him and they hugged. Darian was taking in the room and trying to examine Freya without it being obvious. There were no noticeable marks on her, cuts or bruises, but that confirmed nothing.

Vinny said, 'Are you okay?'

'Yes, I'm okay, bored and frustrated but I'm okay. What the hell took you so long, I was expecting you ages ago?'

'What the hell...? I've been turning the city upside down trying to find you, that's what.'

'Twelve days, Vinny. Some cop you are.'

Darian smiled. 'Come on, let's get out of here.'

Freya said, 'Oh, yes, I could use some fresh air.'

'Won't be that fresh, it's full of smoke out there.'

On the way to the door Vinny paused and looked behind at the basement, saying quietly to Darian, 'Bloody hell, it's bigger than my flat, and a lot better equipped apart from no phone or wi-fi, and even with them my signal's patchy. I mean, I'm not saying I'd ever want to be kidnapped, but if it had to happen this is where I'd want to go.'

'Yeah, they were well prepared.'

They walked up the stairs and through the darkness to the front door. In the vestibule Darian found the keypad to unlock the front gate and they made their way down the lane.

An Caillte

The sea had been rough and that was what they had wanted, had been why they sailed. It calmed as they entered the mouth of the sea loch and continued to sail south, the two men in the thirty-foot open boat wet and cold but filled with nervous optimism. Both were tall and heavily bearded, Ranulf 'Ruadh', twenty-eight, and Tormod 'Ciùin', twenty-seven, and both carried the scars to display the bloody work they had done in their lives, on land and at sea. Battle had brought them relative riches, but had also taught them that respect should be earned and not given, and those who wished to impose laws upon them had earned nothing.

'Further, back to the flat rock,' Ruadh said to his friend, and as he looked over the side of the boat added, 'it's deep, all the way in so far.'

'The hills keep tall on both sides so the loch will be deep,' Ciùin said in his low voice, the same gruff accent of a Leòdhasach as his friend.

They had returned to their island and found the king's men demanding loyalty, demanding a share of their violent earnings to take their coin and use it to further the glory of another man. Gèbennach was a fiercely ambitious man, a king of small throne who wanted more, and expected their help to take from those they had given nothing to. Others on the island accepted it, but others had not travelled as widely as they had, did not know how different the world could look. Others had not learned the hard lessons they had learned. People with titles would always take from them unless they took the titles.

In their previous visit to this loch they had found stones in two spots that might once have been buildings, but small and far apart, no hint that there had been a community. All that still stood to tell of man's time here were the standing stones, tall on the peak of a hill to the east and a reminder of a lost home. The hills protected them from prying eyes on the north coast, those who controlled the lands looking always for an advantage, a way to gain valuable favour or to steal from others. As they sailed towards the southern end of the loch they saw the valley that opened in the hills there, leading into the mountains. Their plan was not to stay so even a break in the ring of high protection was of little concern.

They sailed beyond an outcrop on the east bank and an island towards the west.

'There,' Ruadh said, 'the rock is as good a spot as any.'

On the west bank was a protruding rock, flat on top with a small overhang at the edge of the water. They lowered their sail when they were close and used oars to pull up to the bank, the water shallowing here but their boat built for this. Preparation was most important, and it was why they were here.

They secured the boat and Ruadh used both hands to carry out the cloth bag they had with them, filled heavy as it was, and placed in on the rock. They put two short swords and an axe pressed to the side of the rock, out of view of the water, in case their negotiations went poorly, and were both reassured by the knives they carried. Now they sat on the rock, feet in the heather, in the rain, and waited.

It was hours later when a single boat came into view towards the mouth of the loch, its sail drifting towards them. When it was close enough they could see Egill 'Halfeye' on board, and with him his little brother, Vali 'Two Eyes'. They knew both men well, the blond hair and wide faces and broad shoulders the same, the sibling look marred only by the long scar that ran from the middle of Halfeye's forehead, splitting his eyebrow in half and ending just below the empty red socket where his right eye had been. They reached the rock and Halfeye stepped off the boat onto the bank.

'This is a good place,' he said in his rough and amusing attempt at Gaelic.

Ruadh spoke a little Icelandic but Halfeye's Gaelic was better so it was what they used.

'It will do,' Ruadh said. 'The hills for shelter, deep water all the way to the south bank. We shall make use of it and you should, too.'

'We shall,' Halfeye said, polite to the offer of a thing he didn't need, rainwater dripping from his neat beard. 'And we start today. There are as many as you asked for, as good as you need,' Halfeye said, 'but I tell you again you are wasting time and blood you have little of to spare.

An island on the western edge? What can you build there when others claim it as theirs, all these kings fighting? You will spend a lifetime defending what you have rather than taking more. Look at this place. Here is where you can build a stronghold to call your own. Sail ships north and east, and not a hard sail to Ireland either.'

'This,' Ruadh said, 'is not home.'

'Home is not where you were born; it's where you choose to be.'

Halfeye helped his brother carry out the delivery, dozens of longswords wrapped in thick blankets. Ruadh took the bag of coins across and placed it beside the weapons. This was the moment when a deal could turn rotten. Old friends or not, new priorities could persuade one side they were better off with the swords, the payment and two dead bodies. Halfeye picked up the bag with more ease than Ruadh had and looked inside. All of the coin had come from a man now dead, stolen by Ruadh and Halfeye just months before. It had made both men, and others, rich, but great wealth led to great problems. Halfeye recognised the coin from the chest they had taken.

The Icelander smiled. 'Good fortune to you, friends, I hope you wet the swords.'

As Halfeye put the bag on the boat beside Two Eyes, Ruadh and Ciùin checked what they had bought, the blades sharp and all of the quality agreed. As they drifted north from the bank they saw Halfeye take a coin from the bag and flick it into the water of the loch, offering his payment for good fortune to the sea that had killed so effortlessly so many good men he had known. Never forget to honour its power. Ruadh and Ciùin watched the brothers sail beyond view before they began to count out the swords, sure that the Icelanders wouldn't return. Halfeye was a hard man to trust around money but perhaps his brother calmed him, or the coming winter persuaded him that the easiest money was the best. Ruadh ran his hand along the side of a blade, thinking of the men who would soon arrive from Ireland to be armed, the blood they would spill to name a new king of the isles.

'This is a good spot,' Ciùin said. 'What shall I mark it?'

'We shall call it An Caillte.'

47

VINNY LED THE WAY with Freya by his side, her looking around all the time. Darian could see that she hadn't known where she had been taken and still didn't know where the hell she was because she'd never been on Geug Place before. As they walked the slow tilt of the lane they could see the blue lights flashing and the orange glow, the thick plume of black smoke yawning into the sky. For someone who hadn't been outside that basement room for twelve days it was an assault on the senses and Freya was holding onto Vinny's arm to make sure it didn't overwhelm her.

She said, 'Finn? Is he okay?

'He's fine. Worried witless about you, but he's doing okay. We can go see him, right after this.'

'Where are we going now?'

'To see the person who did this and if he doesn't tell me why he did it I'm going to throw him back into the fire Darian just got him out of.'

Darian already suspected something close to the truth, but he wanted to hear it from Simon. They turned into the drive and walked past the fire engines and onto the grass where Sholto was keeping watch over Simon, Harold and Phil. They stood looking at each other, Simon sheepish, Freya unsure. Harold raised his chin slightly, defiant.

Before Freya could utter a word, Harold said, 'Whatever you are about to accuse my nephew of you should be very careful. He is not a well man, and he has just been through a terrible trauma. Our family has sympathy for whatever has happened to you but we will defend ourselves. I have already contacted people to that effect.'

He spoke fast, breathlessly. He was a man rowing against the waves. Freya glared at him and said, 'I know what happened. I know.'

Sholto said, 'You contacted people? You contacted Noonan? Must have been before we got here, and he hasn't turned up yet. You're about to find you have fewer friends than you thought.'

Vinny looked back and forth and said, 'Hang on, what? This is about Simon, right? It was Simon.'

Freya shook her head. 'Will Dent told me it was Harold behind it all. Dent was the only one I saw and I didn't know if I could believe him, but he was right. Where is he?'

For a few seconds the group fell into an awkward silence before Vinny, with no hint of sympathy, said, 'He died yesterday, probably trying to stop us from finding you. Tried to break into Sholto's office, got chased, ran across the railway lines and had an argument with a speeding train. He lost.'

Simon Sutherland said, 'He did everything because I asked him to. He did it for me, so, I'm sorry.'

Harold grabbed his nephew by the shoulder and said, 'Say nothing, Simon. Not a word. They'll use it against you.'

Simon looked at him. There was a moment where Darian wondered, where it seemed that the strength of his uncle's hold on him might be enough. Not this time. Simon stepped away from Harold and Phil and moved over to stand next to Darian. Vinny was watching, the bulky, menacing presence. When Harold took a step towards Simon, Vinny moved between them.

Freya glared at Harold and said, 'Will told me he was trying to stop me from being killed. He said it had happened before and that him and his friend were going to stop it happening again. I take it you're the friend.'

Simon nodded when she turned to him and said, 'Yes, I'm the friend. Harold is my uncle; he killed a young woman called Ruby-Mae Short. Will was able to tell me about it because he was there. Uncle Harold told him they were going to pick up a girl he was dating but they went to Earmam and picked a drunk girl off the street. Will drove them to a flat Uncle Harold had in Bakers Moor and left them there. He didn't like it, the young woman didn't know what was happening. He didn't stop it. Then Uncle Harold called him two hours later and made him come up to the flat. He took her dead body and dropped it at the railway line. It was only when Uncle Harold put the bra in my house that Will decided to tell me what happened. I know I should have told the police but he's family and the bank needs him. He looked after me when my mother died. When Will told me about you, about the accident and Uncle Harold saying he liked you, we decided to keep an eye on him. If he was going to make a move we would be a step ahead of him. When he started sending you gifts we knew we had to act.'

Harold was shaking his head and laughing. 'This is nonsense. No one believes this. Simon, I know you're ill, God knows I've done more to help you than anyone, but you need to stop talking. We'll get you help, okay. I will.'

While Harold spoke, loud above the shouts and actions of the firemen, the rest of them looked at Simon and at Vinny. Simon held the truth. Vinny held the violence.

There was a short lull before Sholto said, 'Why kidnap her? Why hold her there?'

'I thought if we kept her out of reach for a week or two he would realise what had happened. He would know that we were onto him, or someone was, and it would stop him. Instead, when he found out it was me, he came round and burned down my house. He thought I would stay inside and be burned with it, and that no one would try to rescue me.'

As he spoke he made eye contact with Darian and there was a nod between them.

Vinny, with a snarl, said, 'Why the hell didn't you just tell someone this bastard was on the prowl?'

Harold stepped back at the fury in the look Vinny gave him. The big man was flooded with relief and energy he hadn't had much chance to use yet. When Harold moved back it was Phil who put out a hand and grabbed his uncle by the arm. He held him tight. Harold turned and glared at him. Shocked. Two family members turning on him. Sutherland against Sutherland.

Vinny turned to Simon. 'The police are going to have a lot of questions for you, what you did was still rotten. Kidnapping her and then accusing me to my face of killing her, you wee bastard.'

Phil said, 'Actually, Simon didn't take her, Will Dent did, and there's nothing to prove Simon ordered it or had any control over it. The worst you could say is he knew about it and he did nothing, but he had reasonable motives for that.'

Sholto, in a high whine, said, 'He just bloody said he ordered it and we all heard him.'

Vinny gave Phil a sideways look that suggested he wanted to put a fist through his young partner and said, 'Aye, you're still a Sutherland all right.'

A car turned into the driveway behind them with a screech, drove up towards the house and pulled recklessly onto the grass to avoid going into the back of a fire engine. Harold looked up hopefully. It could have been Noonan. But Harold would never see his pet cop again. Noonan only backed the winning team. You always backed the Sutherlands because they always won, that was common logic. The police knew that. The Sutherlands were in control. Maybe, just maybe, he would have been able to solve the problem. The Sutherlands had bought their way out of plenty of scandals before. Defend the family. Protect the bank. Those were the rules and as long as all the family stuck to them they had a chance of surviving any scandal. Not this time. The car door opened and DC Angela Vicario got out.

48

ANGELA APPROACHED THE group and introduced herself. Harold tried to get his story in first.

'You can't charge Simon with anything. He's mentally ill, demonstrably so, it's care and protection he needs, not this, not a squad of policemen bullying him into lies. And don't think I won't be pressing charges for this…'

It was Vinny who stepped towards Harold and shut him up. 'You're going to let the boy speak and you're not going to say a word.'

Nerves were rising. The flood of relief at finding Freya and now the determination to stop whoever was responsible. The heat from the house and the shouting of the firemen, the roar of the fire, made every word jangle with nerves. Behind them more blue lights as a police car from the local station turned into the drive and found itself confronted with more people and vehicles than it knew what to do with. Behind it an ambulance joined the throng.

Angela introduced herself to the new arrivals and one of them said, 'So who are we arresting?'

Vinny pointed at Harold and said, 'That one.'

The uniformed officers hesitated. One of them said, 'But what for?'

Darian said, 'He set the fire. We got here and the gate was locked, no cars around, but when I went over the railings he was inside, on his own. He slipped in, locked the gate behind him and set the fire.'

Harold was laughing again and shaking his head but Phil said, 'I saw your car round the corner on King Robert Street.'

Another family betrayal. Harold looked with horror at Phil and Simon, but the two uniformed officers stepped in and led him away to the car. There would be many more charges to follow.

Angela turned to Simon and said, 'You're the one who knows what's going on here. Why don't you share it?'

Simon nodded. 'Okay, I'll tell you. It was Will who told me about it. Uncle Harold had always been, I don't know what you would call it, a ladies' man. But he only liked to have short-term relationships. He didn't let Will see the truth until he was sure that he could trust him. Then he could have Will drive other men's wives to one of his flats around the city for the night. He started sending Will to bars to pick up girls for him. He was getting more forceful about it, too. Then he had Will drive him around on weekends, late at night, and would offer drunk girls a lift in his luxury, chauffeur-driven car. When they had gotten into the back he would try his luck. Will said sometimes Uncle Harold got aggressive, and other times the girls were too drunk to know what was happening. Then one night they picked up Ruby-Mae Short. Will dropped them at the flat in Bakers Moor, on Normandy Road, he said, and left. When he was called back she was dead and Uncle Harold told him where to take her, like he'd planned it, told him how to get to the tracks without being seen. Will was convinced they'd get caught but it never happened, the police didn't come after them. He told me everything. Uncle Harold had put the bra in my house, I think as a warning to Will. I should have called the police then but Uncle Harold has looked after me since my mother died and I knew what it would do to the bank. Then there was a while when everything seemed to calm back down to normal, like he had been sated by what he'd done, and then the crash happened. Uncle Harold started sending you gifts after that, and Will found out because he had to go and collect them when you refused them. We had already planned what we would do if we thought it was definitely going to happen again, so we put it into practice. Will was convinced that he would get years in The Ganntair for what happened to Miss Short, and I don't think he believed he could survive that long. I think that must be why he didn't step out of the way of the train. I thought when all this happened

Uncle Harold would speak to me, tell me he wouldn't do it again and everything would be okay. I honestly never imagined that he would try to kill me, too.'

He had spoken quietly throughout, face still smudged by smoke, the group around him straining to hear his voice over the fire and the people fighting it.

Angela said, 'Thank you, Simon, that's helpful. You'll have to tell that again on tape, and you might have to go to court.'

'Oh, yes, I know.'

Phil said, 'He's doing all he can to help and he'll continue to. I'll contact the chairman of the bank, have him send out a legal representative for Simon.'

It was an attempt to negotiate complete honesty in exchange for favourable treatment, no charge of withholding information and, if he could sweet-talk Freya, which seemed unlikely, no charge of kidnap. Phil had spent years steering clear of the upper branches of his family tree and here he was promising to call the patriarch personally. The very mention of the most powerful man in Challaid subdued the aggression Vinny had shown and promised a prosecution-defying defensive wall was about to be built around Simon. Phil was sacrificing a little of his normal life to protect his cousin, who had no one else to look after him now.

Angela said, 'I'll have people head out to the house on Eilean Seud and try to work out what other property in the city he owns, which is probably a lot. The very least we can be certain of convicting him on is setting fire to the house, but I think we have enough to get a whole lot more. We've been trying to get justice for Ruby-Mae for a while, and we will now. I'm going to the station to prepare for the interview. Simon, we'll want to talk to you right away.'

As more police cars pulled up Phil said, 'I'm coming with him. Freya, it's good to see you safe, and Darian, Sholto, well done on everything tonight, you saved Simon and stopped a killer. Thank you.'

There had been a stiffness in Phil's delivery that made it sound obligated and not heartfelt, and he led Simon to a waiting police car. Angela said to Darian, 'They'll take him to Piper Station first, this is their patch. It could be a while before we get to question him. We'll need to talk to you all as well.'

Darian nodded. 'Of course.'

Angela brushed his hand and, before she walked down the driveway, said, 'I'll call you.'

There were four of them left now, Darian, Sholto, Vinny and Freya, and they all breathed a sigh of relief.

Darian looked at Freya and said, 'How are you feeling?'

'Relieved. Tired. A bit hungry. Annoyed it happened. Glad it's over.'

Vinny said, 'All because one bloody Sutherland didn't want to call the cops on another bloody Sutherland.'

Sholto said, 'No matter how good his legal team are and how much your partner wants to help him, Simon Sutherland is looking at a conviction here.'

'He is, but we all know how these things work around here. He's rich and his family will pull strings, he'll go to court and say he was scared of his uncle and that he has mental health issues so if he does get convicted there's almost no chance he'll spend a single night in a cell. They'll send him back to his rebuilt mansion to hide from humanity forever more.'

Darian said, 'Aye, well, the more I see of humanity the more I think he might be onto something.'

It was at that point that Vinny smiled and said, 'Okay, hands up who among you had me pegged as the most likely suspect?'

Sholto slightly raised his hand and then pulled it down again in case Vinny wasn't making a joke of this, and then said, 'DS MacNeith did for sure.'

'I know she did, and she was right to. It's usually the ex.'

Freya looked askance. 'You? They thought you would be able to kidnap me? They thought you had killed me?'

'I know, I could never win a bloody argument with you, let alone get away with bumping you off.'

'The only thing you ever made a half-decent job of was Finn, and now I want you to take me to him.'

'Yeah, let's go. I can smoke out the window of the car. Been desperate for a San Jose for the last hour but I don't want to light up in front of firemen and paramedics. I feel like I'd be on the end of a double-barrelled lecture. Let's go see the boy.'

Vinny and Freya said goodbye to Darian and Sholto and left, knowing Freya should have stayed to talk more to the police but feeling this was more important. Vinny would take her to the station later, but for now they were heading to his flat in Whisper Hill to see their young son. That, Darian felt, was the most gratifying moment of the whole thing, watching them going to give a young kid the surprise he had been praying for. That happened far too rarely. There would be children in the city, other family members, too, desperately hoping that a lost parent or child or sibling would return. Most would be disappointed.

Darian and Sholto walked slowly out to the car, both tired and sore, and Sholto made a three-course meal of making a three-point turn to get them out of Geug Place.

On the way south through Barton, Sholto said, 'A Sutherland will never call the cops on another Sutherland, that's what Vinny said.'

'We knew that, didn't we?'

'I suppose. I just wonder if it applies to his partner, too. He's a Sutherland. How early did he know about his beloved uncle? How early did he know about Ruby-Mae?'

'You think he knew and said nothing, even when Freya was missing? That's a hell of an accusation.'

'I know, that's why I only put it to you in the car instead of in front of the rest of them in the garden. I won't repeat it either, because I'll never be able to prove it, but it's always worth remembering that even people you think are good folk have their own moral code. Everyone does. You think someone is decent because they have most of the same standards as you, but then you spot a difference and it shocks you, but it shouldn't. Nothing would surprise me about the moral code of another person, even if it meant believing Phil could have put a stop to this earlier.'

Darian mumbled agreement but didn't dive into dirty detail. One of the very first pearls of wisdom Sholto had rolled his way was that no case was perfect, and most would leave behind a selection of unconquered question marks, even after the main point of the investigation was solved and the file closed. Nothing as complicated as a Challaid criminal could give you an easy answer.

As they stopped outside Darian's flat, the sun making its lazy way into the sky, Sholto said, 'Go and get some proper sleep. I don't want you in the office before lunchtime. We've got a big report to write and no one to read it, and you'll have to give more statements to the police. If you're lucky it might be to DC Vicario, and you'll want your beauty sleep before you see her again. Go on, get out of my sight.'

'Thanks, Sholto.'

Darian walked slowly up the stairs and took the key from his pocket. He opened the front door and went into his small flat. There were times, sitting at his desk in the office looking down at Cage Street, when he felt jealous of big operators like Raven, and when he resented his father for robbing him of the chance to follow his dream of becoming a real detective. Nights like this one changed it all.

ABOUT THE AUTHOR

Malcolm Mackay was born in Stornoway on Scotland's Isle of Lewis. His Glasgow Trilogy has been nominated and shortlisted for several international prizes, including the Edgar Awards' Best Paperback Original and the CWA John Creasey (New Blood) Dagger award. His second novel, *How a Gunman Says Goodbye*, won the Deanston Scottish Crime Book of the Year Award. Mackay still lives in Stornoway.